"Tell me why you're here," he said.

"I promised Colin." It sounded so archaic when she said it. Lucy pushed back her hair, too aware of herself for her own comfort. "I told him if I ever needed help, I'd come to you. So, here I am. Except I really don't need your help, after all."

"You don't? Good. I'd hate for you to have wasted a trip." Sebastian started back across the worn floorboards toward the porch. "I'm not in the helping business."

She was stunned. "What?"

"Plato'll feed you, get you back on the road before dark."

Lucy stared at his back as he went out onto the porch. In the cabin's dim light, she saw an iron bed in one corner of the room, cast-off running shoes, a book of Robert Penn Warren poetry, a stack of James Bond novels and one of Joe Citro's books of Vermont ghost stories. There was also a kerosene lamp.

This was not what she'd expected. Redwing Associates was high-tech and very serious, one of the best investigative and security consulting firms in the business. Sebastian's brainchild. He knew his way around the world. If nothing else, Lucy had expected she might have to hold him back, keep him from moving too fast and too hard on her behalf.

Instead, he'd turned her down flat. Without argument. Without explanation.

She took a deep breath. The dust, altitude and dry air hadn't given her a bloody nose like they had J.T. They'd just driven every drop of sanity and common sense right out of her. She *never* should have come here.

CARLA NEGGERS

THE WATERFALL

ISBN 1-55166-582-4

THE WATERFALL

Visit us at www.mirabooks.com

Printed in U.S.A.

To Dick and Diane Ballou...
for the house, the clothes, the fun and the friendship.

Many thanks to Corine Quarterman for generously sharing her expertise in adventure travel and introducing me to my first Vermont waterfall. While the waterfall in this book is fictional, there are many wonderful, picturesque waterfalls throughout this beautiful state—I hope readers will get a chance to visit some of them!

Thanks, also, to my husband, Joe Jewell, for not forgetting everything he learned at Castle Heights Military Academy, and to Kate and Zachary for their patience during a particularly long, hot summer of writing. Yes, even Vermont was hot last summer....

Thanks, finally, to my editor, Amy Moore-Benson, for her encouragement and enthusiasm...if not for addicting me to crème brûlée! And to my agent, Meg Ruley, for living up to every word of her incredible reputation.

Enjoy,

Carla Neggers

Carla Neggers

P.O. Box 826
Quechee, VT 05059

One

"The Widow Swift?" Lucy made a face as she absorbed her daughter's latest tidbit of gossip. "Who calls me that?"

Madison shrugged. She was fifteen, and she was doing the driving. Something else for Lucy to get used to. "Everyone."

"Who's everyone?"

"Like, the six people who live in this town."

Lucy ignored the light note of sarcasm. *The Widow Swift.* Good Lord. Maybe in some strange way this was a sign of acceptance. She had no illusions about being a "real" Vermonter. After three years, she was still an outsider, still someone people expected would pack up at any moment and move back to Washington. Nothing would suit Madison better, Lucy knew. At twelve, life in small-town Vermont had been an adventure. At fifteen, it was an imposition. She had her learner's permit, after all. Why not a home in Georgetown?

"Well," Lucy said, "you can just tell 'everyone' that I prefer to be called Lucy or Mrs. Swift or Ms. Swift."

"Sure, Mom."

"A name like 'the Widow Swift' tends to stick."

Madison seemed amused by the whole thing, so much so that she forgot that parking made her nervous and just pulled into a space in front of the post office in the heart of their small southern Vermont village.

"Wow, that was easy," Madison said. "Okay. Into park. Emergency brake on. Engine off. Keys out." She smiled at her mother. She'd slipped into a little sundress for their trip to town; Lucy had nixed the flimsy slip-on sandals she'd wanted to wear. "See? I didn't even hit a moose."

They'd seen exactly two moose since moving to Vermont, neither en route to town. But Lucy let it go. "Good job."

Madison scooted off to the country store to "check out the galoshes," she said with a bright smile that took the edge off her sarcasm. Lucy headed for the post office to mail a batch of brochures for her adventure travel company. Requests from her Web site were up. Business was good to excellent. She was getting her bearings, making a place for herself and her children. It took time, that was all.

"The Widow Swift," she said under her breath. "Damn."

She wished she could shake it off with a laugh, but she couldn't. She was thirty-eight, and Colin had been dead for three years. She knew she was a widow. But she didn't want it to define her. She didn't know what she wanted to define her, but not that.

The village was quiet in the mid-July heat, not even a breeze stirring in the huge, old sugar maples on the sliver of a town common. The country store, the post office, the hardware store and two bed-and-breakfasts—that was it. Manchester, a few miles to the northwest, offered considerably more in the way of shopping and things to do, but Lucy had no intention of letting her daughter drive that far with a two-week-old learner's permit. It wasn't necessarily that Madison wasn't ready for traffic and busy streets. *Lucy* wasn't ready.

When she finished at the post office, she automatically approached the driver's side of her all-wheel-drive station wagon. Their "Vermont car," Madison called it with a touch of derision. She wanted a Jetta. She wanted the city.

With a groan, Lucy remembered her daughter was driving. Fifteen was *so* young. She went around to the passenger's side, surprised Madison wasn't already back behind the wheel. Driving was all that stood between her daughter and abject boredom this summer. Even the prospect of leaving for Wyoming the next day hadn't perked her up. Nothing would, Lucy realized, except getting her way about spending a semester in Washington with her grandfather.

Wyoming. Lucy shook her head. Now *that* was madness.

She plopped on the sun-heated passenger seat and debated canceling the trip. Madison had already voiced objections about going. And her twelve-year-old son, J.T., would rather stay home and dig worms. The purported reason for heading to Jackson Hole was to meet with several western guides. But that was ridiculous, Lucy thought. Her company specialized in northern New England and the Canadian Maritimes and was in the process of putting together a winter trip to Costa Rica where her parents had retired to run a hostel. She had all she could handle now. Opening up to Montana and Wyoming would just be spreading herself too thin.

The real reason she was going to Wyoming, she knew, was Sebastian Redwing and the promise she'd made to Colin.

But that was ridiculous, too. An overreaction—if not pure stupidity—on her part to a few weird incidents.

Lucy sank back against her seat, feeling something under her—probably a pen or a lipstick, or one of J.T.'s toys. She fished it out.

She gasped at the warm, solid length of metal in her hand.

A bullet.

She resisted a sudden urge to fling it out the window. What if it went off? She shuddered, staring at her palm. It wasn't an empty shell. It was a live round. Big, weighty.

Someone had left a damn *bullet* on her car seat.

The car windows were open. She and Madison hadn't locked up. Anyone could have walked by, dropped the bullet through the passenger window and kept on going.

Lucy's hand shook. Not again. Damn it, not again. She forced herself to take slow, controlled breaths. She knew adventure travel—canoeing, kayaking, hiking, basic first aid. She could plan every detail of inventive, multifaceted, multi-sport trips and do just fine.

She didn't know bullets.

She didn't *want* to know bullets.

Madison trotted out of the country store with several other teenagers, swinging her car keys as if she'd been driving for years. The girls were laughing and chatting, and even as Lucy slid the bullet into her shorts pocket, she thought, *Yes, Madison, you do have friends.* Since school had let out, her daughter had been making a point of being miserable, if only to press her case for Washington.

She jumped into the driver's seat. "Saddle up, Mom. We're ready to roll."

Lucy didn't mention the bullet. This wasn't her children's problem, it was hers. She preferred to cling to the belief that she wasn't the victim of deliberate harassment. The incidents she'd endured over the past week were random, innocent, meaningless. They weren't related. They weren't a campaign of intimidation against her.

The first had occurred on Sunday evening, when she'd found a dining room window open, the curtains billowing in the summer breeze. It was a window she never opened. Madison and J.T. wouldn't bother. But Lucy had dismissed the incident, until the next night when the phone rang just before dawn, the caller breathing at her groggy hello, then hanging up. Too weird, she'd thought.

Then on Tuesday, while checking the mailbox at the end of her driveway, she'd had the distinct sense she was being watched. Something had alerted her—the snapping of a twig, the crunching of gravel. It wasn't, she was certain, her imagination.

The next morning, the feeling was there again, while she was sweeping the back steps, and ten minutes later, she'd found one of her tomato plants sitting on the front porch. It had been ripped out of the ground.

Now, today, the bullet on her car seat.

Maybe she was in denial, but she didn't believe there was enough to take to the police. Individually, each incident could have an innocent explanation— her kids, their friends, her staff, stress. How could she prove someone was watching her? She'd sound like a nut.

And if she went to the police, Lucy knew what would happen. They would notify Washington. Washington would feel compelled to come to Vermont and investigate. And so much for her low-profile life.

It wasn't that no one in town knew her father-in-law was Jack Swift, a powerful United States Senator. Everyone knew. But she'd never made it an issue.

She was his only son's widow; Madison and J.T. were his only grandchildren. Jack would take charge. He would insist the Capitol Police conduct a thorough investigation and make sure his family wasn't drawing fire because of him.

Lucy couldn't imagine why anyone going after Jack would slip a bullet onto his widowed daughter-in-law's car seat. It made no sense. No. She was safe. Her children were safe. This was just…bizarre.

"Mom?"

Madison had started the engine and backed out onto the main road without Lucy noticing, much less providing comment and instruction. "You're doing great. My mind's wandering, that's all."

"What's wrong? Is it my driving?"

"No, of course not."

"Because I can get someone else to drive with me. It doesn't have to be you, if I make you nervous."

"You don't make me nervous. I'm fine. Just keep your eyes on the road."

"I *am*."

Madison had a death grip on the steering wheel. Lucy realized she'd scared her daughter, who noticed everything. "Madison. You're driving. You can't allow yourself to get distracted."

"I know. It's you."

It *was* her. Lucy took a breath. She could feel the weight of the bullet in her pocket. What if it had worked its way under the seat and J.T. had found it? She shut off the stream of what-if scenarios. She'd learned from hard experience to stick with what was, which was difficult enough to absorb.

"Never mind me and drive."

Madison huffed, annoyed now. With her blue eyes and coppery hair, her introspective temperament and unbridled ambition, she was so like her father. Even Madison's two-week-old driving mannerisms were pure Colin Swift.

He'd died, suddenly and unexpectedly at age thirty-six, of a cardiac arrhythmia while playing tennis with his father, his life and a brilliant career at the U.S. State Department cut short. Madison had been twelve, J.T. nine. Not easy ages to lose a father. Six months later, Lucy had plucked her children away from the only life they knew—school, friends, family, "civilization," as Madison would say. But if they hadn't moved—if Lucy hadn't done something dramatic to get her bearings—they'd have been in danger of losing their mother, too, and that simply wasn't an option.

There'd been nothing from Sebastian Redwing when Colin died. Not a flower, not a card, not a word. Then, two months later, his lawyer showed up on Lucy's doorstep offering her the deed to his grandmother's Vermont farmhouse. Daisy had died the previous year, and Sebastian had no use for it.

Lucy threw the lawyer out. If Redwing couldn't even offer his condolences, she didn't want his damn house.

A month later, the lawyer was back. This time, she could have the house at a below-market price. She would be doing Sebastian a favor. His grandmother had wanted someone in the family to have the house. He had no brothers or sisters. His parents were dead. Lucy was the best he could do.

She'd accepted. She still didn't know why. Sebastian had once saved her husband's life. Why not hers?

In truth, she couldn't pinpoint one clear, overriding reason. Perhaps the lure of Vermont and starting her own adventure travel business, the stifling fog of grief, her fears about raising her children on her own.

Maybe, she thought, it boiled down to the promise she'd made Colin shortly before he died. Neither had known until that day on the tennis court that he had a heart condition that could kill him. The promise had seemed like one of those "if we're trapped on a desert island" scenarios, not something she would ever need to act on.

Yet Colin had been so sincere, so serious. "If anything happens to me, you can trust Sebastian. He's the best, Lucy. He saved my life. He saved my father's life. Promise me you'll go to him if you ever need help."

She'd promised, and now here she was in Vermont. She hadn't heard from Redwing, much less seen him, since she'd bought his grandmother's house. The transaction had been handled entirely through his attorney. Lucy had hoped never again to be so desperate that she'd feel compelled to remember her promise to Colin. She was smart, she was capable, and she was used to being on her own.

So why was she packing herself and her kids off to Wyoming—Sebastian Redwing country—in the morning?

"Mom!"

"You're doing great. Just keep driving."
With one finger, Lucy traced the outline of the bullet in her pocket. There was probably an innocent explanation for the bullet and all the other incidents. She should just focus on having fun in Wyoming.

The locals still referred to Sebastian Redwing's grandmother as the Widow Daisy and the remnants of her farm as the old Wheaton place. Lucy had learned Daisy's story in bits and pieces. Daisy Wheaton had lived in her yellow farmhouse on Joshua Brook for sixty years as a widow. She was twenty-eight when her husband drowned saving a little boy from the raging waterfall in the hills above their farmhouse. It was early spring, and the snowmelt had made the falls treacherous. The boy had gone after his dog. Joshua Wheaton had gone after the boy. Later, the falls and the brook they were on were named after him. Joshua Falls—Joshua Brook.

Daisy and Joshua's only child, a daughter, couldn't wait to get out of Vermont. She moved to Boston and got married, and when she and her husband were killed in a hit-and-run accident, they left behind a fourteen-year-old son. Sebastian came to live with Daisy. But he hadn't stayed in Vermont, either.

Seven acres of fields, woods and gardens, and the rambling yellow clapboard farmhouse were all that remained of the original Wheaton farm. Daisy had sold off bits and pieces of her land over the years to second homeowners and local farmers, keeping the core of the place for herself and whoever might come after her.

It was said Daisy had never gone back to Joshua Falls after she'd helped pull her husband's body out of the frigid water.

The Widow Daisy. Now, the Widow Swift.

Lucy grimaced as she walked up the gravel path to the small, classic barn she'd converted into office space. She could feel the decades yawning in front of her and imagined sixty years on this land, alone.

She stopped, listening to Joshua Brook trickling over rocks down the steep, wooded embankment beyond the barn. The falls were farther up in the hills. Here, the brook was wide and slow-moving before running under a wooden bridge and eventually merging with the river. She could hear bees buzzing in the hollyhocks in front of the garage. She looked around her, at the sprawling lawn, lush and green from recent showers, and the pretty nineteenth-century farmhouse with its baskets of white petunias hanging on the front porch. Her gaze took in the stately, old sugar maples that shaded the front yard, the backyard with its vegetable garden and apple trees, and a stone wall that bordered a field of grass and wildflowers, with another stone wall on its far side. Then, beyond that, the wooded hills. So quiet, so beautiful.

"You could do worse," Lucy whispered to herself as she entered her office.

She had learned most of what she knew about the Wheaton-Redwing family not from closemouthed, elusive Sebastian, but from Rob Kiley, her only full-time employee. He was parked in front of his computer in the open, rustic space that served as her company's home base. Rob's father was the boy Joshua Wheaton had saved sixty years ago—one of the circuitous but inevitable connections Lucy had come to expect from living in a small town.

Rob didn't look up. "I hate computers," he said.

Lucy smiled. "You say that every time I walk in here."

"That's because I want to get it through that thick, cheapskate skull of yours that we need a full-time person to sit here and bang away on this thing."

"What are you doing?" Lucy asked. She didn't peer over his shoulder because that drove him nuts.

He was a lanky, easygoing Vermonter whose paddling skills and knowledge of the hills, valleys, rivers and coastline of northern New England were indispensable. So were his enthusiasm, his honesty and his friendship.

"I'm putting together the final, carved-in-stone, must-not-deviate-from itinerary for the father-son backpacking trip." This was a first-time offering, a five-day beginner's backpacking trip on nearby trails in the southern Green Mountains; it had filled up even faster than he and Lucy had anticipated. Rob looked up, and she knew what he was thinking. "There's still time for J.T. to join us. I told him I wasn't a substitute for his real dad, but we can still have a lot of fun."

"I know. This is one he has to figure out for himself. I can't decide for him."

He nodded. "Well, we've got time. By the way, he and Georgie are digging worms in the garden."

Lucy wasn't surprised. "Madison will love that. I just sent her to check on them."

Rob tilted back in his chair and stretched. Sitting at a computer was torture for him on a day when he could be out kayaking. "How'd she do driving?"

"Better than I did. She's still lobbying for a semester in Washington."

"Grandpa Jack would love that."

"She's romanticized Washington. It's everything Vermont isn't."

Rob shrugged. "Well, it is."

"You're a big help!" But Lucy's laughter faded quickly as she slipped her hand into her pocket and withdrew the bullet. "I want you to take a look at something."

"Sure."

"And I don't want you to mention it to anyone."

"Am I supposed to ask why not?"

"You're supposed to say okay, you won't."

"Okay, I won't."

She opened her hand and let the bullet roll forward in her palm. "What do you think?"

Rob frowned. "It's a bullet."

"I know it's a bullet. What kind?"

He picked it out of her palm and nonchalantly set it upright on his cluttered desk. He'd grown up around guns. "Forty-four magnum. It's the whole nine yards, you know, not just an empty shell."

She nodded. "I know that much. Can it go off?"

"Not sitting here on my desk. If you dropped it just right or ran it over with a lawn mower or something, it could go off."

Lucy stifled a shudder. "That can't be good."

"If it went off, you wouldn't have any control over where it goes. At least with a gun, you can take aim at a target. You might take lousy aim. But if you run over a live round with a lawn mower, there's no chance to aim at anything. Thing can go any which way.'' He sounded calm, but his dark eyes were very serious. ''Where'd you find it?''

''What? Oh.'' She hadn't considered a cover story and hated the idea of lying. ''In town. I'm sure it's no big deal.''

''It's not Georgie or J.T., is it? If they're fooling around with firearms and ammunition—''

''No!'' Lucy nearly choked. ''I stumbled on it in town just now. I didn't want anyone to get hurt, so I picked it up. I was just wondering if I was panicking unnecessarily.''

''You weren't. Someone was very careless.'' He touched the dull gray metal tip of the bullet. ''You want me to get rid of it?''

''Please.''

''Do me a favor, okay? Check J.T.'s room. I'll check Georgie's. If I find anything, I'll let you know. You do the same. I don't keep a gun at home, and I know you don't, but they wouldn't be the first twelve-year-old boys—''

''It wasn't J.T. or Georgie.''

Rob's eyes met hers. ''If you won't check J.T.'s room, I will.''

Lucy nodded. ''You're right. I'll check his room.''

"The cellar, too. I nearly blew myself up at that age screwing around with gunpowder."

"I don't have gunpowder—"

"Lucy."

"All right, all right."

Rob was silent, studying her. She'd known him from her earliest days in Vermont. He and his wife, Patti, were her best friends here. Georgie and J.T. were inseparable. But she hadn't told him about the weird incidents.

Lucy tried not to squirm. Sweat had matted her shirt to her lower back. So much to do, so many responsibilities. She didn't need some crackpot targeting her. "Just get rid of the damn bullet, okay?"

Rob crossed his arms on his chest. "Sure, Lucy."

She could guess what he was thinking—what anyone would be thinking. That she was on edge, frayed and crazed, more than would be warranted by a rapidly expanding business, widowhood, single motherhood and an impending trip west. That he wanted to call her on it.

Lucy took advantage of his natural reluctance to meddle. "I'm sorry if I seem a little nuts. I have so much to do with this whirlwind trip to Wyoming this weekend. You can hold down the fort here?"

"That's in bold print on my resume. *Can hold down forts.*"

His humor didn't reach his eyes, but Lucy pretended not to notice. She smiled. "What would I do without you?"

He didn't hesitate. "Go broke."

She laughed, feeling better now that the bullet was out of her pocket. These incidents had to be unrelated. It was kooky and paranoid to think they were part of some kind of bizarre conspiracy against her. What would be the motive?

She left Rob to his computer aggravations and bullet disposal, and went outside. She'd ask Rob later what he thought about this Widow Swift business. She had a good life here, and that was what counted.

"I made lemonade," Madison called from the front porch.

"Great. I'll be right there."

Lucy reminded herself it was only in recent months her daughter had come to feel aggrieved by their move to Vermont.

"I'm pretending I'm living in an episode of 'The Waltons,'" Madison said when her mother joined her amidst the hanging petunias and wicker furniture. Indeed, she had filled one of Daisy's old glass pitchers with lemonade and put on one of her threadbare aprons. Sebastian hadn't taken anything of his grandmother's before he'd sold her house.

"Did you ask the boys if they want any?" Lucy asked.

"They're still out back digging worms. It's disgusting. They smell like dirt and sweat."

"You used to love digging worms."

"Yuck."

Lucy smiled. "Well, I'll go ask them. And since you made the lemonade, they can clean up."

The two boys were still hard at work on the edge of the vegetable garden, precariously close to Lucy's tomatoes. Not that she minded. She wasn't as enterprising a gardener as Daisy had been. She'd added raised beds and mulched paths to take up space and had cultivated a lot of spreading plants, like pumpkins, squash and cucumbers. She had little desire, however, to can and freeze her own fruits and vegetables. This was enough.

"Madison made lemonade. You boys want some?"

"Later," J.T. said, too preoccupied with his worm-digging to look up.

He, too, had Colin's coppery hair and clear blue eyes, although his sturdy frame was more Blacker than Swift. Lucy smiled at the thought of her kind, thickset father. She had inherited her mother's slender build and fair coloring, and both her parents' love of the outdoors. They'd recently retired to Costa Rica to run a hostel, leaving behind long careers at the Smithsonian. Lucy planned to visit them over Thanksgiving, taking Madison and J.T. with her and working on the details of a Costa Rica trip she wanted to offer to her clients next winter. It was a long, painstaking process that involved figuring out and testing every last detail—transportation, food, lodging, contingency plans. *Nothing* could be left to chance.

Flying to Costa Rica to see them, Lucy thought, made more sense than flying off to Wyoming to see Sebastian Redwing.

J.T. scooped up dirt with his hands and piled it into a number-ten can he and Georgie had appropriated from the recycling bin. "We want to go fishing. We've got a ton of worms. Want to see?"

Lucy gave the can of squirming worms a dutiful peek. "Lovely. If you do go fishing, stay down here. Don't go up near the falls."

"I know, Mom."

He knew. *Right.* Both her kids knew everything. Losing their father at such a young age hadn't eroded their self-esteem. They had Colin's optimism, his drive and energy, his faith in a better future and his commitment to making it happen. Like their father, Madison and J.T. loved having a million things going on at once.

Lucy left the boys to their worms and returned to the front porch, where Madison had brought out cloth napkins and a plate of butter cookies to go with her lemonade. "Actually, I think I'm more Anne of Green Gables today."

"Is that better than John-Boy Walton?"

Madison wrinkled up her face and sat on the wicker settee, tucking her slender legs under her. "Mom—I really, really don't want to go to Wyoming. Can't I stay here? It's only for the weekend. Rob and Patti could look in on me. I could have a friend stay with me."

Lucy poured herself a glass of lemonade and settled onto a wicker chair. Her daughter was relentless. "I thought you couldn't wait to get out of Vermont."

"Not to *Wyoming*. It's more mountains and trees."

"Bigger mountains, different trees. There's great shopping in Jackson."

She brightened. "Does that mean you'll give me money?"

"A little, but I meant window-shopping. It's also very expensive."

Her daughter was unamused. "If I have to sit next to J.T. on the plane, I'm inspecting his pockets first."

"I expect you to treat your brother with respect, just as I expect him to treat you with respect."

Madison rolled her eyes.

Lucy tried her lemonade. It was a perfect mix of

tart and sweet, just like her fifteen-year-old daughter. Madison untucked her legs and flounced inside, the sophisticate trapped in the sticks, the long-suffering big sister about to be stuck on a plane with her little brother.

Lucy decided to give her the weekend to come around before initiating a discussion on attitude and who wouldn't get to do much driving until she changed hers.

She put her feet up on the porch rail and tried to let the cool breeze relax her. The trip to Wyoming made no sense. She knew it, and her kids at least sensed it.

The petunias needed watering. She looked out at her pretty lawn with its huge maples, its rambling old-fashioned rosebush that needed pruning. She'd just gone to town with her fifteen-year-old behind the wheel, inspected a can of worms and dealt with her daughter's John-Boy/Anne of Green Gables martyr act *and* a bullet on her car seat.

The Widow Swift at work.

Lucy drank more lemonade, feeling calmer. She'd managed on her own for so long. She didn't need Sebastian Redwing's help. She didn't need anyone's help.

J.T. permitted his mother to help him pack after dinner. Lucy kept her eyes open for firearms, bullets and secret antisocial tendencies. She found none. His room betrayed nothing more than a twelve-year-old's mishmash of interests. Posters of Darth Maul and peregrine falcons, stuffed animals, Lego models, sports paraphernalia, computer games, gross-looking superheroes and monsters, way too many Micro Machines.

He didn't have a television in his room. He didn't have a computer. Dirty clothes were dumped in with clean on the floor. Drawers were half open, a pant leg hanging out of one, a pair of boxers out of another.

The room smelled of dirty socks, sweat and earth. A dormer window looked out on the backyard, where she could still see evidence of the digging he and Georgie had done.

"You didn't bring your worms up here, did you?" Lucy asked.

"No, me and Georgie freed them." He looked at her, and corrected, "Georgie and I."

She smiled, and when she turned, she spotted a picture of Colin and J.T. tacked to her son's bulletin board. Blood rushed to her head, and she had to fight off sudden, unexpected tears. The edges of the picture were cracked and yellowed, pocked with tack holes from the dozen times J.T. had repositioned it. A little boy and a young father fishing, frozen in time.

Lucy smiled sadly at the image of the man she'd loved. They'd met in college, married so young. She stared at his handsome face, his smile, his tousle of coppery hair. It was as if she'd gone on, propelled forward in time, while he'd stayed the same, untouched by the grief and fear she'd known since the day his shattered father had knocked on her door and told her that his son—her husband—was dead.

The searing pain and shock of those early days had eased. Lucy had learned to go on without him. So, in their own ways, had Madison and J.T. They could talk about him with laughter, and remember him, at least most of the time, without tears.

"You can pack the extra stuff you want to take in your backpack," Lucy said, tearing herself from the picture. "What book are you reading?"

"A *Star Wars* book."

"Don't forget to pack it."

She counted out shirts, pants, socks, underwear, and debated whether to bother looking in the cellar and the garage. J.T.'d had nothing to do with the bullet in her car.

She set the clothes on his bed. "You're good to go, kiddo. Can you shove this stuff into your suitcase, or do you need my help?"

"I can do it."

"Don't forget your toothbrush."

She went down the hall to her daughter's room.

The door was shut, her music up but not at a wall-vibrating volume. If Madison needed help, she'd ask for it. Lucy left her alone.

Her own bedroom was downstairs, and on the way she stopped in the kitchen and put on a kettle for tea. She'd pack later. It was an old-fashioned, working kitchen with white cabinets, scarred counters and sunny yellow walls that helped offset the cold, dark winter nights. The biggest surprise of life in Vermont, Lucy had discovered, was how dark the nights were.

She sank into a chair at the pine table and stared out at the backyard, wondering how many nights Daisy had done exactly this in her sixty years alone. A cup of tea, a quiet house. The Widow Daisy. The Widow Swift.

It was dark now, the long summer day finally giving way. Lucy could feel the silence settle around her, the isolation and loneliness creep in. Sometimes she would turn on the television or the radio, or work on her laptop, write e-mails, perhaps call a friend. Tonight, she had to pack. Wyoming. Good God, she really was going.

She made chamomile tea and took her mug with her down the hall to the front door, locked up. Shadows shifted on the old wood floors. She had no illusions the ancient locks would stop a determined intruder.

A sound—the wind, maybe—took her into the dining room.

She hadn't touched it since moving in. It still had the old-fashioned button light switch for the milk-glass overhead, Daisy's faded hand-hooked rug, her cabbage-rose wallpaper, her clunky dining room set. A 1920s upright piano stood along one wall.

A breeze brought up goose bumps on Lucy's arms.

Someone had opened a window. Again.

The tall, old windows were balky and difficult to open. Since she almost never used the dining room during the summer, Lucy didn't bother wrestling with them. She'd meant to have them looked at before the good weather, but hadn't gotten around to it.

She felt along the wall with one hand and pressed the light switch. It *had* to be a kid. Who else would sneak into her house and open the windows?

Light spilled into the room, casting more shadows. It could be a great room. One of these days she'd have the piano tuned, the rug cleaned, the wood floors sanded and oiled. She'd hang new wallpaper and refinish the table, and have family and friends over for Thanksgiving. Even her father-in-law, if he wanted to come.

The floor seemed to sparkle. Lucy frowned, peering closer.

Shards of glass.

She jumped back, startled. The window wasn't open. It was broken, its upper pane spider-cracked around a small hole. A triangle of glass had hit the floor and shattered.

Lucy set her mug on the table and gingerly touched the edges of the hole. It wasn't from a bird smashing into her window, or an errant baseball. Too small.

A stone?

A bullet?

She spun around, her heart pounding.

It couldn't be. Not twice in one day.

She saw plaster dust on the chair next to the piano, directly across from the window. Above it was a hole in the wall.

Holding her breath, Lucy knelt on the chair and reached up, smoothing her hand over the hole. The edges of the wallpaper were rough. Plaster dust covered her fingertips.

The hole was empty. There was no bullet lodged there.

She sank onto her hands and knees and checked the floor. She looked under the piano. She flipped up the edges of the rug. She could feel the hysteria working its way into her, seeping into her pores, sending poison into every nerve ending.

She flopped back onto her butt and sat there on the floor. So, she thought. There it is. Some bastard had shot a hole in her dining room window, sneaked into her house, removed the bullet and sneaked back out again.

When? How? *Why?*

Wouldn't someone—Madison, J.T., Georgie, Rob, the damn mailman—have heard or seen *something?*

They'd run up to Manchester last night. It could have happened then, when no one was home.

The windows faced east across the side yard and the garage, the barn, Joshua Brook. A hunter or target shooter could have been in the woods near the brook and accidentally landed a stray bullet in her dining room, panicked, slipped inside and dug it out.

"Ha," she said aloud.

This was no accident.

Lucy was shaking, sick to her stomach. If she called the police, she'd be up all night. She'd have to explain to Madison and J.T. Rob's grandmother had a scanner—she'd call Rob, and he and Patti would come over.

And that was just the beginning. The police would call Washington. The Capitol Police would want to know if the incidents had anything to do with Jack Swift. He would be notified.

She staggered to her feet and picked up her tea.

Now was she desperate enough to ask Sebastian Redwing for help?

She ran into the kitchen, dumped her tea down the sink and locked the back door. She went into her bedroom to pack. "You need a dog," she muttered to herself. "That's all."

A big dog. A big dog that barked.

"A big, ugly dog that barks."

He'd take care of intruders, and she could train him to go fishing with J.T. Even Madison would like a dog.

That settled it. Never mind Redwing. When she got back from Wyoming, she'd see about getting a dog.

Two

Sebastian slipped off his horse and collapsed in the shade of a cottonwood. He was out on the far reaches of his property where no one could find him. Still, the bastards had. Two of them. In a damn Jeep. It was bouncing toward him. He could take his horse through the river, but the idiots would probably come after him.

He sipped water from his canteen, took off his hat and poured a little water over his head. He could use a shower. The air was hot and dusty. Dry. He hoped the dopes in the Jeep had water with them. He wasn't planning on sharing any of his canteen. Well, they could drink out of the river.

The Jeep got closer. "Easy," Sebastian told his horse, who didn't look too worried or even that hot.

A man jumped out just as the Jeep came to a stop about twenty yards off. "Mr. Redwing?"

Sebastian grimaced. It was never a good sign when someone called him Mr. Redwing. Not that chasing him in a Jeep was a good sign.

He tipped his hat over his eyes and leaned back on his elbows. "What?"

"Mr. Redwing," the man said. "I'm Jim Charger. Mr. Rabedeneira sent me to find you."

"So?"

Charger didn't speak. He was a new hire, probably waiting for Sebastian to get up and act like the man who'd founded and built Redwing Associates, a premier international security and investigative firm. Instead he kept his hat over his eyes, enjoying the relief from the Wyoming summer sun.

Finally, he sighed. Jim Charger wasn't going anywhere until he delivered his message. Sebastian liked Plato Rabedeneira. They'd been friends since their early twenties. He'd trust Plato with his life, the lives of his friends. But if Plato had been the other man in the Jeep, Sebastian would have tied him to this cottonwood and left him.

"Okay, Mr. Charger." He tipped his hat back and eyed the man in front of him. Tall, blond, very fit, dressed in expensive western attire that was no doubt dustier now than it had ever been. A Washington import. Probably ex-FBI. Sebastian could feel the blood pounding behind his eyes. "What's up?"

If Sebastian Redwing wasn't proving to be what

Jim Charger had expected, he kept it to himself. "Mr. Rabedeneira asked me to give you a message. He says to tell you Darren Mowery is back."

Sebastian made sure he had no visible reaction. Inside, the blood pounded harder behind his eyes. He'd left Mowery for dead a year ago. "Back where?"

"Washington."

"What's Plato want me to do about it?"

"I don't know. He asked me to deliver the message. He said to tell you it was important."

Darren Mowery hated Sebastian more than most of his enemies did. Once, Sebastian would have trusted Mowery with his life, with the lives of his friends. No more.

"One other thing," Charger said.

Sebastian smiled faintly. "This is the thing Plato said to tell me if I didn't jump in your Jeep with you?"

No reaction. "Mowery has made contact with a woman in Senator Swift's office."

Jack Swift, now the senior senator from the state of Rhode Island. A gentleman politician, a man of integrity and dedication to public service, father-in-law to Lucy Blacker Swift.

Damn, Sebastian thought.

At the reception following Lucy Blacker and Colin Swift's wedding, Colin had made Sebastian promise he'd look after Lucy if anything happened to him. "Not," Colin had said, "that Lucy will want looking after. But you know what I mean."

Sebastian hadn't, not really. He didn't have anyone in his life to look after. His parents were dead. He had no brothers and sisters, no wife, no children. Professionally, though, he was pretty damn good at looking after people. That mostly had to do with keeping them alive and their pockets from getting picked. It didn't have to do with friendship, a promise made to a man who would be dead thirteen years later at age thirty-six.

Colin must have known. Somehow, he must have guessed he would have a short life, and his wife and whatever children they had would end up having to go on without him.

When Sebastian had made his promise, he'd never imagined he'd have to keep it.

"What do you want me to tell Mr. Rabedeneira?" Charger asked.

Sebastian tilted his hat back over his eyes. A year ago, he'd shot Darren Mowery and thought he'd killed him. It was carelessness on his part he hadn't known until now whether Mowery was dead or alive. In his business, that kind of lapse was intolerable. There was no excuse. It didn't matter that Darren had once been his mentor, his friend, or that Sebastian had watched him send himself straight into hell. When you shot someone, you were supposed to find out if you'd killed him. It was a rule.

But this was about Jack Swift. It wasn't about Lucy. Plato would have to handle Darren Mowery. Given his personal involvement, Sebastian would only muck up the works.

"Tell Plato I'm retired," Sebastian said.

"Retired?"

"Yes. He knows. Remind him."

Charger didn't move.

Sebastian pictured Lucy on the front porch of his grandmother's house, and he could almost feel the Vermont summer breeze, hear the brook, smell the cool water, the damp moss. Lucy had needed to get out of Washington, and he'd made it happen. He'd kept his promise. He no longer owed Colin.

He decided to stop thinking about Lucy. It had never done him any good.

"You've delivered your message, Mr. Charger," Sebastian said. "Now go deliver mine."

"Yes, sir."

The man left. Sebastian suspected he hadn't lived up to Jim Charger's expectations. Well, that was fine with him. He didn't live up to his own expectations. Why should he live up to anyone else's?

He'd quit, and that was the end of it.

Barbara Allen fumbled for the keys to her Washington apartment. Acid burned in her throat. Sweat soaked her blouse, her dozens of mosquito bites stinging and itching. Part of her wanted to cry, part to scream with delight. Incredible! At last, she'd acted. At last!

She unlocked her door and pushed it open, gasping at the oppressive heat. She'd turned off the air-conditioning before she'd left for Vermont. Vermont had been cooler than Washington, wonderfully exhilarating. She quickly shut her door and leaned against it, letting herself breathe. She was home.

She had no regrets. None. This surprised her more than anything else. Intellectually, she knew what she'd done was wrong. Her obsession with Lucy was even, perhaps, a little sick. Normal people didn't spy on other people. Normal people didn't stalk and terrorize other people.

But if anyone deserved to live in fear, it was Lucy Blacker Swift. She was the worst kind of mother. Self-indulgent, impulsive, reckless. Colin had provided a necessary check against her worst excesses, but with his death, there was no one to rein her in.

For more than a year, Barbara had taken a secret thrill in sneaking up to Vermont on a Friday night to watch Lucy, heading back to Washington on Sunday. She was Jack Swift's eyes and ears, his confidante, his trusted personal assistant. She'd given twenty years of her life to him, suffered every loss with him. The ups and downs of his political career, the assassination attempt, the long, slow, painful death of his wife, the sudden death of his son.

Then, Lucy's galling decision to move to Vermont. It was the last straw. Barbara knew Jack was appalled at how she was raising his son's children. Madison, aching for a real life. J.T., running wild with his dirty little friends. But Jack would never say anything, never do anything to force Lucy to wake up.

Well, Barbara had. *At last, at last.*

Let people underestimate her. Let them take her for granted. She *knew*. She had the courage and self-discipline to do what needed to be done.

With one foot, she nudged her suitcase into the corner by the coat closet. She'd unpack later. She turned the air-conditioning on high and went into her living room. Like the rest of her apartment, it was simply decorated in contemporary furnishings, its clean lines and clean colors reflecting her strength of character. She despised anything cute or frilly.

She sat in a chair by the vent. Her apartment was in a nondescript building on the Potomac; it was one of the smallest units, with no view to speak of. Not that she spent much time here. She was in the office by eight and seldom out before seven.

She closed her eyes, feeling the cool air wash over her. She'd worn long pants and a long-sleeved shirt to hide her bug bites. Each one deserved a tiny Purple Heart. They were her badges of courage. It wasn't weakness that had made her act—it was strength, courage, conviction.

She'd been meticulous. She wasn't an idiot. She hadn't felt the need to do anything dramatic to conceal her presence. She'd stayed at a Manchester inn and driven a car she'd rented in Washington. She'd had a plausible cover story in case she had been discovered.

Oh, Lucy, I was just stopping in to see you and the kids. I took a few days off to go outlet shopping, do a little hiking. By the way, did you hear gunfire? I saw someone going up the dirt road over by the brook with a rifle. They must have been target practicing awfully close to your house.

It had never come to that. She'd conducted exhaustive surveillance before implementing her plan, even something as simple as the late-night hang-up. Lucy was too self-centered, too stupid, to catch her.

Firing into the dining room had been Barbara's supreme act. It was even better than the bullet on the front seat. That was just the proverbial icing on the cake. Barbara had waited until Lucy and the children left for Manchester. She was parked up on the dirt road, as if she were off to check out the falls. She crossed Joshua Brook, jumping from one rock to another, and dropped down low, working her way up the steep, wooded bank until Lucy's house came into view. She lay flat on her stomach in the brush. Mosquitoes buzzed in her ears, chewed on every inch of exposed skin. Her tremendous self-discipline kept her focused.

If she'd been caught then, at that moment, with her rifle aimed at Lucy's house, she'd have had no cover story. The risk—the challenge—was part of the thrill, more exhilarating even than she'd imagined.

Her father had taught her and her three sisters how to shoot. He had never said he wished he'd had a son, but they knew he did. Barbara was the youngest. The last, shattered hope. She'd become a very good shot. No one knew how good—certainly no one in Jack's office. Not even Jack himself. They knew her only in relation to her work, her devotion to her job and her boss.

Only after she'd fired and lay in the still, hot, prickly brush did she decide to go after the spent bullet. It wasn't concern over leaving behind evidence that propelled her across the yard behind the barn—it was the idea of further terrorizing Lucy, imagining her coming into her dining room and seeing the shattered window, then realizing someone had slipped inside to dig the bullet out of the wall.

The back door wasn't locked. Lucy often didn't

lock all her doors. Perhaps, Barbara thought, this would teach the silly twit a lesson.

The acid burned down her throat and into her stomach, gnawing at her insides. The urge to scare Lucy, throw her off her stride, had gripped her for days, consuming her. With each small act of harassment, Barbara felt a little better. The pressure lifted. The urge subsided. Now, she could think straight.

"So. You're back."

She jumped, suppressing a scream. "Darren, my God, you startled me. What are you doing here?"

He stepped over her feet and sat on the sofa. "Waiting for you."

Even knowing Darren Mowery, Barbara thought, was a calculated risk. She'd heard the rumors in Washington. He'd gone bad, he'd lost his company, he'd been killed in South America. He was dangerous. She knew that much. She smiled uneasily. "You could have turned on the air-conditioning."

"I'm not hot."

"You must be half lizard."

They'd bumped into each other a few weeks ago at a Washington restaurant and ended up having dinner a couple of times, although Barbara had no serious romantic interest in him—or he in her, as far as she could tell. She didn't know where their relationship would lead, but her instincts told her he was important. Somehow, Darren Mowery would help her get off the grinding treadmill that had become her life. Perhaps it was because of him that she'd finally taken action against Lucy.

"You disappeared for a week," he said.

"I didn't disappear. I took a few days off. I told you."

"Where did you go?"

She didn't answer right away. Darren was a man who'd want to believe he was in charge, that he had the upper hand. He was very handsome, she had to admit. Early fifties, silvery haired. He could have stood out in Washington if he'd wanted to. Instead, he chose to blend in with his conservative dark suits and country club casuals, his only distinguishing feature his superb physical condition. He was in better shape than many men half his age, but his reflexes were the real giveaway. This was not a man who'd spent the past thirty years behind a desk.

"I went outlet shopping," she said.

"Where?"

"New England." Let him think she was being evasive. She didn't care. She wanted him to know she was strong while at the same time believing he was stronger. It was a delicate balancing act.

He scratched one side of his mouth; he always looked relaxed, at ease with his surroundings. Yet he was observant, alert to every nuance around him.

Barbara knew she couldn't make a misstep with such a man. He'd probably searched her apartment, she realized; but she'd anticipated as much.

No, she had no illusions. She wasn't yet sure of the exact nature of the game they were playing, but she knew Darren Mowery would kill her if she crossed him. She had to be careful, strong, sure of herself. And smart. Smarter than he was.

"We've been dancing around each other long enough," he said. "Let's put our cards on the table. I want to know everything. No surprises."

What did that mean? Did he know about her and Lucy? Barbara dodged the little needle of uncertainty and suppressed the surge of excitement that finally they were getting down to it. She shrugged, nonchalant. "All right. You first."

He studied her. He had very blue eyes. Stone-cold blue eyes. "Lucy Swift left for Wyoming today."

It wasn't what Barbara expected. Another, weaker woman might have panicked, but she sat back in her chair and yawned. She was the personal assistant to a powerful United States senator, a professional accustomed to managing the unexpected. She already knew about Lucy's trip to Wyoming; she'd found out when she'd checked in with Jack's office yesterday. Lucy must have told Jack, and a member of his staff had left Barbara a routine message. The unexpected was that Darren knew. "Yes, I know.

Something to do with her adventure travel business, I believe.''

"Redwing Associates is based in Wyoming.''

"Ah, yes. Sebastian Redwing sold Lucy her house in Vermont. It belonged to his widowed grandmother. From what Jack tells me, he and Lucy aren't very good friends. Didn't Sebastian once work for you?'' She was tempted to pick at an itchy mosquito bite, but resisted. "I gather his company is doing very well.''

Mowery didn't react. Barbara liked that. It meant he had self-control. According to Washington gossip, there was no love lost between Sebastian Redwing and his old mentor. There was even talk that Mowery blamed Sebastian for the downfall of DM Consultants, Darren's private security firm.

Barbara supposed it was theoretically possible that Lucy would go whining to Sebastian about what had happened to her this week, but she doubted it. Lucy was quite determined to prove herself capable, independent—which, of course, she wasn't. Barbara had already calculated that Lucy wouldn't go to Jack or to the Capitol Police. Lucy wanted no part of being a Swift.

"I get the impression you don't like Lucy Swift very much,'' Darren said.

"I don't see what concern that is of yours.''

He leaned forward. "Cards on the table, Barbie.

I have a bone to pick with your boss. I want to make him sweat. And I want your help."

"My help?"

"I think you've got something on him," Mowery said, smug and confident.

"No. Senator Swift is a man of sterling integrity."

Mowery threw back his head and laughed.

Barbara pursed her lips. "I'm serious."

"Yeah, well, so am I. Barbie, Barbie." He shook his head at her, sighing. "Office gossip says you threw yourself at the old boy a couple weeks ago, and he laughed you out of his office."

Her stomach flipped over on her. "That's not true."

"What part? You didn't throw yourself at him or he didn't laugh?"

"You're disgusting. I want you to leave."

"No, you don't want me to leave. You want to help me settle a score with Jack Swift. You want to see him sweat. You want him to suffer for humiliating you."

"He—he wasn't prepared for the level of intimacy I offered, that's all. He was scared."

"Scared, huh?"

"He knows I've been there for him. Always. Forever."

Mowery's gaze bored through her. "What do you have on him?"

"Nothing!"

"Barbie, I'm going to put the squeeze on Senator Jack. I'm going to bleed him. You're going to watch, and you're going to enjoy the show." He reached over and touched her knee. "Revenge can be very sweet."

She said nothing.

His eyes narrowed, and he smiled. "Only it's not revenge you want, is it, Barbie? I get it now. You want Jack to suffer and come to you, the one woman who loves him unconditionally. This is precious. Truly precious."

"My motives," Barbara said, "are irrelevant."

"In twenty years, has old Jack ever made a pass at you?"

"He wouldn't. For much of that time he was a married man."

Mowery laughed out loud. "God, you're a riot. This is going to be fun."

She was on dangerous ground. Deadly ground.

Her stomach heaved, and she ran to the bathroom and vomited.

Oh, God. I can't do this.

But she had to. She'd given Darren Mowery all the signals. He *knew* this was what she wanted. Not just a chance to get back at Jack for spurning her, but a chance to provide him with the opportunity to come to her for help, to find solace in her strength and wisdom. She'd driven up to Vermont and harassed Lucy, hoping it would relieve the pressure of wanting to hurt Jack, too. But it hadn't. She loved him, and she wasn't one to give up easily on those she loved.

When she'd confided her love to him, Jack hadn't gotten angry with her or shown any passion, any heat, any depth of emotion. He'd been kind. Solicitous. Professional. He gave her the predictable speech about how much he appreciated her, how he felt affection for her as a member of his staff, and how together, over the past twenty years, they'd done so much good for the people of this great nation.

Blah-blah-blah. He'd even offered her a way out of her embarrassment, saying they'd all been under tremendous pressure and she should take a few days off.

Well, she had, hadn't she?

She splashed her face with cold water and stared at herself in the mirror. Her gray eyes were bloodshot from the effort of vomiting, the lashes clumped together from water and tearing. She was just forty-one, not old. She still could have children. She knew plenty of first-time mothers in their forties.

But she couldn't have Swift children. Jack didn't

want her. Twenty years of dedicated service, and what did she have to show for it?

Lucy was the one with the Swift children.

Barbara dried her face. She could have had Colin. She could have had the Swift children. Instead, she'd waited for Jack.

Darren opened the door behind her, and she placed a hand on the sink to steady herself. "I'm sorry. My stomach's a little off. It must be the heat."

He was so smug. "Blackmail's not a game for someone with a weak stomach."

That *was* what they were tiptoeing around—and had been right from the beginning. Blackmail. She nodded, cool. It was to her advantage for him to think he was the security expert with the murky past, the dark and dangerous insider convinced he knew how the "real world" worked better than a super-competent, desk-bound bureaucrat possibly could.

"Colin and I," she began. She swallowed, met Mowery's cold gaze. "We had an affair before he died. Jack doesn't know. Neither does Lucy. No one does."

"And?"

"And I have pictures."

Mowery nodded thoughtfully. "Kinky pictures?"

"You're disgusting."

"Well, if it's pictures of you two on his daddy's campaign trail—"

"By your standards, the pictures would be considered 'kinky.' By mine, they're proof of the physical and emotional bond we shared."

"Uh-huh."

"Do you want to see them?"

He rubbed his chin. "So you fucked the son, and the widowed daughter-in-law and the innocent grandkids don't know it."

"Must you be so coarse?"

"Listen to you, Barbie. You're the one who had an affair with another woman's husband. The boss's son. And this you tell me not two weeks after you threw yourself at the boss, presumably because you'd like to get some of him, too. Let's talk about who's 'coarse.'"

She was silent. Stricken.

"Well," Mowery said, "it's not pretty, but it could work."

"It will work. Jack will pay dearly to keep such information quiet." She straightened, eyed him coolly. She wanted him to think he was in control, not that she was a complete ninny. "If you're not convinced, walk out of here now. I'll forget we ever had this conversation."

He gave a curt laugh and started back down the hall to the living room. Without turning around, he motioned with one finger for her to follow.

Barbara joined him. She had to stiffen her muscles to keep herself from trembling. Goose bumps sprang up on her arms from the air-conditioning. She was cold now. Dehydrated. Not nervous, not afraid, she told herself. She was absolutely positive this was the best—the only—course of action.

"Here's the deal, Barbie. In for a penny, in for a pound. I don't do cold feet."

She raised her chin and met his gaze directly. "I'm not some weak-minded twit."

She sat stiffly on a chair and crossed her legs and arms, steeled herself against the cold of the air-conditioning, the itching, stinging bug bites, the insidious feeling that Mowery knew more about her than she realized. She had to remember the kind of work he did, remain on her guard.

Slowly, her shivering subsided.

"Did you fuck the son," he asked, "or are you just making that up because Jack doesn't want you?"

She remained calm, practicing the restraint she'd learned in twenty years as Jack Swift's most trusted aide. "Men like you don't understand loyalty and service, true commitment."

"Damn right we don't." He grinned, deeply amused by his own wit. "Well, it doesn't matter. You can have whatever little fantasies you want, Barbie."

"I'm not a woman taken to fantasizing."

Indeed not, she thought. She wouldn't have gone to Jack if she hadn't believed with all her heart, soul and mind that he wanted her to speak up, finally, after all these years. She didn't invent this sort of thing, not after two decades in Washington. She hadn't misread the cues. Jack Swift simply wasn't prepared to act on his own feelings. He had run. And now she needed to turn him back in the right direction, back to her.

Darren jumped up, grabbed both her hands and lifted her onto her feet. Her breath caught. What now? What was he doing? He was very muscular and strong. She could never physically overpower him. She had to rely on her wits, her intelligence and incredible self-discipline.

There was nothing sexual in the way he held her. "How long has it been, Barbie? How long since you've had a man?" He squeezed her waist, choking the air from her. "Not since Colin Swift? Not ever?"

"That's none of your business." She kept her tone deliberately cold, in control. "Our relationship is strictly professional. We are partners in a scheme to blackmail a United States senator. That's *all*."

He squeezed harder, painfully. She couldn't move. "No surprises, Barbie. Understand? If this is going to work, I know everything."

"I told you—"

"Did you have an affair with Colin Swift?"

"Yes."

This had to be a test. She didn't know what to do to pass. Run screaming? Beg him to make love to her? Slap him?

No, she thought. Hold your ground. She wanted him to underestimate her, not to think he could roll over her.

"You stereotype me at your own peril, Mr. Mowery," she said. "I'm not some dried-up prune pining for a man I can't have."

"Where were you last week?"

"On vacation. I hit outlet stores all over New England."

"Vermont?"

"What?"

He moved his hands higher, squeezing her ribs. "Did you go to Vermont?"

"I can't breathe—"

"You can say yes or no."

She nodded, gasping. "Yes."

"Did you see Lucy Swift?"

She shook her head, unable to speak.

"She decided to go to Wyoming at the last minute. She paid top dollar for the tickets. She took her kids. I want to know why."

"I can't—breathe—I—"

He eased up, just slightly.

Barbara coughed, gulping in air. "Goddamn you—"

"Tell me about Lucy."

"I don't *know* anything. You'll have to ask her yourself. I went outlet shopping in Manchester one day. That's all."

Lying to him was dangerous, Barbara thought, but telling the truth had to be more dangerous.

He traced the skin just under her breasts with his thumbs. He had no sexual interest in her. His focus on his mission was total. He wasn't that complicated a man, Barbara thought, and she wasn't that undesirable a woman. Obviously his obsession with Jack Swift was something she needed to better understand.

His gaze was cold even as he released her. "Arnica," he said.

She rubbed her sides. "What?"

"Rub in a little arnica oil for the bruises."

She headed back to the bathroom. This time she didn't throw up. She washed her hands, closed the lid on the toilet and sat down. She was risking everything. She had a stimulating career, a nice apartment, a fabulous set of friends. There were men who wanted her. Good, successful men.

She didn't have to let a scummy Darren Mowery fondle her in her own living room.

After Jack had dispatched her, so politely, as if

she were pathetic, she'd learned he was seeing Sidney Greenburg, a curator at the Smithsonian—fifty years old, never married, no children. Why her? Why not Barbara?

Sidney was one of Lucy's Washington friends.

I could have married Colin. I didn't have to wait for Jack.

"Barbara?"

Darren was outside the door. She didn't move.

"Here's how it's going to go down," he said. "I'll approach Jack. I'll put the squeeze on him. He's not going to risk his own reputation or sully his dead son's reputation. He'll pay. And you'll get ten percent."

She jumped up and tore open the door. "Ten percent! Forget it. I'll call the police right now. You'd have nothing without me. *I* had the affair with Colin. *I* have the pictures."

"You won't call the police," Darren said calmly.

"I *will*. You're threatening a United States senator."

"Barbara. Please." He was cold, supercilious. "If you make one wrong move once this thing gets started, I'll be there. Trust me. You won't want that."

Her stomach turned in on itself. She clutched it in silent agony. What if Lucy went crying to Sebas-

tian Redwing because of her harassment campaign?
"Bastard."

"Bingo. You got that one right."

Barbara held up her chin, summoning twenty
years of experience at using other people's arrogance to her own advantage. And to Jack's. "Jack
couldn't survive a week in this town without me,
and he knows it. When he comes to me, you'd better
be far away. That's your only warning."

"Oh, is it? Get this straight, Barbie." Mowery
leaned in close, enunciated each word clearly. "I
don't care if you fucked Swift father and son at the
same time. I don't care if you made up the whole
goddamn thing. We're putting this show on the road,
and we're doing it my way."

Acid rose up in her throat. "I can't believe I let
you touch me."

He laughed. "And you will again, Barbie. Trust
me on that."

He swaggered back down the hall. She spat at his
back, missing by yards. He laughed harder.

"Fifty percent," she yelled.

He stopped, glanced back at her.

She was choking for air. Dear God, what had she
done? "I want fifty percent of the take."

"The take? Okay, Dick Tracy. I'll give you
twenty-five percent."

"Fifty. I deserve it."

He winked at her. "I like you, Barbie. You got the short end of the stick with the Swifts, and you keep on fighting. Yep. I like you a lot."

"I'm serious. I want fifty percent."

"Barbie, maybe you should think this through." He rocked back on his heels. "I'm not a very nice man. I expect you know that by now. My sympathy for you only goes so far."

She hesitated. Her head was spinning. This wasn't a time for cold feet, any sign of weakness. "Twenty-five percent, then," she said.

Jack Swift poured himself a second glass of wine. It was a dry apple-pear wine from a new winery in his home state. He toasted Sidney Greenburg, who was still on her first glass. "To the wines of Rhode Island."

She laughed. "Yes, but not to this particular bottle. I love fruit wines, Jack, but this one's pure rotgut."

He laughed, too. "It is, isn't it? Well, I've never been much of a wine connoisseur. A good scotch—that's something I can understand."

It was a very warm, humid, still evening. They were sitting out in the tiny brick courtyard of his Georgetown home. Rhode Island, his home state, the state he'd represented first in the House, then in the Senate, seemed far away tonight. This was where he'd raised his son, where he'd nursed his wife through her long, losing battle with cancer. They were both gone now. He'd been tempted to sell the house. He'd bought it in his early days in Washington; it'd go for a mint. He'd even debated quitting the Senate. Barbara Allen had talked him out of both. Over twenty years, she'd saved him from many a precipitous move.

"I don't know what to do, Sidney." He stared at the pale wine. He and Sidney had been discussing Barbara Allen most of the evening. "She's been with me since she was a college intern."

"You're not going to do anything."

"I can't just pretend—"

"Yes, you can, and you'll be doing her a favor if you do."

Sidney set her glass on the garden table. That she had such affection for him was a constant source of amazement. He was an old widower, a gray-haired, paunchy United States senator who wasn't eaten up with his own self-importance. She was a striking woman, with very dark eyes and dark hair liberally streaked with gray. She wore little makeup, and she complained about carrying more weight than she liked around her hips and thighs; Jack hadn't noticed. She was intelligent, kind, experienced and self-assured, comfortable in her own skin. She'd worked with Lucy's parents at the Smithsonian and had known Lucy since she was a little girl, long before Lucy had met Colin.

"Listen to me, Jack," she said. "Barbara is not a pathetic woman. You are not to feel sorry for her because she's forty and unmarried. If she's given herself to her job to the exclusion of her personal life, that was her choice. Allow her the dignity of having made that choice. And don't assume just because she doesn't have a husband and children, she must not have a full life."

"I haven't! I wouldn't—"

"Of course, you would. People do it all the time." She smiled, taking any edge off her words. "If Barbara Allen's feeling a little goofy and off-center right now, accept it at face value and give her a chance to get over it."

Jack sighed. "She practically threw herself at me."

"And I suppose you've never had a *married* woman throw herself at you?"

"Well…"

"Come on, Jack. If Barbara's nuts unmarried, she'd be nuts married."

He held back a smile. As educated and refined as Sidney was, she did know how to cut to the chase. "I didn't say she was nuts."

"That's my point exactly." Her eyes shone, and she spoke with conviction, laughing at his frown.

"You are a very dense man for someone who has to go before the people for votes. Jack, the woman made a pass at you. It's been three years since Colin's death, five years since Eleanor's death. You've only just begun dating again. I see her actions as—" She shrugged. "Perfectly normal."

He drank more of his wine. The damn stuff all tasted the same to him, whether it was made from pears, apples or grapes. "Maybe so."

"But?"

"I don't know."

"The unmarried forty-year-old in the office makes people nervous. They never know if she's a little dotty, living in squalor with twenty-five cats."

"That's archaic, Sidney."

She waved a hand dismissively. "It's true. If Barbara were married and made a pass at you, you'd be flattered. You wouldn't sit here squirming over what to do. You'd think she was a normal, healthy woman." She grabbed up his hand. "Jack, I've *been* there."

"No one could ever think you were off your gourd."

She smiled. "I have two cats. I've been known to feed them off the china."

He saw the twinkle in her eye and laughed. That was what he treasured about Sidney most of all. She made him laugh. She was quick-witted, self-deprecating, irreverent. She didn't take her job, herself, or life inside the Beltway too seriously.

But Jack couldn't shake a lingering sense of uneasiness. "There's still something about Barbara."

"Then there's something about Barbara. Period."

"I see what you're saying—"

"Finally!" Sidney fell back against her chair, as if his denseness had exhausted her. "Now, can we change the subject?"

He smiled. "Gladly."

She gave him an impish grin. "Let's talk about my cats."

Sidney didn't stay the night. They both had unusual Saturday meetings, but Jack knew that really wasn't the issue. "I'm just not ready to hang my panty hose in a senator's bathroom," she said breezily, kissing him good-night.

He remembered her counsel the next morning when he arrived in his office at eight and Barbara Allen, as ever, was at her desk. Before he could say a word, she gave him a bright smile. "Good morning, Senator."

"Good morning, Barbara. I thought you were still on vacation."

She waved a hand. "It was a few days off, not a vacation. I always planned to be back for this meeting. I know it's important."

He smiled. "Well, then, how were your few days off?"

"Perfect," she said. "Just what I needed."

She flipped around in her chair and tapped a few keys on her computer. She looked great, Jack thought—relaxed, polished, professional, with none of the wild desperation that had made them both so uncomfortable the week before.

Relief washed over him. A little time away had done the trick. He would follow Sidney's advice and pretend nothing had happened. It wasn't just a question of doing Barbara a favor—he was doing himself a favor, too. He needed her efficiency, knowledge and competence, her long years of experience.

He headed into his private office. Thank God, she was back to her old self.

Three

"Bastian Redwing saved Daddy's life?"

Madison sighed at her brother with exaggerated patience. "It's not *Bastian*. It's *Sebastian*. And he saved Dad *and* Grandpa. Some other guy saved the president."

J.T. frowned. "How come I don't remember?"

"Because you weren't born."

"Madison doesn't remember, either," Lucy said. "It happened before your dad and I were married."

"I read the articles," Madison reminded her mother.

J.T. kicked the back of her seat. They'd rented a car when they'd arrived in Jackson yesterday, and this morning Lucy had dutifully met with the western guides, who were wonderful and all but told her outright she had no business trying to expand out west. No surprise there.

Afterwards, she'd almost talked herself out of following her hotel desk clerk's directions to see Sebastian. Almost. She still had time to turn around and go back to Jackson.

"Was it an assassination attempt?" J.T. asked. "Tell me!"

Madison was horrified. "Mom, how does he know something like 'assassination attempt'? That shouldn't be in a twelve-year-old's vocabulary."

J.T. snorted from the back seat. "Oh, yeah? Then how am I supposed to know about Abraham Lincoln and Martin Luther King? And President Kennedy and Julius Caesar?"

"Julius Caesar?" Madison swung around at him. "You don't know anything about Julius Caesar."

"He was stabbed in the back."

"You're sick."

"*You're* sick."

Lucy gripped the steering wheel. She was on a stretch of clear, straight road, trying to enjoy the breathtaking Wyoming scenery. The mountains surrounding the long, narrow valley, she thought, were incredible. She'd pointed out the different vegetation to Madison and J.T., explained about the altitude, the dry air. But they wanted to discuss Sebastian Redwing and how he'd saved their father's life.

Lucy gave up and told the story. "The president was giving a speech in Newport, Rhode Island.

Someone got in with a gun and started firing. Sebastian knocked Grandpa and Dad to the floor, while the man he worked for at the time, Darren Mowery, tackled the shooter.''

"Was anyone hurt?" J.T. asked.

"Sebastian spotted a second shooter, who'd actually helped the other guy get inside. Sebastian, your dad and another man, Plato Rabedeneira, a parachute rescue jumper who was being honored, went after him. The man shot Plato in the shoulder, but it wasn't serious.''

"What happened to the shooter?"

Lucy hesitated. "Sebastian killed him.''

"Sebastian had a gun? Why?" J.T. was into the story now. "What was he doing there?"

How to explain Sebastian Redwing? All J.T. knew about him was that he'd sold them their house. Lucy slowed the car. "Sebastian was a security consultant. He was very young—he and Darren Mowery, his boss, were after the shooter for some other reason. They had no idea they'd get mixed up in an attempt to assassinate the president of the United States."

"Dad, Plato and Sebastian all became friends," Madison added. "Sebastian was the best man at Mom and Dad's wedding."

J.T. was hopelessly confused. "I don't get it."

His sister moaned. "What is there to 'get'?"

"Sebastian has his own company now, J.T.," Lucy said. "Redwing Associates. It's based here in Wyoming. He and Plato and Dad weren't able to see as much of each other as they'd have liked."

That seemed to satisfy her son.

"At least Sebastian had the sense to get out of Vermont," Madison said.

They came to a cluster of log buildings set in a grassy, rolling meadow. No marker announced this was the base and main training facility for Redwing Associates, an international investigative and security firm with clients ranging from business executives and government officials to high-profile entertainers and sports figures. Many came here, to Wyoming, to learn for themselves how to assess, prevent and manage the risks they faced, whether it was kidnapping, assassination, corporate espionage, disgruntled ex-employees, obsessed fans or computer fraud.

Security was subtle but not unnoticeable. When Lucy came to the end of the long, winding driveway, a man in casual western attire introduced himself. "I'm Jim Charger, Mrs. Swift. I'll take care of your car. Mr. Rabedeneira is expecting you."

She tried to smile. "Plato Rabedeneira?"

Jim Charger didn't return her smile. "That's right, ma'am."

What was Plato doing here? And why was he expecting her? Lucy fought off a rush of uneasiness. "Well, I guess you guys really are that good, aren't you?"

Still no smile. "Your children can stay out here with me or go in with you. Your choice."

"They'll go with me."

He motioned for her to go into the sprawling main house, its rustic log construction deceiving. This was no ordinary ranch house. No expense had been spared in its furnishings of wood, leather and earth-colored fabrics. The views were astounding. Not one square inch of it reminded her of Sebastian's roots in southern Vermont.

Plato joined her in the living room, in front of a massive stone fireplace. He took both her hands and kissed her on the cheek. "Hello, Lucy. I heard you were in the area."

"You must have spies on every corner."

"Not *every* corner."

He laughed, dropping her hands. He was a dark-haired, dark-eyed, intensely handsome man who'd worked his way out of a very tough Providence neighborhood into a very tough profession, where he'd excelled. He'd helped his mother, who'd raised him alone, earn her college degree; she was now a professor at a community college, and one of Jack Swift's constituents.

Colin, Lucy thought, had never been tempted to

jump out of a helicopter into the teeth of a storm to rescue fishermen and yachters. He had been content with his work at the State Department and testing himself on the tennis court—which had killed him.

"When did you start working for Redwing Associates?" Lucy asked.

"I was injured in a rescue jump eighteen months ago. When I woke up from surgery, my summons from Sebastian was waiting for me." He turned to Madison and J.T., both obviously enthralled. "Well, you two have grown up. It's great to see you."

He was so charming, Lucy thought. She would feel safe if she had to dangle from a rescue helicopter over churning seas with him. Colin had been well-mannered and kind, a man people tended to like automatically. Sebastian Redwing, she thought, was none of the above. He wasn't charming, well-mannered, kind or likeable. He wouldn't care about making her or anyone else feel safe. That, he would say, was up to them. He was just very, very good at what he did.

"You kids want a grand tour of the place?" Plato asked. "Go back out front. Tell Mr. Charger I'd like him to show you around."

The prospect of a tour clearly excited J.T. more than it did Madison, who seemed transfixed by her father's ultra-fit, very good-looking friend. But she went along with her brother, and Lucy suddenly felt self-conscious, even a little foolish. Redwing Associates dealt with real threats and real dangers. Kidnapping, extortion, terrorist attacks. Not late-night hang-ups and bullets dropped through an open car window.

"You're looking well, Lucy," Plato said, eyeing her.

"Thanks."

"How's Vermont?"

"Great—I have my own adventure travel company. It's doing surprisingly well for a relatively new company."

"I don't get adventure travel, I'll admit."

She smiled. "That's because you've had to clean up after too many adventures gone wrong. Safety is our first priority, you'll be glad to know."

He moved to the leather chair, and she noticed his slight limp. It would never do in the demanding world he'd left, and at Redwing Associates, it would keep him behind a desk.

He dropped onto the couch, his expression turning serious. "You want to tell me why you're here?"

"I had business in Jackson. I just thought I'd stop in and say hello."

"You didn't know I'd be here," he pointed out.

"I know, but Sebastian—"

"Lucy. Come on. Since when would you or anyone else make a special trip to say hello to Sebastian?"

She sat on the edge of a wood-armed chair, thinking it would be nice if she could just sit here and visit with an old friend, reminisce about the past, forget the bullet hole in her dining room wall.

Of course, Plato would see through her half-hearted story. Cold feet were probably common in both his past and current work.

At least Plato had sent flowers and written a card when Colin died. He couldn't get away for the funeral, he said, but if she ever needed anything, she had only to let him know. He'd be there. Colin had trusted him, too. But, possibly because of the different nature of their work—or their personalities—it was Sebastian he'd made her promise to go to if she ever needed help.

"Has he changed?" she asked.

"That depends on your point of view. Look," Plato said, "why don't you tell me what's going on. Then we can figure out what to do about it."

Meaning, whether she needed to bring it to Sebastian's attention.

Lucy twisted her hands together. At home, in her business, she was at ease, confident, capable. This was foreign ground for her. Sebastian Redwing and Plato Rabedeneira had been her husband's friends. She and Colin had fallen in love so fast, marrying within two months of their first date. Madison had come along the next year. Then J.T. And then Colin was gone.

She really didn't know Plato *or* Sebastian.

"Lucy?"

"It's silly. I'm being silly, and I know it. So please feel free to pat me on the head and send me back to Vermont." She leveled her eyes on him. "Trust me, you'd be doing me a favor."

"Well, before I do any head-patting, why don't you tell me what's going on first. Okay?"

She nodded, gulped in a breath and told him everything. She kept her tone unemotional and objective, and left out nothing except her own reactions, the palpable sense of fear, the nausea.

When she finished, she managed another smile. "You see? Pure silliness."

Plato rose stiffly, his limp more noticeable as he walked to the massive stone fireplace. He looked back at her, his dark eyes serious. "You won't go to the local police?"

"If you're convinced it's the best thing to do, I'll consider it. But they'll call Jack."

He nodded. "That might not be such a bad idea."

"These incidents—whatever they are—have nothing to do with him."

"Maybe not. The point is, you don't know why they're happening."

Lucy ran a hand through her hair. She felt light-headed, a little sick to her stomach. Jet lag, the dry air and the altitude were all taking their toll. So was reliving the events of the past week.

"Either there's no connection at all between these incidents," she said, "or someone's just trying to get under my skin. If I go to the police, it proves they succeeded."

"And if they don't get the desired reaction from you, the incidents could escalate."

"Damn." She sank back against the couch and kicked out her legs. "I don't have a clue what the 'desired reaction' is. Coming out here? Fine, the bastard can declare victory and get out of my life. Running screaming into the night? Forget it." She jumped to her feet. "I won't fall apart for anyone."

"What does your gut tell you?" His voice was quiet, soothing. Plato was very good at caring.

"I don't *know*." Lucy paced on the thick, dark carpet. "Plato, I'm not a normal person. I'm the widowed daughter-in-law of a United States senator. You know damn well Jack will send in the Capitol Police."

"Lucy—"

"I have a business to tend. I have kids to raise. Damn it, I'm all Madison and J.T. have. I'm not going to put myself in undue danger, but I won't— Plato, if I can possibly avoid it, I'd rather not have

Jack and a bunch of feds mucking around in my life.''

Plato placed an arm around her shoulders. ''It's okay. I understand. Look, I have to be in Frankfurt this next week—''

''I wasn't hinting you should drop everything and come to my rescue. I just wanted an expert opinion.'' She smiled a little. ''It felt good to tell someone.''

He smiled back, but shook his head, giving her upper arm a gentle squeeze. ''You didn't come for *my* expert opinion.''

''I would have if I'd known you were here. I'd much rather tell my troubles to you than Sebastian.''

He laughed. ''Who wouldn't?''

''Good. Then it's settled. I'll trust my gut instincts. I'll go home and hope nothing else happens—''

''No, Lucy, you're going to see Sebastian and tell him everything.''

''Isn't he going to Frankfurt?''

''No way. He's…'' Plato frowned, walking her toward the door. He seemed to be searching for the right words. ''He's on sabbatical.''

''Sabbatical? Come on, Plato. It's not like he's some kind of professor. How can he—''

''You'll have to drive out to his cabin,'' Plato said. ''It's not that far. I'll give you directions.''

Lucy slipped from his embrace and stood rock-still in the middle of the hall. He kept walking, his back to her. She was blinking rapidly, as if that might somehow clear her head.

"I don't want to see Sebastian," she said.

Plato turned back to her. "He can help you, Lucy. I can't."

"I told you, I didn't come here for help."

"I know why you came here." His dark, dark eyes seemed to burn into her. "You promised Colin you would."

Her throat caught. "Plato..."

"Colin was right to send you to Sebastian. Lucy, I did rescues, and now I keep this company out of hot water. Sebastian's a son of a bitch in a lot of ways, but he's the best."

Lucy stood her ground. "What if I drive on out of here without seeing him?"

"Then I'll have to tell him what you told me."

She eyed him. "I have a feeling that would be worse."

He gave her a devilish smile. "Much worse."

Plato's directions were simple. He put Lucy on a dirt road and said to keep going until she couldn't go anymore. She'd know when she reached Sebastian.

Lucy wasn't encouraged. However, not finishing

what she'd stupidly started seemed to carry more risks than finishing. If he told Sebastian her story, Plato might exaggerate. Then Sebastian might end up in Vermont, and she'd really be in a mess. Sebastian might be worse than the feds. He might be worse than the occasional stray bullet through her dining room window.

So *why* had she dragged herself and her two children out to Wyoming?

The road was winding, dry, hot and dusty. The scenery was spectacular. Wide-open country, mountains rising up from the valley floor, a snaking river, horses and cattle and wildflowers. Despite its other uses, this was still a working ranch.

J.T. loved it. Madison endured. "I'm pretending I'm Meryl Streep in *Out of Africa*," she said. "That might keep me awake."

"The high altitude is probably making you sleepy," Lucy said.

"I'm not sleepy, I'm bored."

"Madison."

She checked herself. "Sorry."

The road narrowed even more, their car kicking up so much dust Lucy made a mental note to run it through a car wash before taking it back to the rental agency. Finally, they came to a tiny, ramshackle log cabin and small outbuilding tucked into the shade of a cluster of aspens and firs. The road ended.

Lucy pulled in behind a dusty red truck. "Well," she said. "I guess this is it."

"Oh, yuck." Madison surveyed the pathetic buildings. "This is like Clint Eastwood in *Unforgiven*."

From *Out of Africa* to *Unforgiven*. Lucy smiled. Madison kept the local video store in an uproar trying to track down movies for her. It was an interest one of her teachers, in the school she so loathed, encouraged.

Three scroungy, big mutts bounded out from the shade and surrounded their car, barking and growling as if they'd never seen a stranger. J.T., his seat belt off, nervously stuck his head up front. "Do you think they bite?"

"I bet they have fleas," Madison said.

Lucy judiciously decided to roll down her window and see how the dogs reacted. They didn't jump. Possibly a good sign. "Hello," she called out the window. "Anyone around?"

She checked for any venomous, antisocial bumper stickers on the truck, like Vermonters Go Home. Nothing. Just rust.

The dogs suddenly went silent. The yellow Lab mix yawned and stretched. The German shepherd mix plopped down and scratched himself. The smallest of the three—an unidentifiable mix that had resulted in a white coat with black and brown splotches—paced and panted.

"You kids hear anyone call them off?" Lucy asked.

J.T. shook his head, his eyes wide. This was more adventure than he'd bargained for, out in the wilds of Wyoming with three grouchy dogs and no friendly humans in sight. "No, did you?"

Madison huffed. "Plato should have sent us with an armed guard."

Lucy sighed. "Madison, that doesn't help."

"You're scaring me," J.T. said.

"You two stay here while I go see if we have the right place." Lucy unfastened her seat belt and climbed out of the car. The air seemed hotter, even drier. The dogs paid no attention to her. She smiled at her nervous son. "See, J.T.? It's okay."

He nodded dubiously.

"Relax, Lucy." The male voice seemed to come from nowhere. "You've got the right place."

J.T. swooped across the back seat and pointed at the cabin. "There! Someone's on the porch!"

Lucy shot her children a warning look. "Stay here."

She mounted two flat, creaky, dusty steps onto the unprepossessing porch. An ancient, ratty rope hammock hung from rusted hooks. In it lay a dust-covered man with a once-white cowboy hat pulled down over his face. He wore jeans, a chambray shirt with its sleeves rolled up to the elbows, cowboy boots. All of it was scuffed, worn.

Lucy noted the long legs, the flat stomach, the muscled, tanned forearms and the callused, tanned hands. Sebastian Redwing, she remembered, had always been a very physical man.

The yellow Lab lumbered onto the porch and collapsed under the hammock in a *kalumph* that seemed to shake the entire cabin.

"Sebastian?"

The man pushed the hat off his face. It, too, was dusty and tanned, and more lined and angular than she remembered. His eyes settled on her. Like everything else, they seemed the color of dust. She remembered they were gray, an unusual, surprisingly soft gray. "Hello, Lucy."

Her mouth and lips were dry from the long drive, the low western humidity. "Plato sent me."

"I figured."

"I'm in Wyoming on business. I have the kids with me. Madison and J.T."

He said nothing. He didn't look as if he planned to move from the hammock.

"Mom! J.T.'s bleeding!"

Madison, panicked, leaped out of the car and dragged her brother from the back seat. He cupped his hands under his nose, blood dripping through his fingers.

"Oh, gross," his sister said, standing back as she thrust a paper napkin at him.

Lucy ran toward them. "Tilt your head back."

The German shepherd barked at J.T. Sebastian gave a low, barely audible command from his hammock, and the dog backed off.

J.T., struggling not to cry, stumbled up onto the porch. "I bled all over the car."

Madison was right behind him. "He did, Mom."

Sebastian materialized at Lucy's side. She'd forgotten how tall and lean he was, how uneasy she'd always felt around him. Not afraid. Just uneasy. He glanced at J.T. "Kid's fine. It's the dry air and the dust."

Madison gaped at him. Lucy concentrated on her bleeding son. "May we use your sink?"

"Don't have one. You can get water from the pump out back." He eyed Madison. "You know how to use an outdoor pump?"

She shook her head.

"Time you learned." He was calm, his voice quiet if not soothing. "Lucy, you can bring J.T. inside. Madison and I will meet you."

She shrank back, her eyes widening.

Lucy said, "It's okay, Madison."

Sebastian frowned, as if he couldn't fathom what

about him would be a cause for concern—a dusty man in an isolated cabin with three dogs and no running water. He started down the steps. Madison took a breath and followed, glancing back at Lucy and mouthing, "Unabomber."

Lucy got J.T. inside. The prosaic exterior did not deceive. In addition to no running water, there was no electricity. It was like being catapulted back a century to the frontier.

"It's just a nosebleed," J.T. said, stuffing the paper napkin up his nose. "I'm fine."

Lucy grabbed a ragged dish towel from a hook above a wooden counter. The kitchen. There was oatmeal, cornmeal, coffee, cans of beans, jars of salsa and, incongruously, a jug of pure Vermont maple syrup.

In a few minutes, Madison came through the back door with a pitted aluminum pitcher of water. Lucy dipped in the towel. "I think you've stopped bleeding, J.T. Let's just get you cleaned up, okay?" She glanced at her daughter. "Where's Sebastian?"

"Out taming wild horses or hunting buffalo, I don't know. *Mom*. He doesn't even have a bathroom."

"This place is pretty rustic."

Madison groaned. "Clint Eastwood, *Unforgiven*. I told you."

Sebastian walked in from the front porch.

"What's she doing watching R-rated movies? She's not seventeen."

"That's without a parent or parental permission." Lucy stifled an urge to tell him to mind his own damn business, but since he hadn't invited her to come out here, she kept her mouth shut. "Madison's a student of film history. I watched *Unforgiven* with her because it's so violent."

He frowned at her. "I'm not violent."

Lucy had always considered him a man of controlled violence in a violent profession, but before she could say anything, Madison jumped in. "But you live like Eastwood in that opening scene with his two children—"

"No, I don't. I don't have hogs."

That obviously settled it as far as he was concerned. Lucy shook her head at Madison to keep her from arguing her point. For once, her daughter took the hint.

"How's J.T.?" Sebastian asked.

"He's better," Lucy said. "Thanks for your help."

J.T. kept the wet towel pressed to his nose. "It doesn't hurt."

"Good." Sebastian didn't seem particularly worried. "You two kids can go down to the barn and look at the horses while I talk to your mother. Dogs'll go with you."

"Come on, J.T.," Madison said, playing the protective big sister for a change. "The barn can't be any worse than this place."

She and her brother retreated, both getting dirtier with every passing minute. If the dry air, dust and altitude bothered Madison, she'd never admit it.

Sebastian grunted. "Kid has a mouth on her."

"They're both great kids," Lucy said.

He turned to her. She was intensely aware of the silence. No hum of fans or air-conditioning, no cars, not even a bird twittering. "I'm sure they are."

"Plato said you were on some kind of sabbatical."

"Sabbatical? So that's what he's saying now. Hell. I have to remember his mother's a professor."

"You're not—"

Something in his eyes stopped her. Lucy could count on one hand the times she'd actually seen Sebastian Redwing, but she remembered his unnerving capacity to make her think he could see into her soul. She expected it was a skill that helped him in his work. She wondered if it was part of why he was living out here. Perhaps he'd seen too much. Most likely, he just didn't want to be around people.

"Tell me why you're here," he said.

"I promised Colin." It sounded so archaic when she said it. She pushed back her hair, too aware of herself for her own comfort. "I told him if I ever needed help, I'd come to you. So, here I am. Except I really don't need your help, after all.''

''You don't?''

She shook her head. ''No.''

''Good. I'd hate for you to have wasted a trip.'' He started back across the worn floorboards toward the porch. ''I'm not in the helping business.''

She was stunned. ''What?''

''Plato'll feed you, get you back on the road before dark.''

Lucy stared at his back as he went out onto the porch. In the cabin's dim light, she saw an iron bed in one corner of the room, cast-off running shoes, a book of Robert Penn Warren poetry, a stack of James Bond novels and one of Joe Citro's books of Vermont ghost stories. There was also a kerosene lamp.

This was not what she'd expected. Redwing Associates was high-tech and very serious, one of the best investigative and security consulting firms in the business. Sebastian's brainchild. He knew his way around the world. If nothing else, Lucy had expected she might have to hold him back, keep him from moving too fast and too hard on her behalf.

Instead, he'd turned her down flat. Without argument. Without explanation.

She took a breath. The dust, altitude and dry air hadn't given her a bloody nose like they had J.T.

They'd just driven every drop of sanity and common sense right out of her. She *never* should have come here.

She followed him out onto the porch. "You're going to take my word for it that I don't need help?"

"Sure." He dropped back into his hammock. "You're a smart lady. You know if you need help or not."

"What if it was all bluster? What if I'm bluffing? What if I'm too proud and—"

"And so?"

She clenched her fists at her sides, resisting an urge to hit something. "Plato fudged it when he said you were on sabbatical, didn't he? I'll bet Madison was more right than she realized."

"Lucy, if I wanted you to know about my life, I'd send you Christmas cards." He grabbed his hat and lay back in the hammock. "Have you ever gotten a Christmas card from me?"

"No, and I hope I never do."

She spun around so abruptly, the blood rushed out of her head. She reeled, steadying herself. Damn if she'd let herself pass out. The bastard would dump a pitcher of well water on her head, strap her to a horse and send her on her way.

"I'm sorry, Lucy. Things change." She couldn't tell if he'd softened, but thought he might have. "I guess you know that better than most of us."

She turned back to him and inhaled, regaining some semblance of self-control. She was furious with herself for having come out here—and with Plato for having sent her when he had to know the reception she'd get. She was out of her element, and she hated it. "That's it, then? You're not going to help me?"

He gave her a half smile and pulled his hat back down over his eyes. "Who're you kidding, Lucy Blacker? You've never needed anyone's help."

Plato didn't come for Sebastian until early the next morning. Very early. Dawn was spilling out on the horizon, and Sebastian, having tended the horses and the dogs, was back in his hammock when Plato's truck pulled up. He thumped onto the porch, his gait uneven from his limp. It'd be two years soon. He'd have the limp for life.

"You turned Lucy down?"

Sebastian tilted his hat back off his eyes. "So did you."

"She didn't come out here for my help. She came for yours."

"She hates me, you know."

Plato grinned. "Of course, she hates you. You're a jackass and a loser."

Sebastian didn't take offense. Plato had always been one to speak out loud what others were thinking. "Her kid bled on my porch. How am I going to protect a twelve-year-old kid who gets nose-bleeds? The daughter's a snot. She kept comparing me to Clint Eastwood."

"Eastwood? Nah. He's older and better-looking than you." Plato laughed. "I guess Lucy and her kids are lucky you've renounced violence."

"We're all lucky."

Silence.

Sebastian felt a gnawing pain in his lower back. He'd slept in the hammock. A bad idea.

"You didn't tell her, did you?" Plato asked.

"Tell her what?"

"That you've renounced violence."

"None of her business. None of yours, either."

If his curtness bothered Plato, he didn't say. "Darren Mowery's hanging around her father-in-law."

"Shut up, Rabedeneira. You're like a damn rooster crowing in my ear."

Plato stepped closer. "This is Lucy, Sebastian."

He rolled off the hammock. That was what he'd been thinking all night. This was Lucy. Lucy Blacker, with the big hazel eyes and the bright smile and the smart mouth. Lucy, Colin's widow.

"She should go to the police," Sebastian said.

"She can't, not with what she has so far. Jack Swift would pounce. The Capitol police would send up a team to investigate. The press would be all over the story." Plato stopped, groaning. "You didn't let her get that far, did you?"

"Plato, I swear to God, I wish you were still jumping out of helicopters rescuing people. I could sell the company and retire, instead of letting some dipshit busybody like you run it."

"You didn't even hear her out? I don't believe it. Jesus, Redwing. You really are an asshole."

Sebastian started down the porch steps. He was stiff, and he needed coffee. He needed to stop thinking about Lucy. Thinking about Lucy had never, ever done him any good. "I figured she told you everything. No need to make her go through it twice."

"Lucy deserves—"

"I don't care what Lucy deserves."

Sebastian could feel his friend staring at him, knowing what he was thinking, and why he'd slept out on the porch. "Yeah, you do. That's the problem. You've been in love with her for sixteen years."

That was Plato. Always speaking out loud what was best left unsaid. Sebastian walked out to his truck. It was turning into a beautiful day. He could go riding. He could take a run with the dogs. He could read ghost stories in his hammock.

The truth was, he was no damn good. About all he hadn't done in the past year since he'd shot a friend gone bad was kick the dogs. He'd renounced violence, but not gambling, not carousing, not ignoring his friends and responsibilities. He didn't shave often enough. He didn't do laundry often enough. He could afford all the help he needed, but that meant having people around him and being nice. He didn't have much use for people. And he wasn't very nice.

"I can't help Lucy," he said. "I've forgotten half of what I knew."

"You're so full of shit, Redwing. You haven't forgotten a goddamn thing." Plato came and stood beside him. The warm, dry air, he said, helped the pain in his leg. And he liked the work. He was good at it. "Even if you're rusty—which you aren't—you still have your instincts. They're a part of you."

Then the violence was a part of him, too. Sebastian tore open his truck door. "I hate bullshit pep talks."

"Redwing—goddamn it. You've never felt sorry for yourself for one minute of your life, have you?"

He had. The day he watched Lucy Blacker walk down the aisle and marry another man.

Sebastian squinted at the dawn. "Tell me what's going on with Lucy."

Plato told him. He was succinct and objective, and Sebastian didn't like any of it. "It's the kids and their friends," he said. "Maybe just their friends."

"It's Mowery, and you know it."

"Mowery's not my problem."

"I had your plane gassed up," Plato said. "They haven't taken your pilot's license, have they?"

Sebastian smacked the dusty roof of his truck. *Damn.* "I'd rather go through drown-proofing again than fly to Vermont."

"You never went through drown-proofing. That was part of my training. I'm the ex-parachute rescue jumper."

"You are?" Sebastian grinned at his old friend. It had been a bad day when he'd learned Plato Rabedeneira was finished jumping out of helicopters, might not even walk again. "I thought that was me."

Plato grinned back. "Lucy's prettier than ever, isn't she?"

"Shut up, Rabedeneira, before I find a helicopter and throw you out of it."

"Been there, done that." Plato stood beside him. "I'll have someone look after the dogs and horses."

"Damn," Sebastian said under his breath.

He knew what he had to do. He'd known it the minute Lucy Blacker Swift had rolled into his driveway. Arguing about it with Plato was just a delay tactic.

He climbed into his truck and followed Plato out the dirt road.

Four

Jack knew he should call the Capitol Police and have them arrest Darren Mowery and bodily remove him from the premises. There really was no question. The bastard was threatening a United States senator. This was *blackmail*.

But Jack didn't reach for his phone or stand up and yell to his staff. He just glared at Mowery, paralyzed. Like most of Washington, Jack had thought Darren Mowery dead, or at least out of the country for good. Instead, here he was in a senator's office.

"Think hard, Senator," Mowery said. "Think hard before you say anything."

Jack summoned his tremendous, hard-won capacity for self-control. "Damn you. I'd like to wipe that smirk off your face."

Mowery shrugged. "Go ahead and buzz the Capitol Police. They look bored today. I think they'd get a kick out of bouncing a blackmailer from a senator's office.''

"Don't you think walking into my office has raised a few eyebrows already?''

"That's not my concern.''

Jack could feel the pain gnawing in his lower abdomen. Nerves. Outrage. That Mowery had confronted him in his office only added to the effrontery, the sheer insult of the man's presence.

What he did now, Jack knew, would determine his legacy as a United States senator. This was what his thirty years in Washington would boil down to—this moment. How he responded to blackmail.

He glanced around at the framed pictures and the letters of thanks, the awards, all the evidence of his long, proud career in public service. He wasn't an arrogant, power-hungry politician. To him, public service was a high and honorable calling.

"You're a cocky bastard, Mowery.'' He was surprised at how calm he sounded, how restrained. Inside, his guts were roiling. "You'll never get away with blackmailing a United States senator.''

"I don't think of myself as blackmailing a United States senator. I think of myself as blackmailing a father who doesn't want the world to know his son was balling a woman who wasn't his wife, two weeks before he dropped dead on a Washington tennis court.''

Jack felt a sudden, stabbing pain, a hot arrow through him. He took a shallow breath. "I want you out of my office. Now."

"I can arrange to have you see a sample of the pictures." Mowery leaned forward on his chair, confident, his gaze as cold and calculating as any Jack had ever seen. "Go ahead, Senator. Call the Capitol Police. Have them haul me off. I've slipped the noose before. I'll slip it again. And even if I don't, the pictures go out."

"You smug, insolent—"

"Yeah, yeah."

"I won't pay one single, solitary dime to you."

"Okeydokey." Mowery got to his feet. He wore a light gray suit, fitting in with the tourists, lobbyists, press and staff floating around the Senate office building. The perfect Everyman. "Consider the first batch of pictures already on its way to various media outlets and to Lucy Swift, the wronged widow."

Jack couldn't speak. His jaw ached from tension. The stabbing pain in his lower abdomen spread upward. He almost wished he could drop dead of a heart attack right here, right now. He'd watched his son collapse and die. It had been so quick, so unexpected. So easy.

Colin. Dear God. What did a father owe his dead son's memory? What did he, Jack Swift, United

States senator, owe his son's widow, his son's children?

And what did he owe the people of his state? Himself?

"Remember, Senator." Mowery seemed very sure of himself. "Sex scandals are always fresh, particularly when they're about anyone or anything related to a powerful, sanctimonious, squeaky-clean senator."

"How *dare* you."

Mowery ignored him. "And, of course, no matter what the papers do, Lucy will know. You won't be able to stuff that cat back into the bag once she sees her dead husband with another woman's mouth—"

"Stop. Just stop. Colin's been dead for three years. Have you no decency?"

"He didn't. Why should I?"

"It's my decency you're preying on," Jack said, more to himself than to the man standing across from him.

"Look, Jack. You can't change what your baby boy did. You can't change that I know about it and have pictures. You can only decide if it's going to remain between us or if the whole world's going to know."

"I could kill you with my bare hands." Jack could hear his voice cracking; he sounded ancient, pathetic. He was a goddamn dinosaur. "Damn you, if I were younger—"

"Well, my friend, guess what? You're not younger. And you don't have the pictures. I do. And," he added pointedly, "I'm better at this than you are. I have contingency plans. You pay me or you lose. Period."

"I won't sell my vote."

Darren laughed. "What would I want with your vote?"

"And I won't betray my country," Jack said.

"Jesus. That's right out of a World War Two movie. Corny, Jack. Real corny. I don't want your vote, and I don't want state secrets. I want cash."

Cash. It sounded so simple. "How much?"

"Ten grand. It's not even enough to get the IRS interested."

Which meant it wouldn't end here, today. Ten thousand was pennies to a man like Darren Mowery.

Jack was silent, the pain eating away at his insides.

Mowery dropped a piece of paper on his desk. "That's where you can wire the money. With the Internet, it's easy. Shouldn't take two minutes."

"I know who you are. I can find you."

"So? I thought about doing this anonymously. You know, the altered voice on the phone in the middle of the night telling you to stuff twenty-dollar bills in a backpack and leave it at the Vietnam Memorial. I figured, nah, too complicated. Too likely you'd hang up and go back to sleep. This way, you know exactly who you're dealing with.''

''An arrogant lowlife who threw away his own reputation and career—''

''You got it, Senator. That means I have nothing to lose. If I were still an honest man and you were my client, I'd tell you to pay the ten grand and cross your fingers.''

He started for the door.

Jack rose, his knees unsteady. ''I want all hard copies of the pictures and all the negatives.''

''That's pretty old-fashioned. I could have them on computer disk by now. Truth is, Senator, with what we can do on a computer these days, they could be fakes.'' He went to the door, turned and winked. ''Transfer the ten grand into my account.''

He left.

Jack staggered back to his chair. For thirty years, he had refused to succumb to cynicism, venom, temptation or arrogance. He did his best. He was honest with himself and the people he represented. That was all he'd ever asked of himself, all he'd ever expected anyone else to ask of him.

Now, he was facing an impossible choice.

If Colin had cheated on Lucy, she'd have known

about it. That was Lucy Blacker. She looked reality square in the eye.

But this was her secret to keep, Jack thought. His son was dead and deserved to rest in peace. His widow and children deserved to go on with their lives. Maybe the affair was part of the reason she'd moved to Vermont.

Mowery hadn't gone to Lucy with his sordid blackmail scheme because she wasn't the senator; she didn't have the power, the reputation, the money that Jack had.

But what did Darren Mowery *really* want?

Ten grand was a small price to pay for his family's peace. Giving in to a blackmailer, Jack thought, was the bigger price.

If he was lucky, it would end here. But Darren Mowery hadn't walked into Jack's office because he was lucky. He wanted something, and Jack doubted it was ten thousand dollars.

When Darren Mowery walked past her desk in Senator Swift's outer office, Barbara refused even to look up. She didn't dare meet his eye. He was so brazen! Her stomach muscles clamped down painfully. He'd warned her that he believed in the direct approach.

So, the deed was done.

Barbara did her meditation breathing. She wasn't

very good at it. Even at home, with her eyes shut and scented candles lit, she found it difficult to focus on her inhaling and exhaling, to let her obsessive thoughts quiet.

She was not to contact Darren. He would contact her when he felt it appropriate. Even if she wanted to, she had no idea how or where to reach him. That wasn't important, she told herself. It wasn't that she trusted him or felt she had enough hold on him— she simply didn't care if he made off with all their profits. She didn't care about the money for what it could buy. She wanted to see a frightened, desperate Jack turn to her for help. She wanted him to understand just what she meant to him.

Let him suffer for taking her for granted. Let him learn.

She suddenly couldn't breathe. Oh, God! She wanted her life back. She wanted to be herself again. If only she'd never said anything to Jack. If only she'd stayed home this past week and hadn't bothered Lucy to relieve her own tension.

Oh, but it had felt good! And if Lucy came crying to Jack, so be it. Barbara could turn it into another lesson. The only danger was if Darren found out.

And the police.

Acid rose in her throat.

"Good Lord," a staff member said. "What's Darren Mowery doing here?"

Barbara looked up as if she'd been deep in concentration. "Oh, you know the senator. He'll give anyone a few minutes of his time to make their case."

Her colleague shuddered. He'd been on Jack Swift's staff almost as long as she had, but *he* wasn't indispensable. "The guy gives me the creeps."

Barbara returned to her work. It was routine, nothing stimulating. She'd once been so ambitious, determined to become the senator's chief of staff, possibly his press secretary. Secretly, she'd hoped he'd run for the presidency.

She'd had so many goals and dreams. Somehow they had gotten away from her. Now here she was, in danger of becoming the sort of woman she loathed. Obsessive, secretive, in love with the boss. She was pathetic.

Except she *wasn't*.

Her alliance with Darren was a show of strength. It demonstrated a great belief in herself, not cowardice.

When he finally emerged from his office an hour later, Jack looked perfectly normal. He was so understated and mannerly, not a bombastic ideologue. He wasn't a rabble-rouser, which sometimes allowed people the mistaken belief he had weak convictions. The premature deaths of his wife and son only added to his mystique, his appeal. He was the last senator in Washington anyone would think could be the victim of blackmail.

He came to Barbara's desk. Her heart jumped.

But there was no sign of fear or even distraction when he spoke. "Barbara, I've decided to spend the August recess in Vermont with Lucy and the kids."

"You're not going home?"

"It's an easy drive to Rhode Island. I'll manage."

Barbara saw now that he was a little off, not quite himself. Of course. He was a strong man, and he'd want to hold on as long as he could before confiding in anyone, even her. But Vermont. This was not a good development. Darren must have triggered an urge for Jack to see his grandchildren.

"J.T.'s been wanting to show me his favorite fishing spots. Madison..." He breathed in, nodded to himself. "Yes, August in Vermont. That's what I'll do. Do you mind, Barbara?"

"Mind what?" She wondered if she'd missed something, or if Jack's encounter with Darren was making him obtuse.

He ran a hand through his gray hair, and only because she'd known him for so long could Barbara detect his agitation. "I'd like to rent a house in Vermont, close to Lucy. Could you make arrangements?"

She smiled through her agony. This wasn't going at all as she'd calculated. "Of course."

"And don't say anything to Lucy just yet. This is so spur-of-the-moment—I don't want to disappoint her and the children if it doesn't work out, for whatever reason."

Like blackmail? Barbara quickly grabbed a stack of papers, as if she had a million things to do and Jack was just giving her one more easily handled detail. "I understand. I'll start making calls right away."

"I think it might be better if you went up to Vermont yourself," he said.

"What?" She felt so thickheaded, unable to follow the logic of his thinking. Why didn't he pull her into his office and beg her to help him with Darren Mowery's blackmail scheme?

"We don't have much time before the August recess, and you'll need to rent a house and get it ready rather quickly." He smiled, looking a bit less distracted. "Unless you'd rather not seize this as an excuse to get out of sweltering Washington for a few more days."

She made herself laugh. "Oh, no, you don't. I'll tie up a few loose ends here and be off. As I recall, there are several vacation homes above Lucy's house. I'll see if one's available to rent."

Jack seemed to relax. "Thanks, Barbara. I knew I could count on you."

Did he? She wondered if this was a start. Or maybe this was just a way to get rid of her while he coped with blackmail. Why have her around, adding to the pressure on him? Perhaps it was an excuse to get her out of town.

Barbara felt sick. She'd thrown herself at him, poured out her soul. They were pretending nothing had happened, but he knew it had, and she knew. She'd broken the bond of trust between them by saying out loud what she knew they both were thinking. She'd hoped blackmail would jolt him out of his denial about his feelings toward her. *Barbara, I'm so sorry. I need you. You know I do!*

Instead, it was off to Vermont with her.

But this was her job as his personal assistant, she reminded herself. She handled the odd details of Jack Swift's life as a senator, a grandfather and a father-in-law.

He couldn't know that by sending her to Vermont, he was sending her back into the lion's den.

She would leave Lucy alone. She *had* to. If Darren found out, he'd kill her.

"Barbara?"

She smiled. "I was just thinking that Lucy could have picked a worse place to live than Vermont. It'll be fun going up there for a few days. I'll keep you posted."

* * *

Lucy plopped a colander of freshly picked green beans on her lap and sighed happily. Two normal days. She'd been to the hardware store to replace the glass in her dining room window, she'd patched the hole in the wall, she'd reported back to Rob Kiley that she hadn't found any firearms or ammunition in her son's possession or anywhere on her property. He likewise reported that Georgie was "clean."

And after a busy day of office work, she and Madison and J.T. had picked beans.

"Do you think Daisy made Sebastian pick beans?" Madison asked, joining her mother on the porch.

Lucy grabbed a handful of fresh, tender beans and started snapping off the ends. "I don't think anyone's ever 'made' him do anything."

"Well, his horses were beautiful."

That, Lucy allowed, was true. Beautiful horses, mutt dogs, no electricity, no running water. Sebastian Redwing had never been an easy man to figure out. Luckily, she didn't have to. He was in Wyoming on his hammock, coughing dust.

While Madison helped with snapping beans, J.T. was making himself scarce. It was a warm, fragrant, perfect Vermont summer evening. In a way, Lucy thought, asking Sebastian for help and having him turn her down so unceremoniously had been cathartic, forcing her to dig into her own resources. She really was on her own.

Colin couldn't have known, she thought. When he'd extracted her promise, Sebastian Redwing had been a different man from the rude burnout she'd found in Wyoming.

"Mom," J.T. yelled from inside, "Grandpa's on the phone!"

"Bring the phone out here."

Madison dropped a half-dozen snapped beans back into the colander. "Can I talk to him?"

Lucy nodded. "Of course."

J.T. ran out with the portable phone, deposited it in her lap and jumped off the porch, taking all the steps in one leap. Talking to their grandfather, Lucy thought, always perked up both her children. He would never let them know he disapproved of their mother's decision to move them out of Washington. But he'd let her know, in his subtle, gentlemanly way. She got the message. He hadn't lasted in Washington as long as he had by being wishy-washy.

"Hi, Jack," she said into the phone. "What's up?"

"I had a minute and thought I'd give you a call."

"Well, I'm glad you did."

"How are you?"

"Madison and I are snapping beans on the front porch."

"Sounds idyllic."

She laughed, but she detected a slight note of criticism mixed with an unexpected wistfulness. "I don't know about idyllic. How're you? How's Washington?"

"I'm fine. Washington's hot."

"It's summer. Let's talk again when the cherry blossoms are out there and it's mud season here."

"J.T. said you had a good trip to Wyoming."

"It was quick, but we enjoyed ourselves."

"Did you stop in to see Sebastian Redwing?"

Lucy paused. Did Jack know about her promise to Colin? Was he suspicious that visiting Sebastian meant trouble? He didn't sound suspicious, but then, he wouldn't. Jack Swift knew how to keep his emotions in check better than most. "Yes," she said carefully. "It made for an interesting field trip with the kids."

"I gather they're not going to camp this summer."

They hadn't gone to camp last summer, either. "I don't see the need, given where we live and what I do."

Lucy kept her tone light, deciding to take his question at face value and not read any criticism into it. But she knew it was there. Her father-in-law would never openly criticize her parenting skills, but she knew he thought his grandchildren's upbringing lacking. That Madison and J.T. could kayak, canoe, hike, swim in an ice-cold stream, pick their own vegetables, climb trees, fish and wander in the woods of Vermont was all well and good—but they weren't learning sailing, golf, tennis. Their occasional lessons at the town rec department didn't count.

"They need their own lives, Lucy," Jack said softly.

Lucy was taken aback, but forced a laugh. "That's what they tell me every time I insist they clean their rooms. 'Mom, I need my own life.'"

"Do you think Colin would have wanted them raised in Vermont? Snapping beans, running through the woods—Lucy, it's a hard world out there. They need to be ready."

"Colin's not here, Jack, and I'm doing the best I can."

"Of course, you are. I'm so sorry."

He *was* sorry, but he'd said what he felt. He was a man without a wife or son, and Lucy had taken his grandchildren off to Vermont. She wasn't raising them the way he and Eleanor had raised Colin. Lucy understood, but wished he could simply say he missed having them right there in Washington instead of implying she wasn't a good mother.

"Forget it, Jack. Look, Madison and J.T. would love to see you. Any chance you can get up here during the August recess?"

"I hope so."

"We'd like to sneak down to Rhode Island for a few days, if you're available. And Madison's looking forward to her trip to Washington this fall."

Lucy glanced at her daughter, who was listening intently to every word. If there was a way to use her grandfather to convince her mother to let her do a semester in Washington, Madison would jump at it. But as much as he might disapprove of Vermont, Lucy was confident Jack would never undermine Lucy that way.

"She'd love to stay longer than a three-day weekend," Lucy said. "Here, would you like to talk to her?"

"Yes, thanks. Great talking to you, Lucy. Oh, by the way, Sidney Greenburg sends her best."

Lucy interpreted this to mean Sidney and Jack were still seeing each other. She hoped a relationship might take some of the focus off her own shortcomings, and the edge off his loneliness. "Thanks. Tell her the Costa Rica trip is coming along—she wants to be the first to sign up."

"Maybe we both will," Jack said. "And Lucy, I didn't mean to imply—you should go on with your life. I know that."

"It's okay, Jack. We miss you, too. We'll see you soon."

Madison disappeared inside with the phone. Jack was good to both her children, Lucy reminded herself. And they loved him. But if she'd stayed in Washington, they'd have stayed in Colin's world—Jack's world—and Lucy knew she wouldn't have survived. She'd needed to make a clean break.

She grabbed another handful of beans. Rob joined her on the porch, flopping down on a wicker chair. "The Newfoundland trip just filled up. Do you want to start a waiting list?"

"Makes sense."

"And J.T. told me he thinks he wants to come on the father-son trip, after all."

"Did he? Well, good. I hope he does."

They talked business, and Lucy snapped beans. She and her kids had a good life here, she thought. That was what mattered, not Jack's approval—or even Colin's.

Sebastian arrived in southern Vermont late in the day and checked into a clean, simple motel on a historic route outside Manchester. Far enough from Lucy, but not too far.

He'd made a detour to Washington first and checked with Happy Ford, a new hire Plato had put on Mowery. She was ex-Secret Service and very good, but only Plato would hire someone with a name like Happy Ford.

She said Mowery had visited Senator Jack Swift at his office this morning. And disappeared.

Sebastian warned her not to underestimate Darren Mowery. "Assume he's better at what you do than you are."

"Do you think he knows I'm on him?"

"He knows."

Sebastian took his cardboard cup of coffee out onto the small patio in front of his motel room and sat on an old-fashioned, round-topped metal chair. It was painted yellow. The chair for the next room was lavender, then pink, then blue. Cute.

There were brochures in his room for the sites in the area—old houses, covered bridges, Revolutionary War stuff, outlets, inns, resorts. He thought about renting a big, fat inner tube and floating down the Battenkill. It seemed like a better idea than spying on Lucy.

He'd never been much of a tourist or an historian. Or much of a Vermonter. Born here, more or less raised here, generations of family buried here. Daisy had insisted she had an ancestor who'd fought at the Battle of Bennington, which actually had occurred just over the border in New York state. Daisy had liked the aura of being a native Vermonter.

He'd left his boots and his hat in Wyoming. He

was an outsider there, but he really didn't give a damn.

The evening air was warm and slightly humid, but pleasant. The rounded hills were thick with trees, and as he sat with his coffee, he felt as if they were closing in on him. Or maybe it was the memories.

He threw the last of his coffee into the grass. "Lucy, Lucy."

He'd done a lot of dumb things in his life. Falling for Lucy Blacker on her wedding day was one of the dumbest. Coming out here was probably right up there with it. A bullet left on her car seat. It was kids. It wasn't Mowery.

Sebastian walked out into the fading sunlight. Tomorrow, he thought, would be hot.

He'd gotten rid of his guns. No point having one, seeing how he didn't hunt and had no intention of shooting anyone. People thought he was kidding when he said he'd renounced violence. He wasn't. Darren Mowery had been his last victim.

A mosquito landed on his arm. He flicked it off. Who the hell needed a gun? If he was going to find out who was intimidating Lucy, what he needed was some serious bug spray.

Five

Lucy grabbed her binoculars and headed across the backyard, over the stone wall and into the field. She had on shorts, a T-shirt and sneakers. The air was hot and humid for southern Vermont.

Two more days without any incidents. She was in good shape. An early start that morning had caught her up on her work, as well as freed her to agree to a local inn's request for her to lead a family on a canoe trip down the Battenkill. Madison and J.T. had gone with her, and they'd had a great time. She'd felt so...*normal.*

Madison was off to Manchester to see a movie with friends, J.T. at the Kileys to play Nintendo with Georgie and spend the night.

Lucy had the evening to herself.

The field grass was knee-high, mixed with daisies and bright orange hawkweed, black-eyed Susans, frothy Queen Anne's lace. With a line of thunderclouds moving in from the west, she couldn't go too far into the woods. The storm should, however, blow out the heat and humidity that had built up through the day.

An old stone wall marked the far edge of the field; beyond it were woods of oak, maple, hemlock, pine and beech. Lucy climbed over the wall and stood in the shade of a huge maple, her binoculars slung around her neck. It was a perfect climbing tree. Up high in its branches, she would have a tremendous view. She could perch up there and bird-watch, enjoy her solitude.

What the hell, she thought, and with both hands, she reached up and grabbed hold of the lowest branch. She'd always loved climbing trees as a kid growing up in suburban Virginia.

When she lived in Washington, she'd had a job organizing unique trips for a Washington museum, and it had seemed such a natural way to combine her degree in anthropology with her love of the outdoors. She'd discovered a passion and a talent for understanding what people wanted and translating it into trips they couldn't stop thinking about once they opened up one of her brochures, something that had served her well when she'd decided to go out on her own. Many of her Washington clients had followed her into her own business.

She swung onto a low branch and climbed higher, the maple's rough bark biting into her hands. Bark had never bothered her at twelve. She moved carefully, having no desire to fall out of a damn tree on her evening off.

She found the perfect branch and sat down, her feet dangling. Even without binoculars, the view was spectacular—woods, fields, stone walls, brook, her yellow farmhouse tucked on its narrow stretch of reasonably flat land. Not too far from here, Calvin Coolidge was buried in a hillside cemetery so as not to take up precious flat land for farms.

Balancing herself with one hand on the tree trunk, Lucy removed the binoculars from her neck. Maybe she'd see a hawk floating in the hazy sky.

But as she put the binoculars to her eyes, she heard something in the woods around her. She went very still. The noise didn't sound like a squirrel or a chipmunk, or even a deer. A moose? The pre-Wyoming incidents came back to her, making her question what she would ordinarily take in stride. A noise in the woods. Big deal.

Without making a sound, she swiveled around to see what was under and behind her. Brush. More trees.

And Sebastian Redwing.

She gulped in a breath, so startled she lost her

balance. Her binoculars flew out of her hand as she grabbed the tree trunk to keep herself from falling.

The binoculars just missed Sebastian's head. He caught them with one hand and looked up. "Trying to kill me, Lucy?"

"It's a thought." She caught her breath, but was still shaking. "Damn it, Redwing, what the hell are you doing here?"

"You wanted my help. Here I am."

The heat and humidity must have gotten to her. She was imagining things. Sebastian was konked out in his hammock in Wyoming with his dogs and horses. He wasn't in Vermont.

She swooped down to a lower branch and swung to the ground as if she were twelve again—forgetting she wasn't. She dropped in a controlled but hard landing. Pain shot up her ankle. Her shirt flew up to her midriff. She swore.

Sebastian wrapped an arm around her lower back, steadying her. She could feel his forearm on her hot skin.

His gaze settled on her. "Easier going up than it is coming down."

"I've been climbing trees since I was a kid."

He smiled. "That's bravado. You almost sprained an ankle, and you know it."

"The key word is *almost*. My ankle's fine."

If she'd injured herself, he'd have carted her off

to the emergency room. There'd be no end to her humiliation.

"What were you doing up there?" he asked mildly.

"Bird-watching."

"Birds have all hightailed it before the storm hits."

He still had his arm around her. "You can let go now," she said.

"You've got your footing?"

"Yes."

He released her and took a step back. He wasn't dusty. The dirty cowboy hat and scuffed cowboy boots were gone. He had on good-quality hiking clothes, including hiking boots. He was lean, tanned, fit—and alert, Lucy thought. That was the first thing she'd noticed when she'd met him all those years ago, just how alert he was. She could feel him taking in everything about her, from her sneakers to her wild hair.

He was worse than an ex-CIA agent. Maybe he *was* an ex-CIA agent. She suddenly realized she knew very little about him. What if she'd taken her promise to Colin out of context, and Sebastian Redwing was the last person she should have asked for help?

She adjusted her shirt. "I thought you weren't interested in helping me."

"I'm not."

"Then go back to Wyoming." She stepped past him and climbed onto the stone wall. "I didn't mean I wanted your help as in you sneaking around my woods. I wanted your opinion." She looked back at him, breathing hard, fighting for some way to assert her control over the situation. "Do note my use of the past tense."

"Noted."

She took a deep breath. "I sure as hell didn't want you scaring me out of a tree."

"I didn't scare you out of your tree. You scared yourself." He stepped over the stone wall, tall enough he didn't have to climb up over the rocks piled up by long-ago farmers, probably his ancestors. "You should find out what you're dealing with before you react."

"Yeah, well, I'm good with canoes and kayaks and snapping beans. I'm not so good with men jumping out of the brush at me."

He smiled. It was an unsettling smile, not meant, she felt, to reach his eyes. Which it didn't. "You nailed me with your binoculars."

"It wasn't deliberate."

He handed them back to her. "I used to climb that tree when I was a kid."

His words brought her up short. He was, after all, Daisy's grandson. He'd sold this place to her. It was more his turf than hers, no matter whose name was on the deed.

Lucy went out into the field, more comfortable on open ground. "How does it feel to be back here?"

He shrugged. "I'd forgotten how pesky mosquitoes can be."

She slung the binoculars over her neck. "I never meant for you to come here."

"What did you mean for me to do?"

"Tell me I wasn't in any danger."

There was still nothing she could reliably read in his eyes.

"And how was I supposed to know that without coming here?" he asked.

"Instincts and experience."

"In other words, I was supposed to release you from all your worries from the comfort of my hammock." He eyed her a moment, then added in a low voice, "Believe me, that would have suited us both."

"I don't want you going to any trouble on my account—"

"Too late."

With a groan of frustration, Lucy started across the field. She took long strides, hoping to separate herself from Sebastian Redwing as fast as possible.

He didn't say a word. He didn't come after her.

She stopped dead in her tracks and swung around.

He was just a few yards behind her, as tall and immovable as an oak. And she'd all but invited him here. "You can go back to Wyoming now."

"I can do whatever I want to do."

"You're trying to spook me. Well, forget it. I've been living out here, just me and the kids, for the better part of three years. I don't spook easily."

"What about the bullet through your dining room window?"

"That's over. It was nothing. I was wrong."

He shrugged. "Maybe, maybe not. No incidents since you got back from Wyoming?"

"No. None." She frowned, wondering if she'd be less agitated if he weren't so damn calm. She was letting him get to her. She never let irritating people get to her. "When did you arrive?"

"A couple days ago."

She held her fury in check. "Where are you staying?"

"Motel."

"So you've had two days to spy on me."

He smiled. "Why would I spy on you? You're not the one who shot up your dining room."

She searched for a way to rephrase what she knew—what he *knew* she knew—he'd been up to. "You've been keeping an eye on me," she said.

He started down through the field. "Your life's pretty goddamn boring."

His way of saying she was right. "To someone like you, maybe." She marched after him, her binoculars swinging on her neck with each furious step. "Did you follow me on my canoe trip?"

"Nope. Sat up here and watched the woodchucks have at your garden."

"You did not."

He glanced around at her. "Check your beans. You'll see."

She bristled. "I do not need a bodyguard."

"Good, because I'm no good at bodyguarding. I was just getting the lay of the land. Lucy goes to work. Lucy picks beans. Lucy takes care of kids. Lucy runs errands. Lucy has a glass of wine on her porch. Lucy goes canoeing." He yawned. "There you go."

"It's better than lying about all day in a hammock."

"No doubt."

She was so aggravated, she could have hit him. Thunder rumbled in the distance. The sky darkened. The wind picked up. She reined in her emotions. She didn't want to be out here alone with him when the storm hit. "Go back to Wyoming. If I catch you on my property, I'll call the police."

"They won't arrest me."

"They will—"

"I'm Daisy Wheaton's grandson. I'll say I'm here

visiting the ancestral home. They'll probably hold a town barbecue on my behalf.''

She stared at him. "Have you always been this big a jerk?"

He grinned at her. "Nah, I'm a lot worse than I used to be. Plato didn't tell you?" He winked; he gave no indication of giving a damn what she thought or what she wanted. "See you around, Lucy Blacker."

Lucy turned the shower as hot as she could stand it. She scrubbed herself with a lavender-scented gel made by a local herbalist who wasn't, she was confident, related to Sebastian Redwing.

Daisy Wheaton should have willed her place to the Nature Conservancy instead of to her miserable grandson.

Then I wouldn't be here, Lucy thought.

Maybe she'd have moved to Costa Rica with her parents, or stayed in Washington and made her father-in-law happy.

Well, Colin had never said Sebastian was a gentleman or even a reasonably nice guy. He'd said he trusted him. He'd said Lucy could go to him if she needed help. It was a mistake, obviously, but Colin couldn't have known.

She dried off with her biggest, fluffiest towel and shook on a scented herbal powder that matched the gel. The thunderstorm had subsided, but she could still hear rumbling off to the east. The air was cooler, less humid. She was calmer. Her encounter with Sebastian had left her spent, drained…and feeling more alive than she wanted to admit.

She pushed aside that uncomfortable thought and slipped into a dressing gown she'd picked up for a song at an outlet in Manchester. Black satin, edged with black lace. Quite luxurious. She'd sit up in bed and read until Madison got back from her movie.

She started into the hallway, but stopped abruptly, catching her reflection in the mirror above the old pedestal sink. She turned and stared at herself in her black satin. Since Colin's death, she had seldom taken the time to think of herself simply as a woman. As a mother, an entrepreneur, a widow, an individual getting her life back together after sudden tragedy, yes. But as a woman who might attract, and be attracted to, a man, no. Not again. Not after Colin, not after the searing grief she'd endured. Never mind that she was still only thirty-eight.

"Good Lord," she breathed. "Where did *that* come from?"

It had nothing to do with leaping out of a tree at Sebastian's feet. The feel of his arm around her. She'd have to be mad to be attracted to him. Her sanity, her rationality, her common sense had seen her through the ups and downs of the past three years. She wasn't about to throw them out the window because of one little touch.

She headed into her bedroom.

Immediately she spotted something black in the middle of her bed. It brought her up short, and her knees nearly collapsed under her. *No.*

She stepped closer. It didn't move. It appeared to be organic—not plastic or rubber, not one of J.T.'s disgusting toys.

She saw the rough texture of its skin, the bits of fur. Wings.

A bat.

Her stomach lurched. Was it alive?

She tugged on the quilt. The bat didn't move.

And the horror swarmed in on her all at once. She couldn't control it. Madison and J.T. were away, and she didn't have to hold back. She tightened her hands into fists and yelled out in anger, disgust and shock. "Damn it, damn it, damn it. Whoever you are, I am not giving you the satisfaction of going to pieces. Not now, not ever!" She brushed back tears, gulped for air. No one could hear her. She was alone. "Damn it, I will not be afraid!"

She coughed, choking back tears.

A dead bat. In her bed.

She tore around her room for something to use to dispose of it. Fury and horror consumed her. Someone had sneaked into her house, slipped down the hall to her first-floor bedroom and deposited a dead animal in her bed.

She wanted to tear up the place. Rip out drawers, smash lamps, kick doors to pieces. She'd held back for so long. She was tired of being *under control.*

She found a tennis racket in her closet. A knife-cut of pain carved through her chest. Tennis. She hadn't played since Colin had died.

She snatched up the racket. She'd scoop up the bat and fling him into the woods. It wasn't *evidence.* It was a damn dead bat.

She spun around, racket in hand.

Sebastian was there as if she'd conjured him up herself. He jumped back a step. "Easy."

"Don't you believe in knocking?" She didn't lower her racket. "You're like a damn ghost. I can't—I—" She made herself breathe. "I can't have you here."

"I heard you yelling bloody murder." His voice was steady, dead calm. He was slightly damp from the rain. "I called from the back door. When you didn't answer, I came to find you."

She pointed with her racket. "There's a dead bat in my bed."

"So I see. Charming."

"Bats don't fall down dead on wedding-ring quilts."

He said nothing. It was obvious the bat hadn't fallen or crawled there to die.

"Daisy made that quilt," Lucy said. "It was in an old trunk in the attic."

"I remember it," he said softly. His eyes didn't leave her.

Her breathing steadied. Her legs were shaking under her, and she became aware of her appearance. The lace-edged black dressing gown, her damp hair, her bare feet, the spots of white powder on her throat. She remembered her reflection.

Sebastian took the tennis racket. His fingers touched hers, and it was all over. She fell against him, his mouth finding hers, her dressing gown making her feel almost as if she were wearing nothing at all. His body was hard, lean, unrelenting. Desire spilled through her, hot, aching, overpowering. It had been so long. So very, very long.

Then she was standing in the middle of her bedroom carpet, and Sebastian was staring out her window. Just like that.

Lucy quickly recovered. It was the dead bat. It had robbed her of all self-control. "Well. I don't even want to know what *that* was about."

He glanced at her, his gray eyes narrowed into slits. "Pretty obvious to me."

"The lonely widow finds a dead bat in her bed,

and next thing she's throwing herself on the man who swoops in to her rescue? I don't think so."

Sebastian picked up her tennis racket. "Takes two."

"To what? Play tennis, get rid of the bat—"

"Lucy."

He'd meant the kiss. Obviously. It took two to do what they'd done. He hadn't forced her. She obviously hadn't forced him.

She winced, still tasting his mouth on her. "I'm a little addled. Don't worry about the bat. I'll get rid of it."

"I can take it on my way out."

He was leaving. Thank God.

"You'll be all right alone?" he asked.

She nodded. "Whoever left that little present here isn't trying to hurt me or the kids."

"Maybe not yet."

"You didn't see anything?"

He shook his head. If he was irritated with himself for not catching the bat-depositor in his two days of sneaking around, he didn't show it.

Lucy stared at the bat. Bats outside were fine with her. Bats inside, dead or alive, weren't. If nothing else, there was rabies to consider. "It's awfully daring, don't you think, to slip in here, drop a bat on my bed and slip out again?"

"It was daring, yes." He patted the racket with

one hand. She could see his mind working. He knew how someone who wanted to harrass and intimidate operated. "But I'd say your friend here doesn't leave much to chance."

"Meaning he or she, or whoever, plans ahead, knows my comings and goings."

"Let me check out your house. It's unlikely I'll find anything, but we'll both sleep better if we know for sure no one's hiding in a closet. It'll take a few minutes."

"I'll help—"

"You'll make a cup of tea and sit in the kitchen and drink it."

"Madison's due back any minute."

"If I hear her, I'll leave. I don't think your kids need to know I'm in Vermont."

Lucy ran a hand through her damp hair. "I hate this."

"I know," he said, then scooped up the dead bat with the tennis racket, checked under her bed, checked her closet and went into the hall.

She followed him. "What are you going to do if you find someone, beat him over the head with the tennis racket?"

He pulled open the hall closet. She had to remember he knew his way around this house, but found she couldn't picture him as a twelve-year-old like

J.T., digging worms in the backyard. He glanced at her. "I could shove the bat down his throat."

"Do you think it died of natural causes?"

He moved down the hall in the opposite direction from the kitchen, where she was supposed to go and have tea as if nothing had happened. "I'm not planning to autopsy the damn thing," he said.

"I'd hate to think of someone deliberately killing a bat just to terrorize me."

He stopped. "Then don't."

"Am I distracting you?" she asked.

"Yes."

She'd meant by talking. He clearly meant something else. She motioned vaguely toward the kitchen. "I'll make myself that cup of tea. You can finish up."

He went without a word.

When he returned to the kitchen ten minutes later, he didn't linger. "Place is clean." He pulled open the back door. "I'll get rid of the bat and leave the tennis racket on the back steps."

Lucy was at the table with a cup of untouched chamomile tea. She hadn't been able to drink. She kept thinking about the dead bat, about kissing Sebastian. Neither induced calm. "That's fine. Thanks."

He looked at her. In the waning evening light, the soft gray of his eyes was even more unusual, as if warning her he didn't belong here. "Colin was a damn fool for ever sending you to me."

"He made me promise," she said.

"I know." He started out the screen door, stared out at the darkening Vermont sky. "Lucy, you don't have to worry. I won't touch you again."

She smiled and echoed him. "It takes two."

He didn't glance back, just left with her dead bat.

There was an unexpected flash of lightning, a rumble of thunder, and a few minutes later, another downpour. Lucy thought Sebastian might come back in out of the rain, but he didn't.

She ran outside onto the back steps. In seconds, the rain drenched her gown. She could see her nipples outlined against the silky black fabric.

How had he disappeared so fast?

She returned inside, dumped out her tea and walked back to her bedroom. She changed into a prosaic nightgown and jumped into bed with a book, but she couldn't concentrate enough to read.

A few minutes later, a car sounded in her driveway, and Madison dashed in through the back door. "Hi, Mom, I'm home," she called from the kitchen. "Hey—who left the tennis racket out?"

Lucy didn't breathe. Sebastian must have seen her on the back steps, her dressing gown clinging to her against the kitchen light. "It was me." She almost couldn't get the words out.

Madison appeared in her bedroom doorway, and Lucy managed a smile. She would do anything, she thought, to protect her children—even let Sebastian skulk around her woods.

She smiled at her daughter. "So, how was the movie?"

The bat hadn't died of natural causes. Sebastian was no expert on dead bats, but that much was obvious.

And tossing its carcass into the woods in no way made up for kissing Lucy when she was in shock.

"That was pretty goddamn low," he said under his breath as he locked himself into his motel room. He had considered, and dismissed, the necessity of keeping watch on her all night. The bat-depositor had accomplished his—or her—mission for the day. Sebastian had no real sense of who was behind the nasty little deeds—man, woman, coconspirators. He was now inclined to eliminate kids as a possibility.

He wasn't sure if Lucy had initiated the kiss, or if he had. He knew for damn sure she'd wanted it. But that didn't matter. She'd just found a dead bat in her bed, and he shouldn't have taken advantage of the situation.

On the other hand, he really didn't have any regrets. All right, he was low. But he'd imagined kissing Lucy for close to twenty years, and now that he had, he felt better.

He kicked off his hiking boots and flopped on his bed.

Who the hell was he kidding? He didn't feel better. Kissing Lucy hadn't helped.

He pictured her standing on her porch steps in her rain-soaked gown. She was smart and daring, and he didn't know why the hell he'd fallen for her, a woman he couldn't have—a woman he *shouldn't* have.

He called Happy Ford in Washington. Nothing yet on Darren Mowery. "I'm chasing down a few leads," she said.

"Be careful."

"Always."

Sebastian unwrapped the tuna sandwich he'd picked up en route back to his motel. He turned on the television. He hadn't watched TV in months. He found a rerun of *Gilligan's Island* and sat on his bed, watching Gilligan and the Skipper and the gang try to get home. There's no going back, he wanted to tell them. Walking above Daisy's house the past two days, that simple, terrible truth had etched itself on his soul. No going back.

He shut off the television.

Was Mowery in Vermont? Was Sebastian's coming here playing into his hands? Would he use a young widow to lure Sebastian east?

He knew to keep speculation and facts separate. Darren Mowery's reappearance in Washington, DC, might have nothing to do with the dead bat tonight on Lucy's bed in Vermont.

"Don't start a job you don't mean to finish," Daisy had liked to tell him.

When he'd gone after Mowery last year, Sebastian had meant to finish the job. But he hadn't, and now he had to make sure no one but he paid for his mistake.

Six

The house was perfect.

Barbara stood on its rear deck above Joshua Brook. She loved being right. She'd known she'd find something close to Lucy. It was the last house on the dirt road above the stupid twit's house. Barbara had rented it on the spot. Jack would be pleased.

The house had two bedrooms, a living room with a fireplace, a full kitchen, a study and lots of glass. There was a screened porch in case of rain or too many mosquitoes. The furnishings were contemporary country, suitable should an emergency press conference be required. The landscaping needed work—it was a little woodsy for Barbara's taste.

The brook was visible through a steep bank of hemlocks and pine, its clear, ice-cold water washing over silvery-gray rocks. She closed her eyes, letting the rhythm of the water absorb her. She could feel a slight breeze on her face.

Darren doesn't know I'm here. Should I tell him?

The thought was an unpleasant intrusion. It was almost as if he'd beamed it to her, just when she was about to relax and attempt to forget she'd colluded with a dangerous man in a scheme to blackmail a senator, the man she'd loved for twenty years.

What if Darren were out there in the woods, watching her?

She shuddered. He couldn't possibly know about her longtime obsession with Lucy. If he did, he'd have killed her by now.

"Just do your job and let me do mine," he'd told her. "You screw this up, you'll answer to me."

She'd intended to leave Lucy alone. But she hadn't, she couldn't—and she didn't understand why. Barbara was a woman of great strength and willpower. She wasn't stupid or weak. She didn't lack self-discipline.

She dropped onto an Adirondack chair. It was Lucy's fault she was even here. If Lucy had stayed in Washington where she belonged, Jack wouldn't have had to send his personal assistant to Vermont to rent a house so he could see his grandchildren. Barbara wouldn't have been tempted to leave a dead bat for his ungrateful wretch of a daughter-in-law to find. She and Lucy might even have become friends.

Her cell phone trilled.

"The money's in the bank," Darren said without preamble. "We're on our way. How's Vermont?"

"How do you know I—"

"Barbara."

She licked her lips. "Jack sent me. He asked me to rent a house for him for August recess. He wants to spend time with Lucy and his grandchildren."

"Blackmail'll do that to a guy."

"He suggested I stay an extra day or two."

"Of course he did. Come on, Barbie. Can't you feel the noose dropping around your neck? He's easing you out. You won't even know what hit you." Darren laughed. "Wishing you hadn't thrown yourself at him after all, aren't you?"

"You're disgusting, and Jack isn't easing me out. This is my job." She drew on her strength of character—*no one* intimidated her. "I don't want you to call me again."

"I don't care what you want, Barbie. Just keep your nose clean. I'll be in touch."

He disconnected.

Barbara slid the cell phone back into its designated slot in her tote bag. She could handle Darren Mowery. He just liked to play games with her to show her how smart he was. Well, she was smarter—

"Barbara? It *is* you!" Madison Swift suddenly

appeared, running up the steep bank from the brook. "I can't believe it! My friend Cindy said her mother showed this place to someone from Washington, and I was hoping—" The girl laughed, delighted. "Barbara, it's *me*. Madison Swift. Senator Swift's granddaughter."

Barbara had recognized the girl immediately. She just needed a moment to recover from the shock. Surely Madison was too polite to eavesdrop—she couldn't have overheard Barbara's conversation with Darren. The girl bounded onto the deck. She had grass stains on her knees, briar tracks on her shins. Her pretty face was freckled from the sun. Her dark, copper hair was in a messy, unfashionable single braid down her back.

She was so like Colin, Barbara thought. Cleaned up and raised properly, Madison Swift would be an asset to Jack, a tribute to his son's memory.

Now, she was a reminder that Barbara's campaign against Lucy was the right thing to do. It had nothing to do with her alliance with Darren Mowery and her frustration with Jack's denial of his love for her. It was an act of courage and self-sacrifice on her part. Someone had to wake Lucy up. Someone had to force her to take responsibility for her children.

Barbara smiled at the excited girl. "Of course, it's you, Madison, Senator Swift's granddaughter. How are you, sweetie?"

"Bored out of my mind," she said cheerfully. "That's okay, I'm used to it. Is Grandpa coming up this summer?"

"You're a sly one, Madison. This is supposed to be a secret. Your grandfather doesn't want to create a circus for him or your mom."

"Does she know?"

Barbara shook her head. "He wanted to make sure he had a house before he told her. He wouldn't want to disappoint you all." The words almost made her sick. Madison and J.T. would have been disappointed if their grandfather had to cancel his visit, but not Lucy. Lucy Swift didn't care if she ever saw her father-in-law again. "He really should be the one to tell you."

Madison crossed her fingers and pressed them to her lips. Her vivid blue eyes sparkled. "Mum's the word."

"What do you think of the house he's rented?" Barbara asked, gesturing. "Isn't it wonderful?"

"This is my favorite house up here."

"It's a beautiful setting."

The girl shrugged. "I guess. Most of Vermont's beautiful. I don't know how much 'beautiful' I can take."

Barbara laughed. "Well, well. Now there's an attitude."

Madison scooted up onto the rail, paying no heed

to the long drop. "I'd rather go to Washington to see Grandpa than have him come here. I'm going for a long weekend this fall, but it's not enough."

"Aha. You're one who'd like to have your cake and eat it, too."

"Yep." She grinned. "Aren't you?"

"Of course." Barbara glanced around at the wooded, isolated landscape. "You're alone? J.T. didn't come with you?"

"No, I'm escaping him. He and his friend want me to take them fishing. I refuse. I *hate* worms. I liked them when I was twelve, but not anymore."

"Not a country girl, are you?"

She seemed to take that as a compliment. "It's not that I hate Vermont—I just prefer the city." She jumped off the rail, a bundle of restless energy. "How long are you staying?"

"A few days. I'm taking a bit of a vacation and making sure everything's set for your grandfather. I'll stock the pantry, lay in some reading material, that sort of thing."

"He could stay with us at the house," Madison said.

And feel about as welcome as a roach. Lucy no longer thought of herself as a Swift—that much was obvious. But her children were Swifts, and there was no changing that fact, much as it might annoy her.

"This will work out beautifully," Barbara said

neutrally. "Would you mind not mentioning to your mother and brother that I'm here? I hate to ask you to keep anything from them, but they'd put two and two together."

"J.T. wouldn't. Mom would, though."

With the memory of the dead bat fresh in her mind, Lucy might start asking the wrong questions and jumping to dangerous conclusions. As much as Barbara hated to ask a child to keep secrets from her mother, under the circumstances it was the only practical option.

The girl laughed. "This'll be great. Of course, I won't tell anyone about you. I wouldn't want to get you into trouble with Grandpa."

"Oh, no, that's not your concern. I just don't want to spoil his surprise."

Madison nodded. "He's always liked to surprise us."

She swung around, asking abruptly, "Have you seen the falls yet?"

Yes, on her illicit visit last week, Barbara thought. She shook her head.

"Oh, you have to see them. They're not far. Do you have time? I can show you. It won't take long."

"I'm not dressed for a hike—"

"There's a short path off the road. It's a little longer than the path along the brook, but it's easier."

The girl seemed so eager. It was because of this pitiful life she led when she should be at a quality summer camp or studying abroad for the summer. Barbara had to contain her fury. If she could get Jack to tear down his wall of denial and see what she offered him, she could have influence over his grandchildren. She *knew* he hated to see them turning into country bumpkins.

She manufactured a smile as she got to her feet. "Go on, then," she said. "Lead the way."

Madison skipped down the deck steps, Barbara following at a slower pace. As a senior staffer of a United States senator, she was dressed professionally, appropriately, in dark slacks, a crisp white shirt and loafers.

They took a gravel path to the front of the house and walked along the edge of the dirt road. Since the house was the last on the dead-end road, Barbara didn't worry too much about a passing car spotting them. This was a risk. But it was a tolerable risk, another act of strength on her part. Madison needed a break from the dull rituals of her summer life.

Barbara knew her way around the woods and paths of the hills above Lucy's house better than she dared let on.

Last night, she'd returned to the rented house alone, even before she'd completed the paperwork with the real estate agent and gotten the keys. The screened porch was unlocked, and when Barbara slipped inside, a bat flapped in front of her face.

It was very early in the evening for bats, and she'd thought it might be rabid.

Then she'd thought of Lucy.

Barbara didn't know anything about bats. She wasn't a killer of helpless animals. She could have left it alone, coaxed it outside in case it meant to make a home for itself on the porch.

But the impulse had taken hold of her, refusing to let go until she'd found a stick, dealt with the bat and tucked its carcass into a bakery bag from her morning coffee.

She'd parked her car under a pine tree on the side of the dirt road and slipped across the brook to her perch on the opposite bank, then looked out across the yard behind the barn. She saw Madison leave with friends, J.T. go off with his grubby little friend. When Lucy finally took off across the field with her binoculars, Barbara weighed the risks and the pleasures. She knew she wouldn't stop thinking about the bat until it was deposited in Lucy's house for her to find, wonder about, scream about. But what if Lucy spotted her with her binoculars?

She came up with a foolproof cover story. *Lucy! You caught me. Jack sent me to rent a house for him for August, and I couldn't resist peeking in on you and the kids. I thought I heard something, but it was nothing.*

If she'd already deposited the bat, she could argue it was the intruder she'd heard. If not, who would ask about her bakery bag?

Lucy hadn't caught her.

She'd found the dead bat and screamed.

Barbara, lurking in the woods on her way back to her car, had heard her. Her satisfaction was almost physical. She'd acquired seven mosquito bites. More little purple hearts.

Barbara and Madison came to a massive hemlock, its roots spreading like thick, spidery veins over the ground. The girl scooted down the narrow path, turning and motioning to Barbara with one hand. "This way," she said. "We're almost there."

Yes, Barbara thought. The risks were necessary, and she had the courage to meet them. Colin's children—Jack's grandchildren—deserved a better life.

Jack Swift sank into a quiet corner booth at his favorite restaurant. The past few days had been excruciating. He hadn't asked Sidney Greenburg to join him for lunch. They'd argued last night when she'd realized something was wrong and he'd insisted there wasn't. Now, he just wanted a martini, a plate of Maryland crab cakes, a good salad and the dark comfort of the traditional, no-nonsense restaurant.

He knew, at least figuratively speaking, he was a man hanging over the abyss by his fingernails. Blackmail. Dear God.

And Colin. His only son, his only child. Had he been the sort of man who fooled around on his wife? Jack had never thought so, but who knew what went on between two people? And the truth really didn't matter. He didn't want to see any "proof." He just wanted this sordid business to go away.

"Senator Swift." Darren Mowery greeted him with a warm, phony smile. "Fancy meeting you here."

Jack called upon his many years of public service to manufacture a return smile, even as every muscle in his body seemed to twist in agony. "Mr. Mowery."

"Mind if I join you?"

The restaurant was also a favorite with reporters and senior congressional staff, all perpetually at the ready for good, fresh gossip. There was no graceful way out. Darren had known it when he'd walked in here. Jack felt his smile falter. "Please do."

Mowery dropped onto the opposite red leather-covered bench. "Did you order the crabcakes?"

Jack nodded. Mowery was making the point that he knew the senator's habits, his likes, his dislikes, and that the supposed information he had on Colin was only the beginning. Which was exactly what Jack had feared—what he'd *known*—when he'd transferred ten thousand dollars into Mowery's specified account.

"I did as you asked," Jack said in a low voice.

"You sure did. And in short order, too. Much appreciated."

The waiter appeared. Darren ordered a beer. No time for lunch, he said. Jack felt no relief.

"Here's an address and a password." With one finger, Mowery passed his business card across the table. "They're for a secure Web site. You might want to take a look."

Jack snatched up the card and dropped it into his suit coat pocket. "Mowery, for God's sake, if you've posted pictures of my son on the goddamn *Internet*—"

"Relax, Senator. It's not that simple. Nothing ever is, you know."

"People are already asking questions about your visit to my office the other day. This won't help."

The beer arrived. Darren took a sip. He shrugged. "So?"

"What do you want from me?"

He drank more of his beer. "Check out the Web site. Then we'll talk."

* * *

Lucy relished the mundane routine of deadheading the daylilies and hollyhocks in front of the garage. After the dead bat incident, she'd loaded up everyone with chores. J.T. and Georgie were pulling weeds, Madison was cleaning the kayaks and canoes and wiping down the life preservers. Lucy had asked both her children to stick close to home today. She was still debating sitting down with them tonight and telling them why. But she didn't want to act precipitously, scare them unnecessarily.

A shadow fell across her, and she looked up at Sebastian. "God, you keep materializing out of thin air."

He touched her elbow. "I came across the side yard. I don't think anyone saw me. Lucy, I need to talk to you."

"In here."

She ducked into the garage and moved to the back, among the shadows, out of view. The room smelled of old wood and grease and was exactly as Daisy had left it. Lucy hadn't touched a thing, from the half-century-old wooden wheelbarrow to the cleaned, oiled tools hanging from rafters and lined up on shelves.

Sebastian seemed attuned to every nuance of his environment. He'd grown up here, Lucy reminded herself, and knew this place and its history better than she did. She was aware of his closeness. He could move with such silence and speed, his presence immediate and overwhelming. She never had a chance to brace herself.

"What's going on?" she asked. "Is something wrong?"

"Did you let Madison go off into the woods on her own?"

Lucy was stunned. "*What?* No! She and J.T. are both doing chores today. She's out behind the barn cleaning canoes and kayaks."

"No, she isn't. She skipped out. I just saw her up in the woods."

Lucy clenched her hands into fists. "That little *shit*."

"Kid's got initiative," Sebastian said.

"She didn't tell me. I had no idea."

"I thought about going after her." His eyes seemed distant, calculating. "I decided to check with you first. I don't like coming between parents and their children."

"She got a phone call from one of her friends. I debated making her call back after she finished—" Lucy huffed, furious with her daughter. "Where is she?"

"On her way back. I got ahead of her."

"You wanted to make sure I wasn't letting her and J.T. run around on their own when I've got some bat-killing lunatic on my case." Frustration and fear welled up in her, and she kicked at an oil stain on the concrete floor. "I'm not an idiot."

Sebastian stayed calm. "I can get a counter-surveillance team in here by morning. Plato can spring a few guys loose. If someone's conducting surveillance on your place, they'll know it."

"Oh, come on."

"Lucy, whoever put that bat in your bedroom knew you weren't around. That means you're being watched."

She crossed her arms over her chest, tapped a foot in nervous frustration. She wore a sundress today, with sandals and tiny gold earrings. Her hair was pulled back with a twisted red bandana as a headband. Madison had liked the look, said it was "retro." Retro what, Lucy didn't know.

"I hate this," she said.

Sebastian didn't answer.

"If I have a 'counter-surveillance' team in here, I might as well call the Capitol Police and be done with it. I don't care how discreet your guys are, Sebastian. People will notice. You know they will. We don't get many guys with no necks and earpieces skulking around the woods."

"Is that a no?"

She dodged his question. Wasn't this why she'd gone to him in the first place? So he could be the judge? She didn't know anything about surveillance, counter-surveillance, dangerous lunatics.

She headed to the front of the garage, then turned back to him. "Do you know what route Madison's taking?"

"The brook path."

"I'll intercept her. She can find out what cleaning a kayak with a toothbrush is like."

Sebastian grinned. "Good. I was beginning to think you were too soft on those kids."

"If I want your opinion, Redwing, I'll ask for it."

"You did, as I recall."

"And as *I* recall, you sent me packing—and it had nothing to do with my parenting skills."

He moved to the front of the garage, but still in the shadows. She was in full sun and couldn't make out his eyes. His expression was serious, and she wondered if he ever really laughed. "No," he said, "it was about who'd leave a dead bat in your bed."

She clamped her mouth shut. The dead bat, somehow, bothered her more than the bullet hole in her dining room window.

"It didn't die of natural causes," Sebastian added.

"Big surprise."

"Lucy..."

She faced him. "No counter-surveillance or whatever-it-is team."

"I can't be everywhere."

She nodded. "I know. I have to think. Give me..." She squinted, warding off an oncoming headache. "Let me find my daughter."

"Stay with J.T. and his friend. I'll see to it Madison gets back okay."

"She's a good kid, Sebastian. She's just fifteen—"

But he was gone, and Lucy walked out back to the vegetable garden, where J.T. and Georgie were busily weeding the rows of beans. They'd picked up their pace when they saw her. They hadn't touched the pumpkins. She went over to the raised bed, little green pumpkins hanging from their prickly vines. She started pulling weeds, the big scraggly weeds. She'd yank them out, shake off the excess dirt, toss the cast-off plant into a pile. One after another. Not breathing, not thinking.

"Mom, geez," J.T. said.

She didn't break her pace. "I'm mad at Madison. Steer clear."

He didn't need to be told twice. "Come on, Georgie, let's go down to the brook—"

"No!" Lucy swung around at the two boys, a pigweed in one hand. "Not now. Go into the kitchen and get yourselves something to drink. I bought Popsicles."

"What kind?" Georgie asked dubiously. "My

mom always buys the fruit juice popsicles. They stink."

Lucy forced herself to smile. "These are the gross, disgusting kind with added sugar and artificial color."

He laughed and clapped his hands. "Okay, J.T., let's go!"

In another minute, she saw Madison walking up from the brook. She came in behind the barn, looking oblivious to the trouble she was in. Lucy abandoned her weeding and made herself take three deep, cleansing breaths before she confronted her daughter.

The air was warm, with a light breeze. A gorgeous summer afternoon, the grass soft under her feet. She made herself pay attention to everything her senses were taking in, not just her anger and frustration and fear.

Madison was in a good mood. "Hi, Mom. I only have two more canoes, then I'm done."

"Where have you been?"

"I took a break after I finished the kayaks. I walked up to the falls. Don't worry, I didn't get too close."

"Madison, I asked you to do a job. You didn't do it." Lucy took another breath, tried to be direct, firm, reasonable. "If you wanted to take a walk, you should have told me."

"Mom, what's the matter with you? I always go off into the woods alone."

"Not today. I specifically asked you—"

"I *know*. I'm getting the stupid job done. It's boring, that's all. I thought you'd be happy I wanted to go into the woods. I mean, it's not like I could go to a mall for a break."

Not that old song today. Lucy gritted her teeth.

Madison kicked the ground. "There's no pleasing you."

"Look, this isn't getting us anywhere."

Lucy blinked up at the sky, trying to figure out what to do. Lock her daughter in her room? Level with her about the intimidation? She didn't know. There was no playbook for this one. She wanted to protect her children. That much she knew. But how?

She looked back at Madison, noticed the scratches and dirt on her arm from thrashing through the woods. Two weeks ago, Lucy would have been thrilled at the idea of her daughter making an effort to enjoy her surroundings. "I want to be kept informed on your whereabouts, that's all. And for the next few days, I don't want you or J.T. in the woods alone."

"Okay, fine. Fine! I'll just stay here and rot."

"Madison—"

But she stormed off to the house, pounding up the back steps, yelling at her brother and Georgie in the kitchen. A minute later, loud music emanated from her room.

Lucy resisted the urge to march up there and turn down the music herself, lace into her daughter about her behavior. But that wouldn't make either of them feel any better, and more important, it wouldn't help the situation. She'd overreacted to Madison's understanding of her transgression. And then Madison had overreacted.

Lucy started back to the house. Had Sebastian witnessed that little mother-daughter scene?

Just then, Rob and Patti Kiley's ancient car pulled into the driveway, and Patti jumped out, waving happily. She was an active, smart woman with graying hair and a bright, crooked smile that inevitably soothed those around her. "We brought dinner. We decided you were looking just a tad stressed. So, dinner on the porch, then a walk to the falls. Maybe we'll throw caution to the wind and take a dip."

Lucy couldn't hide her relief. "You're a godsend."

Rob got out of the car and nodded at Madison's room, the house practically vibrating with her music. "You want me to go up and agree with her that her mother's a crazy bitch and doesn't understand her?"

Patti glared at him. *"Rob."*

He grinned. "Well, isn't that what all teenagers think of their mothers?"

"No, it's not. That's pure prejudice."

"Okay." He shrugged; it was often impossible to know when he was serious and when he was pulling everyone's leg. "I'll just go up and offer to take her driving. Lucy?"

Lucy could feel herself beginning to relax. It wasn't just Madison and whoever was trying to get under her skin. It was Sebastian, too. His intensity, his seriousness. He was one for worst-case scenarios. She understood—her business required her to plan for worst-case scenarios. But that's not how she wanted to think right now.

She smiled. "Great idea, Rob. Thank God for good friends."

Seven

The path along Joshua Brook hadn't changed much since Sebastian was a boy. He preferred this route. When he'd visited his grandmother, he'd always made a point of walking up to the falls. Daisy never joined him. For her, the falls were a place of tragedy, danger and loss, not beauty and adventure.

He remembered visiting her late in her life, when the strenuous hike up to the falls was beyond her capabilities. "I sometimes think I'd have been better off if I'd gone up there right after Joshua died," she'd told him. "But I waited too long. Sixty years."

"You've had a good life, Gran."

"Yes, I have."

But she'd never remarried, Sebastian thought now as he ducked under the low branch of a hemlock. What she'd tried to tell him—he'd been too thickheaded to see it—was that by refusing to go to the falls, she'd allowed at least a part of herself to stop time and refuse to acknowledge that Joshua Wheaton was dead. She'd buried him, she'd gone on with her life. But there was still that place deep inside her where her husband was on his way up into the woods on a wet March day after a boy and his dog. He was the young man she'd married—and she wasn't a widow, even sixty years later.

The path narrowed and almost disappeared as it went up a steep hill. Sebastian had to grab tree trunks and find his footing on exposed roots and rocks. The brook was fast-moving after last night's thunderstorms, coursing over gray, smooth rock down to his right. He was below the falls, close now.

He had made sure Madison Swift was back with her mother. As she'd sneaked back from the woods, he'd noticed the kick in the girl's step and wondered at its source. He doubted it was the beauty of the Vermont woods that had her in such a good mood. A boy? Friends? A fifteen-year-old could get into a lot of mischief on her own in the woods.

The air was drier than yesterday, not as buggy, even close to the water. Sebastian went past a huge boulder almost as tall as he was, the path disappearing with the thin, eroded soil.

He was near the falls now. A large, upward sloping boulder blocked his view, but below it, he could hear the water rushing over the series of slides, pools and cascades it had carved into a huge monolith of granite.

The falls were beautiful, intimate, deceptively treacherous. Sebastian worked his way methodically up the steep hill, eased out to the edge of the granite wall. Above him, the brook started its precipitous, downward journey over, through and into the massive rock, shaping it into long, curving, picturesque slides and cascades that dropped into a series of three pools. The first was deep and unforgiving with its surrounding sheer rock wall. It was directly below him, impossible to reach except by a risky dive out over the protruding rock. But he could understand the appeal of its clear, cold water, the thrill of the dangers it presented.

Water from the pool funneled over another slide that formed a second smaller, shallower pool farther down the falls, before cascading to a final large, shallow pool. The water in this last pool went from ankle-deep to, at most, three-feet deep this time of year; swimmers were in no danger of being swept up in the current or bashed against rock. A proper Vermont swimming hole. Below it, the brook re-formed, quietly continuing downstream past the Wheaton farm.

Sebastian caught himself. It was Lucy's place now.

He ducked past a scraggly hemlock, half its roots protruding out over the falls, and peered down, imagining his grandfather coming up here sixty years ago. With the snowmelt, the water would have been high, raging. Had Joshua Wheaton even noticed the power and beauty of the gushing waterfall? Was he that kind of man?

Sebastian remembered wanting to be as brave and heroic as his grandfather. Now, he wondered if Joshua had gone over the falls because he'd screwed up, because he just didn't know what else to do and was flat out of options.

A noise…

Rocks, sand, a movement. Sebastian reacted instinctively, but already he knew he was too late. He'd let his mind wander. Now, there was no time to adjust, no room to maneuver. Rocks, sand and dirt gave way on the steep hillside above him, cascading onto his narrow ledge. There wasn't enough room for him and the small landslide coming at him.

He grabbed for the hemlock, but a softball-size rock struck him on the back of his knees. He thought he heard a grunt, an exhale, above him. Then another rock hit him in the small of his back, throwing him completely off balance.

His body pitched forward, and for a timeless moment he was suspended in air. He was the grandfather he never knew, about to tumble to certain death.

Only his would be an ignoble death, Sebastian thought. Knocked off his feet while his mind was elsewhere.

His training and experience took over, forced out all thought. He tucked his chin into his chest to protect his head and let his butt and shoulders take most of the fall. He hit rock, bounced, hit more rock, bounced again and hit water.

He went in hard in a sprawling dive that stung, and the water was cold, cold, cold. His mind flashed on Plato, who'd done this sort of thing for a living and would have his own commentary if Sebastian survived.

His momentum took him under. He tried not to suck in water. He smashed into the gravel bottom, scraped his face raw, banged his knees. He found his footing and pushed up through the water, gasped in the cool air.

The landslide fell into the pool—small stones, pine needles, black soil. Sebastian didn't wait for another rock to come flying at him. Painfully, as quickly as he could manage, he swam to the opposite bank of the deep pool. He felt along the vertical rock wall, barely able to see, until it gave way just above the next water slide. He hoisted himself onto the rock slide, blood pouring down his face, his head spinning, the thirty-foot drop to the next pool directly beneath him.

If the water had been any higher, the current any stronger, he'd have gone over. Instead, the rock slide, smoothed and curved from the endless stream of water, came at him fast. He was passing out. He couldn't stop himself.

Grandpa.

He collapsed, and the blackness took him.

He knew he'd been unconscious only seconds. Long enough. He moved his shoulders, just a twitch, and pain erupted through his head. He ignored it. Water flowed under him. He eased up onto his hands and knees, scraped and cut and bruised from the fall.

He remembered the grunt, the exhale of air as whoever was on the hill above him had hurled those rocks at him. It wasn't kids. It wasn't an accident, fate. It was deliberate, and it meant he was still in the open, in the line of fire. Anyone above him on the ledge could see him. A well-aimed rock could finish him off.

He hadn't actually seen anything. And his mind hadn't been on the job, on the moment. It had been in the past, proof he should never have come back here. He should have sent Plato or Jim Charger or Happy Ford. On paper, he was still the damn boss even if Plato really had run things for the past year.

He grabbed for handholds along the rock, cursing himself for his inattention. Lucy, memories. A toxic combination.

He moved off into the shade and shadows, reached up with both hands and caught hold of the protruding roots of a thin pine. His head pulsed with pain. He had one chance. If he didn't pull himself up the first time, he'd end up back down in the water. Either he or the skinny tree would give out. Maybe both.

Ignoring the pain, the blood, his spinning head, he heaved himself up, pulling hard on the root. It gave way, and he quickly shot one hand out and grabbed a thicker section of root, hoisting himself up over the rock and onto dry, soft ground. He fell in the shade of the pine.

His hands and arms were bloody and badly scraped. He could feel more blood dripping down his temples. His back was at least bruised.

He swore viciously.

Then he heard voices below him, from the shallow, pleasant swimming hole at the base of the falls. Kids. Tourists. Lucy. He couldn't tell.

He dropped his face onto the dried pine needles. Screw it. He wasn't moving. The path on this side of the falls was seldom used. He'd take his chances. If someone found him and called the rescue squad, so be it. He'd think of some reason for being here besides removing dead bats from Lucy Swift's bed.

"I'll be right back," he heard a woman's voice saying not too far away. Lucy. It was almost as if he'd imagined her voice, as if it weren't real. "I *know* I heard something."

It was real. She hears something, Sebastian thought, and goes off to investigate by herself. No wonder someone had gotten away with shooting up her dining room.

"Who's the one lying here half-dead?" he muttered out loud.

He sounded terrible. *Half-dead* was an understatement.

Above the rush of the waterfall and his own pain, he could hear more laughter, kids squealing. Adult voices. At least she hadn't left Madison and J.T. on their own.

"It was probably just a squirrel," a man's voice called up to her.

"I know. I'm just curious."

Sebastian shivered, the water evaporating on his skin making him colder. He wondered if the cold was what had killed his grandfather. Joshua had gone into the falls in March, not mid-summer.

A fat mosquito landed on his bloodied arm. Sebastian didn't have the strength to swat it, but watched it crawl in the red ooze. He swore some more, under his breath this time.

He could hear Lucy thrashing her way up the narrow, difficult path on his side of the falls. It would take her along the ledge above his head, about four feet up. If he stayed quiet, she might walk right past him, assume her friend was right, that she'd heard a squirrel, and go back to the swimming hole.

Which left the problem of how he'd get the hell back to his motel. His car was tucked out of sight down the dirt road. A long way off in his condition. He'd probably pass out a few times before he made it. In the meantime, whoever had created the little landslide and thrown rocks at him could return and finish him off. It wouldn't take much, and he deserved it. On the other hand, what good would he be to Lucy?

"You're not much damn good now," he muttered.

Suddenly she was there, standing on the path above him. All she had to do was look down through the trees.

He should have followed his instincts and stayed in Wyoming. Ridden his horse. Slept in his hammock. He hadn't gambled in months, so that was out. He could play solitaire and read poetry.

He sighed, even his eyeballs aching. "Hello, Lucy."

She jumped, although not as much as he'd have expected. Maybe she was getting used to having him around. "Sebastian? What are you—oh, *Jesus.*"

Without hesitation, she slid down the hill on her butt—intentionally—and crouched next to him, the adventure travel expert at work. She had on shorts and a T-shirt. She hadn't, mercifully, bothered with a swimsuit for her dip in the brook with the kids. The water was only up to her knees.

Sebastian tried not to look as bloody and beaten as he was. He grinned. Or thought he did. "I could use some dry clothes."

"You could use an ambulance. What the hell happened?"

"Landslide. I fell."

The pretty hazel eyes narrowed. He could see doubt. And fear. She touched a finger to a spot above his right eye. "You need a doctor. You could have a concussion."

"Nah."

"You could need stitches."

"I don't mind scars, and I'm not going to bleed to death."

She stared at him for a few beats. "A landslide, huh?"

"Yep."

"It wasn't an accident," she said.

"It could have been. Theoretically."

She nodded. "Sebastian, tell me. Do I need to call an ambulance?"

He shook his head. A mistake. Her face swam in front of him, and all that stopped him from throwing up was the thought of it landing in her lap. She'd pitch him back in the water or get her friends up here and call an ambulance. There'd be a scene.

He shut his eyes, let the world get still again. "No," he said, eyes shut, "I'll be fine."

"I should call the police."

"They won't find anything. I didn't see anything." He'd only heard the grunt, the exhale—not enough.

"Sounds familiar," she said in a low voice.

Sebastian opened his eyes. "I just need water and a few Band-Aids."

"Bullshit."

"Lucy!" her friend called from below. "You find anything?"

She stood up, yelled down over the falls, "I'll be right there!" She crouched back beside Sebastian. "That's Rob. He's a friend. He knows first aid better than I do. I could ask him—"

"No."

"God, you're stubborn. All right. He and Patti can go back with the kids. I'll make up some excuse and help you get to my house and patch you up." She eyed him. "Unless you can't make it. If you collapse on me, I'm getting a rescue team in here and having you hauled out on a stretcher.''

Sebastian grimaced. He had limited choices, none good. "I'll make it. I don't need your help.''

"Ha,'' she said, and scooted back down the hill.

Sebastian was a slab of meat—cold, wet, bloody. Lucy had to catch him twice on their way down to her house. He would walk fifteen or twenty feet, crash against a tree or grab uselessly at ferns to steady himself, walk another fifteen or twenty feet. He was lucky he'd survived his fall.

They took a longer but easier path up from the brook and slipped in through the back door of the house. Madison, J.T. and the Kileys had arrived ahead of them and were in the side yard playing volleyball.

Lucy knew she'd have to explain Sebastian at some point. But not right now.

He sank against the kitchen counter. He was very pale, his eyes shut. Blood crusted on the gash above his right eye. He looked awful. Lucy wondered if she could sneak in a call to 9-1-1 while he was half out.

"World spinning on you?'' she asked.

His eyes were slits. "Just catching my breath.''

"Ha.''

"Florence Nightingale, you're not.''

She eased her shoulder under his arm. "Lean on me. I still have a little *oomph* left."

"I'll crush you."

"No, you won't. I'll take most of your weight in my legs. Come on, let's get moving before you pass out. It'd be harder having to drag you by your feet."

"Where are we going?"

"My bedroom."

He managed a faint, ironic smile. She slipped an arm around his back, taking more of his weight. She saw him wince in pain. Bruises. More scrapes. Possibly a cracked rib or two. He was a mess.

"You're not going anywhere for a while," she said.

He didn't answer. He was too far gone to argue. Lucy half coaxed, half dragged him down the short hall to her bedroom. Just inside the door, he collapsed onto his knees on the flat-braided rug. She debated leaving him there. Just shut the door and hope for the best when she opened it again.

"Come on." She caught up one arm and tugged. "We're almost there."

"I like it here." He slumped onto his stomach, and, without raising his head, said, "I'll be fine— you can go."

He stopped moving. Lucy, exhausted and hot, knelt beside him. He was either asleep or unconscious. "Sebastian?"

"I'm not dead yet."

She ran to the window overlooking the side yard west of the house, opposite the barn and garage, where the volleyball game was breaking up. She'd called down from the waterfall and had told Rob and Patti and the kids to all go ahead of her, that she'd go on to the house in a bit. No explanation. Rob had looked faintly suspicious, well aware from recent days that she wasn't herself. This was just more evidence.

"Hi, guys," she called through the screen. "I'll be out in a minute."

"Forget it," Madison said. "The bugs are eating us alive."

Patti tucked the ball under one arm. "You okay, Lucy?"

"Oh, yeah. I just slipped and got my feet wet." That would explain her damp clothes from leaning against the soaked, dripping Sebastian. It didn't explain the streaks of his blood. "I'll put on fresh clothes and meet you out front."

She dashed back to Sebastian, who was still prone on her rug. "Are you conscious?"

"Unfortunately."

"I'll be right back. Don't try to get up without me."

"Don't worry."

She stepped over him, grabbed a T-shirt out of

her drawer, and debated ducking down the hall to the bathroom. Forget it. Sebastian's eyes were pointed in the other direction, and he wasn't in any condition to make any unnecessary movements. She whipped off the wet, blood-spattered shirt and pulled on the fresh one. The clean, dry cotton against her skin instantly made her feel better.

When she got outside, Rob and Patti had the leftovers packed into the cooler. Lucy was breathing harder than she should be from an ordinary trek down from the falls.

Rob, who knew her capabilities, noticed. "Did you eat enough at dinner? You look whipped."

She *hated* lying. The trust she'd built among herself and her children, her friends, her staff, was based on being honest and straightforward. They might not like what she had to say, but it was always truthful. These, however, were extenuating circumstances. She had a bloodied Sebastian Redwing in her bedroom.

"I pushed it more than I realized," she said. "Thanks for dinner. My turn next."

He didn't look appeased. "Lucy..."

Patti touched his arm. "Come on, Rob, let's go. We don't want to outstay our welcome." She smiled at Lucy. "You take care. Call us if you need anything."

They both were suspicious, Lucy decided. Patti

probably suspected a romantic tryst; Rob, something to do with the big, fat bullet Lucy had yet to adequately explain.

They collected Georgie, and Lucy waved as they backed out of the driveway.

"I wish Georgie could spend the night," J.T. said from the porch.

Lucy joined him, her legs heavy and aching with each step. J.T. was hogging the wicker settee. Madison was flopped in a wicker chair, her long legs hung over one side. Both kids looked beat. Good, Lucy thought. They'd sleep well tonight.

"I'll explain more later," she said, "but I want you both to know that Sebastian Redwing is here."

Madison nearly fell off her chair. *"What?"*

J.T. was instantly excited. "He is? Where?"

"He's the noise I heard up at the falls. He took a nasty fall, and I helped him back here. He doesn't want it to get out that he's in town. That's why I didn't mention him to Rob and Patti." She should have, she thought. She should have just gotten it over with. There was no way J.T. wouldn't blab.

"Why wouldn't he want anyone around here to know he's in town?" Madison asked.

"Because he's from here."

"Oh. Actually, I get that."

"He'll need to recuperate a day or two," Lucy went on. "If you two will make up the guest room upstairs, I'll sleep up there. I need to get back to him. You two can manage?''

''We'll be fine, Mom.'' Madison was already on her feet, her face flushed. In her dull, deprived world, Lucy thought wryly, the sudden appearance of Sebastian Redwing passed for excitement. ''Let us know if there's anything else we can do.''

''I will. Thanks.''

When Lucy got back to her bedroom, Sebastian was on his feet, his shirt off. His jeans hung low on his lean hips. His arms, shoulders, back and chest were scraped and raw, bruises forming. His injuries aside, Lucy noted he was in impressive physical condition. He couldn't have spent all his time in his hammock.

''You can stay here tonight,'' she said. ''I'll throw your clothes in the wash. The kids and I can run out to your motel room tomorrow and fetch anything else you need.''

''I can drive myself back to my motel.''

''*Don't* argue with me. I'm not in the mood.''

He gave her a ghostly smile. ''Yes, ma'am.''

This wasn't a man who took easily to injury and incapacity, Lucy thought. ''Sit down before you fall down.'' She tore open the closet door, pulled out a shoe box that contained her medical supplies. ''Do you need help getting your pants off?''

''No. No help required.''

Something in his voice caused heat to surge up her spine. But she concentrated on the task at hand, rummaging in the shoe box. Her work required first aid training. Rob had full wilderness EMT qualifications, but she'd sent him home. She'd have to make do.

She grabbed antibiotic ointment and her wilderness medicine manual, leaving the rest for now.

Sebastian had crawled under the wedding-ring quilt his grandmother had made. His jeans were neatly hung over the foot post. He pointed to them. "They can dry right there. I'm not giving up my damn pants."

"I can run them through the wash in no time—"

"Not without a backup pair, you're not. I don't see anyone in this house who'd wear my size."

Lucy shrugged. "Suit yourself."

"What's the book?"

"My wilderness medicine manual. I want to double-check and make sure I'm treating you properly."

"Lucy." His look was dark. "You're not treating me at all."

She ignored him and turned to the page that described falls on rocks. She didn't think she needed to bother with the stuff on near drownings. "First we have to make sure the bleeding's stopped and you don't have any broken bones."

"Done. Next?"

"Your head. It's possible you have a concussion."

"If I do, it's mild and there's nothing to be done about it. So." He shifted position, wincing. "That's it. You can scoot."

Her eyes pinned him down. "I could have left you to the mosquitoes."

"And you think that would have been worse?"

"Your bravado must be exhausting. Why don't you just shut up and let me do this? I have basic first aid training. Except for minor scrapes and bee stings, I've never really had to use it. Rob has more experience." She sat on the edge of the bed. "Are you sure you don't want me to have him take a look at you?"

"Speed counts, Lucy."

She laid her manual on the bedside stand, open to the appropriate page. "You're sure you didn't puncture a lung or break a couple of ribs?"

"Ribs're fine," he said. "Lungs're fine."

As annoying as he was, she could see that talking was an effort for him. She examined the nastiest gash, the one above his eye. "It probably could use a couple of stitches." But he didn't answer, and she assumed any discussion of stitches was over. "I'll need to clean your wounds."

"Brook did that."

"Brook water is not a proper disinfectant."

His eyes darkened, their many shades of gray helping to communicate in no uncertain terms the low ebb of his patience. This was not a man who liked being at anyone's mercy.

Lucy decided to trust him on the ribs and lungs. "Let me get a few more supplies. I'll only be a second."

She was all of half a minute looking through her shoebox, but when she turned back to him, he was asleep. Or unconscious. "Sebastian?"

She sat on the edge of the bed and leaned close. His breathing seemed normal enough. She decided he'd dozed off. Just as well. Trying to be as efficient as possible, she quickly dipped sterile gauze into disinfectant and cleaned the gash and the worst of his scrapes, leaving the more minor injuries. She dabbed on antibiotic ointment. The gash on his head had to be bandaged. She was as gentle as possible, touching him only where she absolutely had to.

When she finished, he opened one eye. "Nurse Lucy."

"You were awake?"

"I figured pretending to be asleep would make it easier on both of us. You wouldn't be so nervous, and I wouldn't have to sit here forever."

She stiffened. "You don't make me nervous, Redwing."

That amused him. "Sure."

"Well, I see the fall didn't knock the jackass out of you." She slid off the bed. "Should I give you a couple of Tylenol or let you macho out the night in pain?"

"So long as I can see Tylenol clearly written on the tablets."

They were extra-strength capsules, and he checked.

Lucy stared at him. "You don't think *I* pelted you with rocks and pitched you over the falls, do you?"

He didn't answer. She told herself it was because of his injuries. Even a man whose professional life could reasonably make him cynical and paranoid couldn't think she was capable of injuring or killing anyone.

She felt the blood draining out of her, shock settling now that the immediate crisis was over. "Do you really think this wasn't an accident?"

"Yes."

"But you don't *know*. It could have been kids messing around, or a spontaneous landslide—"

"Could have."

But Lucy saw that wasn't what he believed. Of course, he wouldn't. His life and the work he did had conditioned him to believe the worse. "Do you think whoever did this wanted you dead?"

"I don't think it mattered."

He drifted off. Either he was asleep, or too out of

it to talk. Lucy stood at his bedside. Bruises were forming, and there was swelling, although nothing looked alarming. He was in no position to stop her from calling the police.

She turned on the fan and went into the hall, shutting the door behind her. She listened at the door, just to make sure he hadn't stirred. If he tried to get up and collapsed again, she'd have to leave him on the floor. She didn't have enough strength left to get him back in her bed.

She bit her lip at the rush of heat she felt, remembering last night's searing kiss. Well, that was over. The man couldn't even stand up tonight.

She headed upstairs. Madison and J.T. had the twin bed in the guest room made up with one of Daisy's ubiquitous quilts. It was a small room with simple furnishings and a dormer window overlooking the front yard.

"How's Sebastian?" Madison asked.

"He'll be fine. He really took a nasty fall." She pulled out a painted yellow chair at Daisy's old pedal-operated sewing machine and sat down. Her legs were twitchy from exertion and nerves. "Madison, when you were up in the woods this afternoon...did you see anyone?"

Madison shook her head. "No."

Lucy went very still, her parental instincts telling

her that her daughter was hiding something. "Are you sure?"

"Of course, I'm sure."

"Not even the summer people?"

"I saw the optometrist in his car." A Boston optometrist owned one of the vacation homes on the dirt road up on the ridge. "I thought you meant while I was out walking—"

"I did."

J.T. jumped up from the bed. "Me and Georgie saw a truck turn around in the driveway."

Lucy stayed focused on her daughter. "If you remember seeing anyone else, let me know."

Madison nodded. No argument. No sarcasm. No impatience with her mother for interrogating her. This struck Lucy as suspicious. Either she looked more done in than she realized and Madison was giving her a break—or her daughter wasn't telling the truth.

"Listen a minute," Lucy said, "both of you. I've got a lot on my mind, and I need you both to cooperate. Sebastian got hurt in a landslide up at the falls. I don't want you two going out in the woods alone until further notice."

"Mom, I'm fifteen—"

"That's the way it is, Madison."

Lucy debated telling them about the strange incidents, but she knew it would frighten them. This was her burden, not theirs. She needed to tell them enough to keep them safe, not paralyze them with fear.

J.T. gave her a hug. "Do you like Sebastian?"

"I don't know. I haven't thought about it. He got hurt, and I'm trying to help out." She patted her son's back; he was sweaty from volleyball, but still, at twelve, a little boy. "I guess he's okay."

"Is he doing his Clint Eastwood act?" Madison asked.

"I don't think it was an act. Anyway, he's not wearing his cowboy hat and boots."

J.T. untangled himself from her. "Can I see him?"

"In the morning." Lucy got to her feet. "Now, I think showers are in order. I'll go first. Find a good book to read. Relax. Okay?"

She hugged and kissed them both, then, in spite of her own fatigue, went back downstairs to check on Sebastian. "Are you asleep?" she whispered from the door.

"No."

"Is there anything I can get you?"

She could feel his eyes on her. He was half sitting up, his face lost in the shifting shadows of the en-croaching night. The fan whirred. "Your instincts were right. Something's going on around here." He fell back against his pillow. "You should call Plato."

"What can he do that you can't? I told you, I don't want to call in the cavalry if I don't have to."

"Plato isn't rusty. I am. He still carries a weapon." He paused, and his voice lowered. "I don't."

"Sebastian, if we're to the point you're worried about having to *shoot* someone, I'll call the police. I won't hesitate."

"I'm through with violence, Lucy."

She stared at him. "What?"

"Last year I had to shoot a man I once considered a friend. I intended to kill him—I thought I had."

"Jesus," Lucy breathed.

"I turned Redwing Associates over to Plato and quit the business." His gaze seemed to bore into her. "I came out of retirement for you, but I won't kill again."

Lucy straightened, trying to shake off a sudden sense of gloom. "Good heavens, Madison's right. You *are* like Clint Eastwood in *Unforgiven.*"

She thought she saw a small smile, but with the fading light, she couldn't be sure. "I was never a drunk."

"Rest. We'll talk in the morning. I don't want you to kill anyone. Although," she added with a smile, "you could wing the bastard."

* * *

Jack Swift typed in the information on the card Mowery had given him at lunch. It was late, quiet in his second-floor study. Only the brass lamp on his desk was lit. With Sidney attending a function at the Kennedy Center, he was alone.

He waited for the images to download. His computer was old and slow, but he was from a generation that didn't "upgrade" until something stopped working, whether it was a toaster or a damn computer. He thought he was doing well having one in his house at all.

The images slowly appeared on his screen. He braced himself. He expected illicit, pornographic pictures of his dead son and another woman.

Lucy.

Jack sat up straight, pain shooting through his chest. "Dear God," he whispered.

She was standing in front of the barn at her house in Vermont. She wore shorts and a T-shirt; flowers bloomed in a nearby garden. The picture had been taken recently.

The next pictures formed. Madison. J.T. His grandchildren together with their mother. All could have been taken last week.

"Bastard," Jack said, clutching his chest. *"Bastard."*

At the bottom of the screen, in big, black, easy-to-read letters were the words "The lovely family of United States Senator Jack Swift."

The pictures were Mowery's way of proving he could reach Jack's family. Of proving he *had* reached them.

Jack shut off the computer. He waited a few seconds for the pain in his chest to subside. If he dropped dead of a heart attack, would Mowery stop? Would he go after Lucy and the kids, anyway, out of frustration and vengeance?

He couldn't call the Capitol Police. It was too late now for official channels. For doing what he should have done in the first place.

Calming himself, Jack reached for his Rolodex. He flipped to a card, dialed the number scrawled on it. His instructions had been to call anytime, day or night.

"Redwing Associates."

"Yes," he said in his best senatorial voice. "This is Jack Swift. I'd like to speak to Sebastian Redwing."

Eight

⤜⟡⤐

Barbara was sick with fear and disgust.

Sebastian Redwing hadn't seen her. She was *sure* of it. But if he hadn't lost his balance—if he hadn't gone into the falls—he would have come after her. As it was, she'd had to pelt additional rocks at him to get him into the water.

A close call. Too close.

Thank God for her instincts. They'd warned her someone was nearby, and she'd ducked off the path and spotted him at the falls. Otherwise, she'd have bumped into him. She'd have had to scramble for an explanation.

He was still thrashing about in the water when she'd heard Lucy, the children and their low-life friends at the bottom of the falls. Barbara had crouched in the brush and ferns, itching and sweating as she'd waited, motionless, before finally creeping back up to the dirt road.

A very close call, indeed.

Now, pacing on the deck of the house she'd rented for the senator, she couldn't believe the risks she'd taken. She was calculating and intelligent, not one to succumb to impulse. If her friends and colleagues in Washington learned of this obsession of hers, these risky escapades, they would be shocked. They wouldn't understand. *She* didn't understand. She imagined what a bulimic girl must feel like, eating away at dinner, then throwing up in secret—the satisfaction, the disgust, the inability to stop herself.

Except she didn't have a disorder, Barbara thought. She could stop herself, if only she would.

She leaned against the deck rail, listening to the brook, the cool early-morning breeze gusting in the woods. Such a peaceful, beautiful spot. She'd chosen well. Jack would enjoy his time here, even if he should be seeing to his constituents in Rhode Island.

What if you'd killed Sebastian Redwing?

Once she'd spotted him lurking in the woods, she'd known Lucy had contacted him on her trip to Wyoming. Lucy had gone crying to him about the few little things that had happened to her over the previous week. Barbara hated whiners. And Sebastian was Colin's friend, not Lucy's. Lucy had no right.

Now Barbara had to worry Darren would find out. "God *damn* you, Lucy."

Well, Sebastian Redwing had survived. Lucy had helped him down to her house. Barbara had seen them as she'd hid in the woods like a madwoman.

Would Madison tell her mother—and Sebastian—about their visit yesterday?

It didn't matter. No one would make the connection between Sebastian's accident at the falls and Barbara's presence in Vermont. She breathed deeply, reminding herself she was the only one who knew—who could even imagine—she could do such a thing. To everyone else, she was the competent, professional, longtime personal assistant to a United States senator.

She sighed, feeling better, calmer. Sebastian Redwing was here in Vermont, and maybe she should tell Darren—but she wouldn't.

Sebastian awoke to a pounding head and the sounds of J.T. and his buddy playing *Star Wars* outside his window. He moaned, not moving, not even opening his eyes. "I hate kids."

The boys were throwing things—his guess, green tomatoes—and pretending they were bombs exploding on impact, with appropriate sound effects. Sebastian remembered playing similar games with his grandmother's green tomatoes.

"Boys!" Lucy yelled, probably from the back steps. "Those are my tomatoes!"

Explanations followed. They were the knobby tomatoes. They'd fallen off the vine. It was good to weed out the weaker tomatoes so the strong could get big and ripen.

Lucy wasn't buying. "Stay *out* of the tomatoes. Why don't you go pick blackberries? I'll make a cobbler."

"What's a cobbler?" J.T. asked. Apparently his mother didn't make too many cobblers.

She threatened to put them to work in the barn sorting mail. They grabbed cans from the recycling bin and vanished. Welcome silence followed.

Sebastian carefully rolled out of bed. It had been a hellish night. The pain and humiliation of falling into the water. Thoughts of kissing Lucy. And memories. So damn many memories. At fourteen, in shock from his parents' sudden deaths, he'd never wanted to leave here.

He reeled, reaching out for a bedpost to steady himself.

"Mom! Sebastian's dying!"

Two boys' faces popped into the window screen facing the backyard. The little bastards were spying on him. He banged on the screen as if they were a couple of pesky moths, and they gasped and cleared out.

Lucy burst in. Her mistake. He was hanging on to the bedpost in his shorts. "Oh," she said, grinding to a halt in the doorway. "I thought—J.T. said—"

He grinned. It was a damned nasty thing to do, but he felt like it. "Be glad I still have my shorts on. Those kids need to learn some manners."

"They know their manners. They just don't always employ them." She had a portable phone in one hand. "I should have remembered to pull the shades."

"Should have thought of it myself."

"You're all right?"

"A pot of coffee and a bottle of aspirin would help."

She nodded and retreated, shutting the door behind her. Sebastian sank onto the bed. He wasn't up to catching bad guys today. He was sore as hell with a mood to match.

He reached for his pants on the footboard, and realized instantly they'd been washed. His shirt was folded next to them. Lucy had managed to sneak in and out of his room at least twice—once to get his clothes, again to return them freshly laundered. He hadn't known. This did not improve his mood.

He got dressed and found his way to the bathroom. Except for fresh paint and towels in bright, vibrant colors, it hadn't changed since Daisy's day.

A look in the mirror told him why J.T. and his friend thought he was dying—and why they'd run off when he'd growled at them. Dried blood, raw scrapes, purple and yellow bruises.

And he needed a shave, but the only razor around was pink. He decided to wait.

He staggered out to the kitchen, where Lucy was at her laptop at the table. She had on a white top and shorts—simple, sexy. She barely looked up at him. "Coffee's made."

"Thank you." He moved slowly to the counter. "You stole my pants in the middle of the night."

"Actually, it was only about nine o'clock. You were dead to the world."

"What if bad guys had stormed the house?"

"I could dial 9-1-1 as easily as you could."

She kept the mugs in the same place Daisy had. He dragged one out and poured his coffee. "I hate going after bad guys in my shorts. I like having my pants. It's one of my rules." He leaned against the counter with his coffee. "Lucy Blacker, are you laughing at me?"

"Me? No way." She tapped a few keys. "Anyway, since you've renounced violence, you wouldn't have gone after the bad guys even if you were up to it."

The coffee was hot and strong, and made him feel almost human again. He took note of Lucy's bare arms and legs, their smooth muscles. She was strong and fit. No wonder she'd been able to help him down from the falls.

"The best thing to do in a dangerous situation," he said, "is to get out of it. Having a gun can give you a false sense of security. And just because I've renounced killing," he added, "doesn't mean I can't still catch bad guys."

She licked her lips. "Have you renounced all violence or just deadly force?"

"I don't carry a gun. I don't own any firearms. When I did, I only fired my weapon when I believed deadly force was the only option." He sipped more of his coffee. "You don't shoot to wound someone. You shoot to kill."

"Uck," she said.

"Yes. It's too often too easy to see shooting as your only option when you're armed to the teeth."

"But would you hit someone?"

He smiled, which made his face ache. "As in spanking or beating the shit out of someone?"

She flushed slightly, whether out of annoyance or embarrassment, he couldn't tell. Probably annoyance. He didn't think Lucy embarrassed easily. She looked at him. "What would you have done if you'd caught whoever knocked you into the falls yesterday?"

"I don't deal in hypotheticals." He dropped onto

a chair across from her. "I've done enough killing. That's my only point."

She nodded. "I understand."

"No, you don't, which is good. Can you point me to breakfast?"

"I can even fix you breakfast."

"You pulled me off the rocks and washed my clothes. That's enough."

She got up and opened the refrigerator. "I don't need you collapsing on my kitchen floor. A cheddar cheese omelette okay?"

"It would be wonderful. Thank you."

The kitchen quickly filled with the smell of eggs, butter, Vermont cheddar cheese and toast. Sebastian remembered countless sunny summer mornings here in his grandmother's kitchen. In Wyoming during the past year, while he gambled, rode his horses, walked with his dogs, bided time in his hammock and otherwise did nothing, he'd found himself haunted by his childhood in Vermont. Images, memories, smells, the hopes and dreams of the introspective boy he'd been. He'd assumed it was because of Lucy, knowing she was here. But maybe not.

He refilled his mug and reached for the bottle of Extra-strength Tylenol.

Lucy turned a lightly browned omelette onto a

plate. "Why didn't you go to the funeral?" she asked quietly.

At first he thought she was talking about Daisy, but he pulled himself out of his own depths and realized she meant Colin. "I was in Bogotá. A kidnapping case."

"You didn't call, write, send a flower—"

"Would it have made you feel better if I had?"

She buttered the toast, not looking at him. "No. That's not the point."

He knew it wasn't.

She placed his food in front of him and walked out of the kitchen, leaving him to his breakfast. And her laptop. Sebastian slid it over with one finger and poked around her hard drive while he ate. Lucy Blacker Swift was a very busy lady, he decided. Her adventure travel company was an attractive mix of active sports, education and relaxation. He called up a draft of her new brochure. Autumn inn-to-inn canoe trips ranging from a long weekend to ten days. Sea kayaking on the coast of Maine. A nature and history hike in Newfoundland. And on it went. Each trip was described with the kind of rich detail that made Sebastian realize he hadn't been that many places just for fun. Tracking down kidnappers in Colombia wasn't the same as enjoying its fascinating culture and scenery.

Madison plopped onto the chair across from him. "Are you spying on my mother?"

No good-morning. No polite enquiry into the state of his health. He eyed her over the laptop's screen. "I'm checking my e-mail."

"No, you're not. The modem's not hooked up."

"Okay. I'm spying on your mother."

She gave him a direct, no-nonsense look. "Why?"

The kid was a pain. "You're fifteen. Why don't you have a job?"

"I do have a job. I work for Mom's company."

"That's not a job. That's working for your mother."

She made a face. Probably if he weren't so bloodied and bruised and dangerous-looking, she'd have told him what was what. The kid had spirit. He shut down Lucy's money file and a financial spreadsheet he'd pulled up. Taking a look at her new brochure was easier to explain. He'd have to talk to her about password protection.

"I figure you can drive me out to my motel," he said. "I need to pick up a few things if I'm going to be laid up here."

"Me?"

"Yeah, you. You drive, right?"

"I have my learner's permit. I can't drive without an adult—"

"I'm an adult."

Her mouth snapped shut.

"Go ask your mother while I finish my breakfast."

The girl seemed taken aback. "Are you serious?"

He sighed. "Don't I look serious? I fell off a flipping cliff last night. I'm not in the mood to joke around."

She mumbled something about asking her mother, and fled. If nothing else, Sebastian figured he'd given her a good excuse to make her retreat. He'd always made kids nervous. He didn't know why.

Madison returned in a few minutes, breathless. "Mom said absolutely not."

"How come?"

She shrugged. She was a pretty kid, looked a lot like her father.

Sebastian grinned at her. "You mean you didn't put up a fight? I thought all fifteen-year-olds snapped up every opportunity to drive."

"I have things to do," she said quickly, and disappeared.

A teenager who didn't want to get behind the wheel. He had to look bad.

At least his head was clearing, if slowly. He felt better after eating. He cleaned up his dishes and poured himself a third cup of coffee, staring out at the backyard. Birds twittered in the garden, and he could hear the hum of bumblebees in the still summer air. A Japanese beetle had made its way onto the kitchen windowsill.

The air, the feel of the light, the vegetation—everything was so different from Wyoming. This was more like a dream, or an elusive memory.

"What do you need at your motel?" Lucy asked behind him.

He pulled himself back into the moment. This wasn't Daisy's house anymore. This was Lucy's house, and Lucy was in a kind of trouble that still didn't make sense to him.

He turned and leaned against the counter, avoiding any sudden movements that could send his head or stomach into a tailspin. "I want to check out."

"And go back to Wyoming?"

"And move in here for a few days."

She didn't react. She wasn't twenty-two anymore, the happy and ambitious young woman starting a life with Colin Swift, the son of a senator, a decent human being who wanted to make the world a better place. Sebastian didn't have such high hopes for himself. Now she was the mother of two children, he realized, and a thirty-eight-year-old widow. She was making a name for herself in the competitive world of adventure travel. If the years had made her stronger, they'd also taken some of the spark out of her. She knew life could kick her in the head.

"I've been thinking," she said. "If your fall yesterday wasn't an accident—"

"Which we don't know."

"Granted. But if it was deliberate, why you? Why not Rob or Patti or me?"

"Two immediate possibilities. One, our little friend saw me checking on you and your place, didn't know who I was and worried I'd mess up their fun. Two, our little friend recognized me."

"How?"

"I grew up here, and I have my share of enemies from my work."

"But your work has nothing to do with me," Lucy said.

Sebastian chose not to tell her about Darren Mowery. "True."

"Could it be someone I'd know, too?"

"Maybe."

Her brow furrowed. "Who?"

"If I knew who," he said, "this'd be over."

She gave herself a small shake. "This'll make me crazy. All right. I'll go check you out of the motel. You can bunk in my room. I'll move upstairs to the guest room."

"I don't mind the guest room."

"Are you kidding? If someone leaves another dead animal in my bed, I'd much prefer you be the one to find it." She grabbed her keys off a wall hook. "You'll look after the kids while I'm gone? Rob's putting Madison to work this morning, and J.T.'s hanging out with Georgie. They have chores to do."

"My childhood revisited," Sebastian said dryly.

She smiled over her shoulder at him. "A little normalcy will do you good."

She pushed open the screen door, felt the morning air warming up fast. "I don't like the idea of you going out to my motel by yourself," he said.

"Oh, sure. Big help you'd be." She turned and shook her head at him through the screen. "Sorry, Redwing, but you look as if you took a header off a waterfall. I know, even beaten and broken, you can probably still take half the men on the planet, but—" she flipped him another smile "—I'll take my cell phone and call 9-1-1 if I run into trouble."

"Have the desk clerk go into my room with you."

She trotted down the back steps, calling back, "Why? If anyone's hiding under your bed, I wouldn't want to endanger some poor innocent desk clerk. If not, then there's no reason to worry."

He went to the door. "Lucy."

She looked up at him. "I'll be fine, Sebastian. Back in an hour." She frowned suddenly. "Oh, wait."

For a moment, he thought she'd changed her mind about going alone. But she ran back into the kitchen, grabbed her laptop, and, as she walked past him again, said, "I'll remove temptation."

Two minutes after she left, J.T. and Georgie made their way into the kitchen. They kept their distance, checking him out like a couple of wary dogs.

"He looks scary," Georgie half whispered to his buddy.

J.T. licked his lips and asked Sebastian politely, "How are you feeling this morning?"

"All in all, I'd rather be in Wyoming. What're you boys up to? I thought you had chores."

"We're done," J.T. pronounced.

"I'll bet. Let's go take a look at your mother's garden, see if it's weed-free."

They didn't like that idea, but they weren't going to tell him. They scampered back outside, Sebastian following at his own reduced speed. He hurt like hell. Pure, dumb luck had saved him worse injury. He couldn't afford to let his mind wander again.

But when he stepped into Lucy's garden, it was as if his past reached up out of the ground and grabbed him by the throat. The feel of the warm dirt under his feet, the sounds of the birds and the wind, the smell of flowers and earth and mown grass. Skinny beans hung from bushy plants. Green tomatoes slowly ripened in the sun. Five varieties of lettuce were at various stages of growth, and prickly vines of cucumbers, summer squash, zucchini and pumpkins spread in their raised beds.

Daisy hadn't had raised beds or mulched paths. She'd planted more vegetables. Her garden hadn't been just a hobby, it had been a way of life for her. What she couldn't use herself, she'd given away. And she'd always had garden work for Sebastian. It wouldn't have occurred to her not to.

She'd never assumed he didn't want the place. Even when she was old and dying, and he was starting his own business and buying a ranch in Wyoming, she'd told him, "You'll get the farm after I die."

"I don't want it," he'd said.

"So what? Once you get it, you can do with it as you please. I don't have anyone else."

"You could donate it to the Nature Conservancy."

She'd scoffed at that idea. "If you get yourself killed before I die peacefully in my sleep of natural causes, then I'll consider giving it away. I worked too hard to hang onto this place. If I'd wanted to give it away, I'd have done it fifty years ago."

He hadn't tried to follow her logic. Daisy Wheaton had a mind of her own, and she'd do what she meant to do, regardless of what he thought. She'd lost a husband and her daughter, her only child, and gone on without them, living by a code that made sense to her.

"You'll know what to do with the place, Sebastian," she'd told him later, when she walked with a cane and could no longer tend her gardens. "I know you will."

He'd sold it to Lucy.

"Can we go fishing?" J.T. asked.

Sebastian shook off the onslaught of memories. This was why he'd gotten rid of the damn place. It stole his mind, invaded his senses. "No. Weed the squash. Then you can go fishing."

"Mom didn't say we had to—"

"I'm saying it."

J.T. stood his ground. "You're not our boss."

Sebastian smiled. It was about the first time the kid had impressed him. "So? You're still weeding the squash. I'll sit up on the back steps and watch you."

"Mom trusts us."

"Good for her. I don't. First chance you get, you boys'll be sneaking off to the brook. Did she tell you no fishing without adult supervision?"

They didn't answer, which meant she had.

"Yeah," Sebastian said, smug, and headed stiffly to the back steps.

Madison appeared in the back door. "Sebastian,

there's a call for you. Your friend Plato Rabe—I can't say his last name."

"Rabedeneira."

"He was calling for Mom. I told him you were here, and he said he'd talk to you."

She looked at him expectantly, as if he'd explain, but he took the portable phone from her without comment. Being her mother's daughter, she stayed in the door. He sat on the steps and glanced up at her. "You going to listen in?"

She blushed. "I wasn't—"

"I thought you were working in the barn."

"I was. I'm on break."

These kids. "Your brother could use help weeding."

"I don't weed," she said. His look must have done the trick because she added quickly, "But I will today. It's not like I don't have chores in the garden. I picked beans the other night."

"That was the other night." He pointed with the phone. "Weeds're waiting."

She slid off down the steps, and Sebastian put the phone to his ear. "I'm here."

"I don't even want to know what that was all about," Plato said. "Sounds like goddamn *Rebecca of Sunnybrook Farm.*"

"Tell me you've ever read *Rebecca of Sunnybrook Farm.* What's up?"

"Jack Swift called for you."

Sebastian was silent.

"Blackmail," Plato said.

"Mowery."

"He wouldn't give me the details, just that someone's blackmailing him and he wants to talk to you."

"Did you tell him where I was?"

"No."

It was a stupid question. Of course, he wouldn't. Plato was a talker, but he wasn't indiscreet. "No details on the blackmail?"

"None."

What could the intrusive and determined Darren Mowery find on a squeaky-clean senator like Jack Swift?

"The girl said something about you slipping into a waterfall?"

Sebastian sighed. No secrets in this family. "I had help."

"Let me know when you need me," Plato said. "I'm scheduled to leave Frankfurt in the morning. I can leave tonight."

"I'll let you know. Thanks, Plato."

"Happy Ford hasn't picked up Mowery's trail. I put her on Jack Swift."

Sebastian nodded. "We won't find Mowery unless he wants us to."

"You found him a year ago."

"Yes," Sebastian said, "but I didn't finish the job."

Lucy parked in front of Sebastian's motel room and let herself in with his key. The room was hot and dark, the curtains and shades pulled, and she felt as if she were meeting a lover. She quickly reminded herself the man who'd occupied this room was in no condition for a romantic tryst or whatever it was her mind was conjuring. And besides, he was Sebastian Redwing.

"Enough said," she muttered and got to work.

His clothes and personal items were simple, functional and obviously expensive. He was a man accustomed to travel. There was nothing frivolous, just exactly what he needed for a few days or even a few weeks.

Nor, Lucy thought, was there anything to satisfy her growing suspicion that he had other reasons for being in Vermont. It wasn't just her. It wasn't just some sense of obligation to Colin. She wasn't sure what had triggered her doubts, but last night, waking up in her guest room with the eerie sounds of an owl in the nearby woods, she'd latched onto the idea that Sebastian was holding back on her. He knew things, he had suspicions that he was keeping to himself.

She was so convinced last night she almost marched down to his room to demand an explanation. But common sense intervened, and this morning her suspicions seemed a little more far-fetched. Not that Sebastian wouldn't withhold information, but that he had anything to withhold. What could he possibly know that concerned her? Certainly nothing *bad,* not at the level he was used to. Assassinations, bombings, kidnappings, extortion. This was just someone trying to spook her.

Pushing back the flood of questions, Lucy dashed into his bathroom for his shaving gear. She was struck by the intimacy of her chore. Sebastian must have known what she'd be handling. Maybe he was too out of it to care.

"Sebastian is never too out of it," she said out loud.

That was his job. Staying alert, on task. Even, she thought, if he had managed to fall into Joshua Falls.

She wished she could call her friends in Washington for the scuttlebutt on him. What did they know about his "sabbatical"? What rumors had they heard? But she didn't dare, because her questions would give them something to gossip about, and it could get back to Jack.

She stuffed everything into her car and walked over to the small building housing the front desk. The clerk was a no-nonsense woman in her sixties.

She wouldn't have been much help with any desperadoes hiding under Sebastian's bed.

The woman complained about her bad knee while she flipped through handwritten cards for the appropriate bill. "I hurt it last winter cleaning out Mother's attic. It's been a year since she died, but I couldn't bring myself to do it." She found the right card and set it on the counter, adjusting her reading glasses. "The owner keeps threatening to computerize, but I don't see the need myself. Well, I'll be! Sebastian Redwing. Daisy Wheaton's grandson?"

"That's right," Lucy said. "Do you know him?"

"Not since he was a boy. I don't know if I'd recognize him now. He came to live with Daisy after his parents were killed. That was horrible. Just horrible. I'll never forget it. That poor woman outliving her husband and her only child." She shuddered. "I was just a little girl and didn't really know what was going on when Joshua Wheaton died, but I've been afraid of waterfalls ever since. I've never even been to Joshua Falls."

"Really? They're very beautiful."

She pursed her lips in disapproval. "I thought it was morbid to name the falls after him. If I get run over by a truck, I don't want anyone naming the truck after me!"

Lucy smiled. "I think it was to honor him because he saved a little boy from drowning."

"He was reckless. He didn't think about his wife, his own little girl."

"Maybe not, but in that situation—I don't know, it would be hard not to try to do something to help. I imagine Joshua thought he could handle the risks he was taking. You can't stand by and watch a little boy drown, but you can't be totally reckless, either. That's suicide."

The clerk nodded grudgingly. "People do say Joshua knew what he was doing, and it was just one of those things. The conditions were worse than he expected, and there he was, committed, with no way out."

"Yes," Lucy said, distracted, wondering if in a way that explained her situation with Sebastian. Committed, no way out.

"Well, it's a sad story. Mother said Daisy never really got over Joshua."

"They were friends?" Lucy asked. She was curious about Daisy Wheaton, whose spirit was so much a part of her life. But she'd never asked many questions of townspeople about her for fear of seeming too nosy, prying into the life of one of their own. And she'd never considered asking Sebastian.

"They were in the quilting club together." The older woman sighed wistfully, tears coming to her eyes. "But that was a long time ago. Mother was ninety-two when she died."

And her daughter missed her, Lucy thought, touched. Would her own children still miss their father when they were in their sixties, after all those years without him? They'd think about him, remember him. That much she knew.

"What did you do with her quilts?" she asked suddenly.

"I saved them, of course. I gave one to each of my children and grandchildren. What else would I do with them?"

Sell them with your mother's place, Lucy thought. That's what Sebastian did. She didn't think he'd saved even a single one of Daisy's quilts.

With all the memories and tragedies associated with Vermont, and specifically Joshua Falls, he could have been distracted yesterday, the landslide thus catching him by surprise. It could have been an accident, after all. Under the circumstances, how reliable a witness was he?

Lucy paid his motel bill and thanked the clerk for her time. "I'm Lucy Swift, by the way. I bought Daisy Wheaton's house from her grandson a few years ago."

"Yes! I've heard of you. You've got that adventure travel business, right?"

"That's right. I hope you'll stop in one day. The house came with a bunch of Daisy's quilts. I'd love to have you tell me about some of them."

"I'd be happy to. I'm Eileen, by the way—Eileen O'Reilly. I'll take you up on your offer one of these days."

"Soon, I hope."

Lucy headed straight home. When she turned into her driveway, she stopped at the mailbox and stared down at Joshua Brook. It was wide and easy here, its water clear and coppery. Placid, beautiful. Soothing. She loved to sit on a rock on a warm afternoon and watch the water course over her feet. It was always cold, and even amidst a mid-summer dry spell, it had never gone dry.

And yet upstream, these same waters had claimed Joshua Wheaton's life and made his wife a widow. The Widow Daisy.

The Widow Swift, Lucy thought again.

She dumped Sebastian's stuff in her bedroom and found him stretched out on a blanket in the shade of an old apple tree in the backyard. J.T. and Georgie were playing checkers on the far edge of the blanket. Lucy pushed aside any lingering thoughts of Sebastian's motel room.

"Boys," she said, "would you mind getting me something cold to drink?"

"Can we have something, too?" J.T. asked.

"Of course."

"Milk shakes?"

"Not right now. Just whatever's in the fridge."

They scooted off. Sebastian eyed her, his head propped on a couple of pillows. "Madison's in the barn. She's pissed at me. Now she says I'm more like Humphrey Bogart in *The African Queen*." He squinted up at Lucy. "Do you think I'm more Bogie than Eastwood?"

"I think my daughter has an active imagination."

He sat up, wincing. In the midday light, she could see that his wounds, while unpleasant and painful, really were superficial and would heal quickly. He narrowed his eyes at her, again giving her that sense he could see into her soul.

"What's on your mind, Lucy Blacker?"

He'd always called her Lucy Blacker, from the day they'd met. "Nothing."

She realized she was pacing, and stopped. She stared out at her garden. It was lush and healthy, and it had her stamp on it. Yet it still felt like Daisy's garden. People in town thought of her as stepping into Daisy's life. Exchanging an old widow for a young widow.

Was that what Sebastian thought?

Suddenly Lucy couldn't breathe, and she knew he was watching her, trying to read her mind. Possibly succeeding.

She turned to him. "Did Daisy ever go back to the falls?"

She could see he knew what she meant. He didn't

react in any obvious way, just seemed to slide deeper inside himself. His past must have taught him that—to stay in control, bury his feelings, choose what he wanted someone else to see. The past three years had taught her similar skills.

He shook his head. "No, never."

"The falls must not be an easy place for you to be."

"My grandfather died long before I was born. Daisy never liked me going up there, but she didn't stop me, except in winter." The unusual gray eyes stayed on her.

If he could read her mind, penetrate her soul, she didn't have the slightest idea how to read him, get inside his soul. She wasn't sure she wanted to.

He added, enigmatically, "It's a beautiful spot."

"Then you weren't distracted yesterday?"

He shrugged. "No, I was distracted."

"And?"

"And what?"

She groaned. "You know damn well what I mean."

"You're fishing, Lucy. What else is on your mind?"

"You didn't come here just because of me." She spoke without thinking, analyzing, debating. Enough already, she thought. She stepped closer to his blanket, knew that what her instincts were saying to her were right. "You had other reasons, too."

"Such as?"

The man was maddening. "Why should I guess when you can just tell me?"

He gave the smallest of smiles. "I don't know, I like the idea of seeing how far-fetched your guesses are."

"Is that a yes, you do have other reasons for being here?"

"You think too much."

And here she was, not thinking at all. She gave him another few seconds, but that was the end of it. Lucy crossed her arms on her chest, considered a moment. "Okay. Fine. Well, here's how it is. From this point forward, you are to keep me informed of where you are and what you're doing, what you know, what your plans are. This is my house, my town, my family—*my* life. Understood?"

"Sure, Lucy." He clasped his hands together behind his neck and settled back on the blanket. He shut his eyes and yawned, making himself comfortable. "By the way, your son cheats at checkers. When Georgie figures it out, there'll be hell to pay."

Nine

◈◈◈◈

Sidney pressed both hands on Jack's shoulders to keep him in his chair in the courtyard. "You sit," she told him. "I'll make the martinis."

He smiled up at her, could smell her fresh perfume as she stayed close behind him. She was so beautiful, so kind. "You don't need to wait on me."

"This isn't waiting on you." She headed off toward the kitchen, laughing over her shoulder at him. "This is snapping you out of your funk. You have one chance—one martini—then I'm out of here, and you can wallow."

In another minute, Jack heard her humming, clinking glasses. His eyes welled with tears. She was such a good woman. Smart and decent, comfortable with herself. He wished he had the courage to tell her about Darren and the blackmail. About Colin. About how he'd sniped at Lucy for living in Vermont, as if somehow the blackmail, his loneliness, was her fault.

But he couldn't bring himself to tell anyone. It was as if speaking the details out loud made them real and true, unavoidable. He supposed he was still in denial, as the pop shrinks would say. Yet his silence ate at him, chewing away at his gut like an acid leak. Except for the day he'd stood over his son's body, he'd never felt so isolated and alone, so goddamn helpless.

Sidney blamed his work. His schedule was jammed with last-minute political jockeying before the August recess. He was using every ethical tactic he knew to garner support for legislation he and another two senators were sponsoring.

To have it all end like this, he thought. He tried to be optimistic. He wanted desperately, horribly, to believe that Darren Mowery would give up his blackmail campaign without bleeding Jack completely dry or asking him to compromise his oath of office. He could only afford another ten or twenty thousand before someone started to notice, before someone talked. It could be anyone—a bank teller, his accountant. Word would get out, questions would be asked. What secrets was Senator Swift hiding? His political enemies would jump. The media would be overzealous in their watchdog role.

Truth would mix with gossip and rumor, and the politics of personal destruction.

And that was the best-case scenario. The worst was if Mowery asked Jack to compromise his oath of office, the ethics by which he'd tried his damnedest to live and work his entire adult life, even before he'd taken public office. Then, who knew what would happen.

He was on his own. Sebastian Redwing hadn't returned his call. Jack wished he hadn't given in to impulse and contacted Redwing Associates. Plato had warned him Sebastian probably wouldn't call back if Jack wasn't willing to be more forthcoming. "Call me back if you want to talk details," Plato said. "I'll get word to him."

He'd refused to say where Sebastian was or to put Jack's call through to him, and finally Jack hung up in frustration. Admitting he was the victim of blackmail had made him physically ill. What difference did the details make? It was Mowery. Sebastian knew Mowery's tactics, had been Colin's friend. The honorable course of action would be to go get the bastard and never mind the sordid details.

So, here he was. Waiting.

Sidney swung out from the kitchen with two martinis. He smiled. "I'll make the next round."

"You're on." She sank onto a chair and tasted her handiwork. "Marvelous, if I do say so myself."

She raised her glass to him. "To love, friendship, the United States Senate, and getting out of this town in one piece."

Jack laughed. "Amen." He had to agree, it was a superb martini. "Imagine, in just a few days, we'll be sitting on a deck in Vermont sipping martinis and looking at nothing but trees."

Her dark eyes flashed. "We?"

"You can sneak off for a week or so at least, can't you?"

"Yes, but—" She set her martini on the table. "I realize Lucy knows we're seeing each other, but you and she and your grandchildren—it's just been the five of you for the past three years."

"Lucy's parents—"

"Are in Costa Rica. Yes, I visited them in January. But you're Colin's father. You're their only connection to him—and they're the only family you have."

"They live in Vermont now," Jack said, wincing at how bitter he sounded. "It's not as if it's been 'just the five of us' for the past three years."

"Ah," Sidney said knowingly.

He managed a smile. "'Ah' what?"

"You're angry with Lucy for moving away. Jack, she's not responsible for your happiness. She's had to get on with life without Colin, just as you have.

It's different for you. Colin was your son, not your husband."

"I lost everyone, Sidney. Eleanor, Colin, my grandchildren."

"Your grandchildren are in *Vermont*. It's not the end of the earth." Sidney shook her head—so kind, so indulgent. She disagreed with him, but wouldn't belittle him. "Oh, Jack. Jack, their moving isn't a rejection of you any more than Lucy's parents' move to Costa Rica is a rejection of her."

"I know that intellectually, but in my gut—" He sighed. "Sidney, in my gut they rejected me."

"That must feel awful."

He smiled, rallying. "Thank God for you. Lucy likes you, you know."

"As a friend and a former colleague of sorts. I don't know about as your lover. And," she added seriously, "I'm not just talking about how Lucy would react having me in Vermont. I'm talking about you, too, Senator Jack Swift."

He frowned. "I don't understand."

"Of course, you don't. You haven't had a 'girl-friend' in forty years."

"Ouch."

Sidney leaned forward in her chair and brushed her fingertips across his chin. "Think hard, Jack, before you invite me to Vermont with your family.

I like what we are together. I don't want that to change."

"Why would it change?"

"Just think, okay?"

"Okay."

She laughed. "You are so thickheaded. But never mind." She swept up her martini and took a big sip. "Whether it's to Vermont or the beach, I'm getting out of the city for a few days. I love Washington, but summers do get trying."

With the martini, the quiet, steamy evening and Sidney's gentle, intelligent company, Jack felt more comfortable. When it came to Washington, he understood what she meant. For all its problems, dangers and frustrations, he loved living and working here. Although Rhode Island was home, Washington was where he was at his best.

He couldn't imagine how Lucy lived in Vermont, no matter how beautiful. Was she at her best there? Or was she just hiding from reality? That, he could understand. He would do anything to hide from reality now, was trying his damnedest to get away with it. Losing Colin had been a terrible blow for all of them. But a short-lived frenzy over senatorial blackmail and a sordid affair could drive Lucy even farther away from her dead husband's father.

Sidney was right. Lucy, Madison and J.T. were his only family. He couldn't act in haste.

"Jack—oh, Jack." Sidney smiled and pretended to knock on his forehead. "You're distracted tonight, aren't you?"

"Just tired," he said. "Barbara reports she's rented a house on the ridge above Lucy's farmhouse. It's within easy walking distance, just above a notorious waterfall."

"Ah, and how is Barbara?"

He shrugged. "Back to her old self."

Sidney looked dubious. "Don't count on it."

"She's worked in my office since she was a college intern. She's not going to rock the boat again. She lost it for a second, that's all. It happens. With the pressure we're under, people lose it every now and then."

"Jack, Jack," Sidney said, incredulous, shaking her head. "The woman's in love with you."

"No, she isn't. She just got carried away. And, even if she is, what can I do about it? She's a valuable member of my staff."

"Oh, God. You sound as if you're talking about your favorite pen."

"I don't mean to. Sidney, I'm not going to fire Barbara Allen because she got a little goofy on me. If she becomes a problem, I'll deal with it."

"I'm sure you will. Excuse me for meddling."

She was matter of fact, not hurt. Jack smiled. "Meddle away. It's nice to have someone with your clear eye to talk to." He sighed; the martini was relaxing him. Or maybe it was just Sidney's company. "I suppose I should tell Lucy I'm coming. She knows I want to come up for a visit, but she thinks it's just for a day or two, not the entire month."

"She and Barbara haven't run into each other?"

He shook his head. "Barbara says not. We spoke earlier today. I want this to be my surprise."

Sidney got to her feet, kissing him lightly. "You're an odd man, Senator Swift."

And jumpy, Jack thought when his cell phone rang and he nearly fell off his chair. Sidney sank back into her chair, obviously assuming his startled response was a result of his distraction over her kiss.

"Hey, Jack." Darren's voice, instantly recognizable. "How's Ms. Sidney tonight?"

Jack ignored the twist of pain in his gut. He kept his voice calm, professional. "We're both fine, thank you. What can I do for you?"

"Remember the number I gave you that day in your office?"

"Yes."

"Let's do another ten-thousand-dollar transfer. Keep things nice and friendly, build a little trust between us."

"I thought—"

"That's your problem, Senator. Don't think. Just

do.'' Mowery gave a sick little laugh. ''Didn't Yoda say something like that?''

And he disconnected.

Jack shakily set the phone back on the table. He knew he was pale. He could feel it. Sidney watched him, brow furrowed. ''Jack?''

He managed a small smile. ''July is always ulcer time in Washington. Another martini?''

Lucy woke up early and made sure she was out of the kitchen before Sebastian wandered in. He was on his own this morning. His presence in her house was throwing her off in unexpected ways. She didn't sleep well, she had unsettling dreams when she did sleep, and she felt constantly on edge—not irritable, just aware, alert, as if her senses were on overdrive.

This morning, she was scheduled to conduct a canoe lesson with local kids on a nearby pond. She had no intention of canceling, or, she thought, of getting Sebastian's okay. That was the other thing about having him around. She was used to being in charge. She didn't like the idea of him thinking he was in control just because she'd asked for his help. She hadn't abdicated any responsibility for herself and her children.

J.T. helped her get together paddles and life vests. Some of his friends were in the group, but he liked to think of himself as a co-teacher more than a student. "Remember," Lucy warned him, "no one likes a know-it-all."

"But if I know something, I know it."

"That doesn't mean you have to be obnoxious about it. We all have our gifts," she said, hoisting paddles into the back of her car, "and yours is to have a mother who taught you how to paddle when you were a tot."

"*Mom.*"

She grinned at him. "Was I being obnoxious?"

Madison floated across the lawn. "Do you mind if I join you? No point hanging around here. Sebastian will just put me to work."

"He could use the time to rest," Lucy said.

His bruises had blossomed, making him look worse, although he was actually doing much better. He hadn't taken any Tylenol yet today. Lucy wondered if having him around was a deterrent, sort of like having a big, mean dog lying in the shade.

Except he was sexy, and last night she'd tossed and turned imagining him in her bed. Not good. Dangerous thinking. *Crazy* thinking.

He came out to the car before they left, wearing jeans and a dark polo shirt, no shoes. Lucy's mouth went dry at the sight of him.

"I'm just making sure both kids are in the car with you," he said. "I don't want any surprises."

"We thought you could use some quiet time."

His mouth twitched. "Toddlers get quiet time. You going to the pond or the river?"

"The pond."

"How many kids?"

"About a half-dozen, not counting my own. It's a very public spot."

He peered into the car, and both J.T. and Madison tried not to stare. His face wasn't as bruised as it could have been, but ugly purple and blue splotches had formed around the cut above his eye. He seemed more energetic and focused this morning, less as if he might pass out at any second. He'd gone to bed early. Lucy had sat up in the living room reading, wondering what it might be like to have him to talk to.

Not that he talked, she reminded herself. He was succinct, closemouthed or antisocial, depending on one's point of view—or mood. In his work, no one cared about his personality, just his competence.

"All right," he said, straightening. He swept her with a humorless glance. "Don't be late."

Lucy bristled. "I answer to myself, Redwing."

His voice lowered so Madison or J.T. wouldn't hear. "You don't want me coming after you."

Actually, she didn't. A hot, almost electric current ran up her spine. She thought she concealed it well, but Sebastian smiled knowingly before retreating to the house. The man noticed *everything*.

A couple of hours on the pond renewed her spirits. The kids she taught were eager to learn, and Madison and J.T. were skilled enough Lucy didn't really have to worry about them. She relished the feel of the paddle dipping into the water, the occasional small splashes on her arms and legs, the sounds of birds and laughter. Her doubts and questions receded, and the heightened state of awareness—almost frenzy—finally quieted. By the time they packed up and headed home, she felt centered again.

But it all went to hell when she pulled into her driveway and saw Sebastian and Rob Kiley chatting on her front porch.

It was as if her two lives—the one in which she was in control versus the one in which she had lost control—had collided in a blinding crash. The two men waved and smiled, but she could see Rob's smile was forced.

"How's the pond?" Sebastian asked, sounding calm, not as pain-racked.

Lucy faked a smile of her own. "Probably much the same as when you two were kids. Catching up on old times?"

Rob got to his feet stiffly, his normal easygoing demeanor lost to obvious tension. "Sebastian never knew my grandmother gave Daisy a fruitcake every Christmas in honor of Joshua Wheaton for saving my father's life.'' He managed a faint glimmer of humor. ''Daisy always fed it to the birds. Sixty years of fruitcakes literally out the window.''

''It was good seeing you, Rob,'' Sebastian said. He, too, rose, and, without even a glance at Lucy, he retreated inside.

Rob sat back down. ''Okay, Lucy. Talk.''

So, she was right. The two men had colluded. ''Talk about what?''

''Sebastian Redwing.''

She sighed.

Rob shook his head, biting off any irritation. If he hated one thing, Lucy knew, it was feeling any kind of negative emotion toward anyone. ''Okay, here's what I know so far,'' Rob said. ''He's Daisy's grandson, his grandfather was killed rescuing my father from the falls, his parents were killed in a hit-and-run accident when he was fourteen. He went on to become some kind of shadowy security guy. He saved your husband's and father-in-law's lives during that attempt to assassinate the president a bunch of years ago, and he sold you this place.'' Rob settled back in his chair; he was so tall and lanky, he barely fit. ''He lives in Wyoming. And you were just in Wyoming. As I recall, you went at the last minute.''

Lucy sighed again, wishing she could be back out on the water. Maybe that's what she should do—

pack up the kids and head to Canada, paddle lakes and streams and coastlines and just wait out whatever was going on here. Hide. Retreat. The passive approach, she thought.

"Rob, I'm sorry." She shook her head, her voice tight and tense. "I should have told you what was going on before now."

"Lucy, I deserve to know. My kid hangs out here."

"You're right." She leaned back in her chair and gave him a direct look. "Rob, the truth is, I'm not sure what's going on. *Something,* yes, but I could be putting incidents together that are unrelated—"

He held up a hand, stopping her. "Start at the beginning and take me through it, step by step. I'm not good at piecing things together and reading between the lines. Just give it to me straight."

She told him everything, start to finish. She only left out the volatile chemistry between her and Sebastian. "If you want to pack up Georgie and clear out—"

"No. It has to be business as usual. We're not going to let this sick bastard win." Rob was adamant, if a little shocked. "I'm just sorry you've put up with this for so long on your own. Why the hell didn't you say something? You didn't suspect me, did you?"

"No! I just—" She threw up her hands, at a loss.

"I guess I'm just used to handling things on my own."

"Maybe too used to it," Rob said quietly.

Lucy didn't answer.

"This Redwing character's good?"

"He used to be. He's been retired or on sabbatical or something for the past year."

"Why?"

She frowned. "That's a good question. I'll ask him."

"I'm not much on cloak-and-dagger shit myself. Look, I don't blame you for not wanting to bring in the police, but if you get any hard evidence—you have to take it in, Lucy."

She nodded. "I will. I promise."

He smiled a little. "Grandpa Jack will calculate his political advantage and decide whether to keep the lid on this thing or not."

"That's so cynical."

"Practical."

Lucy laughed, feeling better. "Thanks, Rob."

"For what?"

"For not jumping down my throat for keeping this to myself for so long."

He waved a hand. "I figure your just punishment was helping Redwing down from the falls the other night. Serves you right when you could have had a strapping guy like me carry him down on my back."

"You'd have called the EMTs."

"He was in that bad shape, huh?"

She nodded.

"Think he fell?"

"I don't know. It was his first time back to the falls since his grandfather's death. He was distracted."

"Mini-landslides don't just happen up there. Maybe after heavy rains, but not this time of year when it's this dry." He got to his feet. "I think I'll go check on the boys."

Sebastian decided to make dinner. He got Madison and J.T. to pick whatever was ripe in the garden. What he didn't steam or throw into a salad, he chopped up and grilled. He found some chicken in the refrigerator and tossed that on the grill, too. It was a charcoal grill, and he had a couple of false starts before he got the damn thing lit. His life-style had never called for much charcoal grilling.

The smell of the charcoal, the feel of the heat on his face, the long, quiet day in a place he loved and yet had tried to forget—all helped him to feel more centered, calmer, steadier. He could go deep inside himself, where he was still and balanced, and think. Darren Mowery. Jack Swift. Blackmail. Lucy and her weird goings-on. They all fit together. He just had to find out how.

And he had to keep his mind on the job, not on what it felt like to be back home, definitely not on what it felt like to be with Lucy. He didn't know what it was about her, but she'd crawled under his skin and buried herself there fifteen-plus years ago. There was nothing he could do except live with it. Last year, he'd let emotional involvement cloud his judgment with Darren Mowery. He hadn't seen the changes in Darren, the creeping cynicism, the loss of empathy. Maybe they'd always been there, buried under a veneer of professionalism, and only last year had they surfaced, taking over.

Sebastian flipped a piece of chicken. Maybe it was like the way seeing Lucy again had taken him over, made him capable of doing who knew what. Thinking about her while grilling chicken and vegetables, for one.

He needed to think about what to do about Jack Swift. Understanding his leverage was the first step. In his experience, United States senators didn't like to talk about what a blackmailer had on them.

The screen door creaked open and banged lightly shut, and Lucy joined him, plopping down in an old Adirondack chair. She had two bottles of Long Trail beer and handed him one as she stretched out her legs, crossing her ankles. She had very good legs, tanned, slim, strong.

She smiled. "Smells good."

"That's the charcoal and barbecue sauce. I could grill up a pile of skunk cabbage and it'd smell good."

"I don't think I'd like skunk cabbage. I haven't even worked up the courage to try dandelion greens. People in town tell me they were a favorite of Daisy's."

Sebastian remembered his grandmother pointing out the tender leaves, instructing him how to pick them without bruising them. "They were," he said.

"Did you eat them?"

"With salt, pepper and vinegar."

"Gross."

He laughed. "Daisy and one of her old friends used to make the occasional batch of dandelion wine. God, it was awful."

Lucy smiled again, watching him as she sipped her beer from the bottle. It was a move that struck him as incredibly sexy. Her eyes seemed darker, even more vivid, against the deepening blue of the early evening sky. "So," she said, "did you ever think you'd stay here when you were a kid?"

"I never thought I'd leave."

"Then you didn't hate it here?"

"No, never." He looked around at the fields of tall grass and bright flowers, the wooded hills, the apple trees and maples and oaks. He could hear the brook and the wind, and remembered thinking that here, it was as if he were inside his own soul. He shook his head. "I couldn't imagine not being here."

"Why did you sell, then?"

"Things change."

He flipped vegetables, and he could feel her watching him, wondering what kind of boy he must have been. The orphan. Daisy's grandson. A child of tragedy and incalculable loss.

"What changed?" Lucy asked quietly.

"I did."

She was silent, but he knew she wasn't letting him off the hook. Not Lucy. She would dig in, probe, commit for the long haul. He'd known that about her the day she married his best friend.

He glanced back at her, drank some of his own beer. "Daisy lived here. It was her home. For me, it was a refuge, a place to hide. And one day I knew I couldn't hide anymore."

"You had to go out and learn how to save people. You couldn't save your grandfather—he died before you were born. And you couldn't save your parents. You weren't there."

He looked at her. "No. I was there."

She almost spilled her beer. She paled slightly, then whispered, "I'm sorry. I didn't know. No one's ever said. Did Colin know?"

"We drank too much one night after the assassination attempt, and it came out.'' Sebastian shrugged. ''We were young. We never spoke of it again.''

Lucy rallied, but he could see she was touched. ''Nothing like bullets and booze to bond a couple of guys together. Was Plato there?''

''He drank wine. Merlot. We never let him forget.''

She smiled, and Sebastian remembered how much she'd loved her husband, how much Colin had loved her. She was different now, and yet the same. Strange. Impossible to articulate.

She set her beer in the grass. ''So, you saw your parents get killed, and you came here to live with your grandmother. Then you left. You went into security and investigative work, started your own company, made a lot of money and retired for the past year to a hammock and a shack without electricity or running water.''

''My life in a nutshell.''

She studied him, eyes narrowed. ''And you renounced violence.''

''Yes.''

''Why?''

''A man named Darren Mowery.''

''I know the name. You worked for him when you and Colin first met. DM Consultants. He saved the president's life.''

"That's who Darren was. He changed."

"Tell me," Lucy said quietly.

"There was a kidnapping case a year ago. A Colombian businessman—a client—and his wife and their three children, all under ten. I took on the case myself."

"What happened? The children weren't—"

He shook his head. "They lived. DM Consultants had just gone bankrupt. I knew Darren blamed me. I knew he was desperate. Tempted."

"He was involved in the kidnapping?" Lucy said.

"He helped engineer it. He damn near got off with thirty million dollars."

Her eyes widened. "My God!"

"It was a wealthy Colombian businessman," Sebastian said with a small smile.

"What happened?"

"I foiled their plans. I had to shoot three of Mowery's Colombian cohorts in front of the children." He could hear their screams now, see their horrified faces. Children. Little children. "The men were pawns."

"Would they have killed the family?"

"Yes. And Darren would have taken the money. I caught up with him in Bogotá. He went for his gun, and I shot him. Pretty straightforward. The Colombian authorities arrived, and I went back to Wyoming."

Lucy's face had gone pale again. There was a slight tremble to her hands. "Do you know if he's alive or dead?"

She was unnerved enough. Sebastian didn't need to tell her Darren Mowery was sneaking around her father-in-law's office. "He's alive."

"But in prison," she said. "The Colombians must have—"

He shook his head. "There was no way to prove his role in the kidnapping. I knew that when I left him for dead. Lucy, I didn't finish the job. There's no excuse."

"So that's why I found you in a hammock."

"That's why. I leave operations to people Plato and I have hired and trained, men and women we trust. The company requires a lot of attention at what Plato likes to call the 'desk level.' I've ignored that, too, for the better part of the past year."

"No wonder Plato was glad to get you out of Wyoming," Lucy said, obviously struggling to insert some humor. "What are you, Sebastian—forty, by now?"

"About."

"No wife, no kids? Ever?"

"Never as yet."

"Almost?"

He thought of her in her wedding gown so long ago—young, pretty, beaming with a kind of hope and optimism he wasn't sure he'd ever felt. "Not quite."

"I guess 'not quite' and 'almost' are two different things."

He let his gaze settle on her until she uncrossed her ankles and sat up a little straighter. "I haven't been much good to anyone in a long time, Lucy. If you want Plato to come out here and see to whoever's trying to get under your skin, I'll get him."

"No," she said, "I want you."

He grinned and drank more of his beer. "Well, finally we're on the same wavelength."

"In your dreams, Redwing." But he could see she was twitchy, aware. She jumped up, obviously needing an outlet for her restless energy. "Where are Madison and J.T.?"

"In their rooms." He scooped zucchini onto a chipped Bennington Pottery platter left over from Daisy's day. "I was going to have them sweep the porch, rake the yard, caulk the windows and deadhead the flowers, but I figured I'd give them a break."

"Daisy never made you work that hard, and you know it."

"How do you know?"

"Because I live in her house. Some nights...I don't know, it's as if her spirit's still here. I imagine she was hardworking and frugal, but I also think she was very kind and knew how to have fun.''

"She was a hard-bitten old Yankee.''

"Ah,'' Lucy said, not taking him seriously, ''so that's where you get it.''

He pointed his spatula at her. ''I could have sold this place to a Boston lawyer.''

"Why didn't you?'' she asked evenly.

"Because I sold it to you.''

She dropped back into her chair and stared out at the vegetable garden. Everything about her, Sebastian thought, was a mix of strength and femininity, and he knew he'd be stupid to underestimate her.

She turned, squinting at him. ''The locals are starting to call me the Widow Swift. They used to call your grandmother the Widow Daisy.''

"That bothers you?''

"I don't know. I have a good life here. I like to think she did, too.''

"She did because she stayed here so she could live, not so she could hide. She never married again, but she had a good, full life.''

"Do you think I'm hiding out here?''

He shrugged. ''It doesn't matter what I think.''

"That's true, it doesn't.'' She grinned at him, taking the edge off their conversation. ''At least not about my life. Dead bats in my bed—that's another story.''

He slid the chicken onto the platter with the vegetables. He hadn't done anything this domestic in years. Maybe ever. It felt good. If he didn't keep busy, his mind would spin off in too many directions. He'd start thinking things about Lucy that he'd been repressing for more than fifteen years. Kissing her the other night might have been low, but he couldn't bring himself to regret it.

She was frowning at him.

"What is it?" he asked.

"Something about your face. You haven't found anything else in my bed, have you?"

He looked at her, and she slid down a bit in her chair, one foot twitching madly. And he knew. She was thinking about their kiss, too—and more. "Lucy, I promised it wouldn't happen again. It won't."

"I don't mind that it did happen."

They were on dangerous ground. "Good."

But she jumped up, avoided his eye. "We should get dinner on the table."

Ten

After dinner, J.T. slipped off. Lucy and Madison were out driving, and Sebastian made the mistake of not locking the kid in his room. J.T. had been quiet through dinner, eating his chicken and salad and pushing the grilled vegetables around his plate. Then all of a sudden—no J.T.

Sebastian checked the garage. The kid's fishing pole was missing.

He went around the back of the barn and took a gently sloping but more roundabout footpath down to the brook. There was a steeper path on the other side of the barn that led straight down the embankment. It was short and direct, and if he hadn't fallen into a waterfall yesterday, Sebastian would have taken it because it would get him more quickly to the brook's best fishing spot.

The air was cool, damp and still, the brook shaded

with hemlock and pine, the coppery water shallow and clear. He headed downstream. He was sore and stiff, but it felt good to move.

He spotted J.T. on a rock at the edge of the brook. His fishing pole lay on the ground beside him. He glanced up as Sebastian came toward him, then quickly tucked his face back in his hands.

Sebastian swore under his breath. What did he know to say to a crying kid?

"Catch anything?" he asked, coming closer.

J.T. shook his head without looking up.

"Mind if I share your rock? Tramping down here's given me a headache. Blood's rushed to my head."

The shoulders went up and down again.

Sebastian took that as a yes, and lowered himself onto the rock. It was big, unchanged from when he was a boy. The trees and undergrowth were thicker, reminding him of the passage of time.

"This was my favorite fishing spot as a kid," he said. "I never caught much. Mostly, I came down here to get away by myself."

No response.

"J.T." Sebastian sighed. He hated this. "It's this father-son canoe trip, isn't it? Rob told me about it. He wants to take you. But he's not your father."

The boy looked up. Tears streamed down his cheeks, carving a path through the dirt. He smelled like Deet and sweat, and he'd been crying for a while. "I want—I want to go with Rob."

And therein lies the rub, Sebastian thought. "Then why don't you? Your mother would let you."

The kid cried harder.

Damn, Sebastian thought. This time, he hated being right. He leaned back against his arms and gazed at the constant stream of water over rock and mud. "J.T., your father was my friend. We didn't see as much of each other as we'd have liked before he died, but one thing I know. He would want you to have men like Rob in your life."

"I know—that's not it."

Sebastian knew it wasn't. He said quietly, "You won't forget him, J.T. You won't ever forget him."

The kid tucked up his knees and buried his face in them, sobbing loudly. Sebastian had known such inconsolable grief. As a boy, he, too, had come here to cry, where no one could find him, where no one could ever know.

"If I stop missing him..."

He couldn't finish. Sebastian sat up and brushed a mosquito off a scab on his forearm. This was why he avoided victim work. He never knew what the hell to say. Daisy had pretty much left him alone to sort things out.

J.T. Swift was a deceptively intense and intro-

spective boy, already thinking deep thoughts at
twelve. Sebastian hadn't thought such deep thoughts
at that age. He'd cry his heart out and then push the
deep thoughts away, as far away as he could.

"Wounds heal," he said lamely. "If they're deep,
like losing a father, they take time, and they leave
a scar. After a while, the scar may not hurt anymore,
but it reminds you of what you lost. And of your
courage in facing that loss."

The boy shook his head. "I'm not brave."

"J.T., I've done a lot of things. I've been shot
and shot at, and I've gone after kidnappers, extor-
tionists, terrorists and every kind of creep and scum
and mad zealot you can imagine." He paused, then
gave it to the kid as straight as he could. "But I
think the hardest thing I ever did was watch my
grandmother cry after my parents died."

J.T. sat up, sniffled. "How did they die?"

"They were hit by a car right in front of me. That
was hard, too, but it was Daisy's tears that did me
in, that reminded me of what I'd lost. My grandfather was killed when she was young, and she only
had me left."

"What happened to your grandfather?"

"His name was Joshua," Sebastian said.

"He was named after the falls?"

"No, the falls were named after him. He fell into

the falls and drowned saving a little boy—Rob's father.''

"He did? Georgie never said!"

"Georgie might not know. People around here are pretty stoic. They don't like to talk about these things, dump it on kids. It was March, in the midst of the snowmelt. The water was high and cold. The kid was going after his dog. He fell in. My grandfather jumped in and saved him.''

"My mom won't let us near the falls in the winter.''

"You listen to her,'' Sebastian said.

"Did your grandmother blame Rob's dad for killing your grandfather?'' J.T. asked in a hushed voice. His eyes were wide and fascinated in a good way, taking on the best of both his parents.

"He was an eight-year-old boy, and he made a mistake. Joshua had two choices. He could let the boy drown, or he could do what he could to save him.''

"Mom knows about swift-water rescue. She's going to teach me someday. I don't think you're supposed to jump in after someone.''

Sebastian nodded. ''Sometimes life doesn't present you with a good choice and a bad choice. Sometimes you just have bad choices. You do the best you can.''

The boy gave that some thought. Finally, he

jumped to his feet and grabbed his fishing pole. "Bugs're bothering me."

And that was that. Their conversation was over.

J.T. bounded up the steep path. Good, Sebastian thought. He was exhausted. If someone had tried to talk to him at twelve the way he'd just talked to J.T., he wouldn't have known what the hell he was talking about. J.T. had followed right along.

Neither he nor J.T. mentioned their conversation to Lucy when she and Madison returned. "If it's run over the chipmunk or lose control of your car," Lucy was saying, "you run over the chipmunk."

"I couldn't," Madison said. "I'd just *die.*"

J.T. leaned toward Sebastian and whispered, "Two bad choices?"

"Tougher to have to run over a chipmunk than go on a father-son canoe trip with Rob and Georgie, don't you think?"

J.T. grinned, and Sebastian retired to his room. Lucy's room, he amended. He surveyed the bed, the furnishings, the rug for anything out of the ordinary—dead bats, bullet holes, live rounds. He dropped down and checked under the bed. Nothing.

He kicked off his shoes and fell back onto the worn, soft quilt.

Lucy knocked. "I need to get a few things."

"Be my guest."

She went straight to her dresser and opened drawers, discreetly pulling out a nightgown—no black silky thing tonight—and underthings, socks, an outfit for tomorrow. Her back was to him. He observed the curve of her hips, the shape of her legs, the way her hair fell carelessly past her shoulders. Without looking at him, she said, "I hope today wasn't too deadly for you."

"I've had worse. You could use a couple of horses, though."

She turned to him. "I can barely manage two kids, a company and this place. What would I do with horses?"

"Loan me one. I'd rather ride a horse than pick squash." Except he'd enjoyed picking squash. He couldn't explain it and didn't want to try.

"You're in no condition to go horseback riding."

"Nah." He was stretched out on her bed, watching her. The scene struck him as scarily intimate. "I'm right as rain. Or close to it."

"Sure," she said dubiously, and breezed to the door. But she stopped, one hand on the knob. "Thank you."

"For what?"

"J.T. He told me he's decided to go on the father-son canoe trip."

"That was his doing, not mine."

"You talked to him."

He sighed. "I should have just fished with him.

Kids are too intense these days. It's this damn therapeutic culture.''

"Right. Nevertheless, thank you."

"Lucy." He let his gaze settle on her, felt her change in mood. "Don't let today fool you. I needed a day or two to recover from my fall. I talked to J.T., picked squash and fired up the grill to kill time."

"Are you trying to tell me you're not a nice man?"

He said nothing, and she smiled.

"I already knew that," she said, and left.

Moron, Sebastian thought. He'd had her right here in his room, thinking kindly toward him, and he'd had to remind her of what a son of a bitch he was. It was Daisy's ghost, he decided.

Back in Wyoming, he'd have had Lucy Blacker Swift in bed with him by now.

A noise woke Sebastian early, just after daylight. It came from outside. He glanced at the bedside clock: five-twenty. This was an early family, but not a crack-of-dawn family. So who—or what—was in the backyard?

He rolled out of bed and peered through the window as he pulled on his pants.

Madison was climbing over the stone wall on the

other side of the vegetable garden. She jumped down and, ducking low, ran up through the field.

Sebastian swore under his breath. What would get a fifteen-year-old out of bed at five in the morning?

"A secret," he said to himself.

He ducked down the hall and made his way soundlessly up the stairs to Lucy's room. The door was open a crack. He slipped inside and dropped beside her bed. "Lucy."

She bolted upright, sank her fingers into his arm. "What is it?"

"Madison's sneaking out across the field," he said. "You know how teenagers love their secrets. I'll go after her. You stay here with J.T."

"What?" She was half asleep, trying to figure out what was going on. "Madison's *where?*"

She pushed back the covers. Sebastian felt his mouth go dry. Her nightgown wasn't silky, but it was little. The *V*-neckline was askew, revealing almost her entire breast. The fabric was pulled tight across the nipple. He tried not to stare, but something in his expression tipped her off—she looked down, sucked in a breath and adjusted her position.

"She doesn't have much of a head start," he said. "We'll probably be back before you and J.T. are even up. I didn't want to chance your waking up and not finding us."

The covers dropped off her legs; the nightgown

just barely covered her hips. Her thighs were smooth and tanned. If her daughter wasn't charging off to God-knew-where, there'd be no stopping him. Desire fired through him, stealing his breath, his senses.

"It'll be okay, Lucy," he whispered, and kissed her, but held back, giving just a hint of how badly he wanted her. She fell against her pillow, her short nightgown riding up to her hips. He pulled away, every fiber of him throbbing with the need to make love to her, now. It was all he could do not to leave Madison to whatever mischief she was making. "I'll be back."

She slipped her sheet over herself. "You'll find her?"

"Yes. Lucy—"

"Go."

He nodded without a word and went.

The morning dew was cold, soaking his shoes and pants below the knee as he tore up through the field. He could distinguish mourning doves and crows in the flurry of bird calls, saw a bluebird swoop toward a bluebird house he'd put up for Daisy years ago at the edge of the field.

He felt better. A good night's sleep and a morning kiss had helped. His head was clear, and the pain of his bruises had lessened. He was stiff, but the soreness wasn't as raw-edged.

He wasn't worried about following Madison's

trail. He knew the route she was taking, and wasn't surprised when he found her footprint in a low, muddy spot just into the woods beyond the stone wall. He took the narrow path up a hill, moving carefully and quietly but not making an effort to make no sound at all. If Madison heard him and scurried home, all the better.

The path ended at the dirt road. Sebastian had already investigated the occupants of the homes up on the ridge: a Boston optometrist, two New York florists. A local real estate woman rented out the third.

He found Madison at this last house, a glass-and-wood contemporary.

She was talking to someone on the screened porch. Sebastian couldn't see who it was as he crept under the sweeping branches of a huge, gnarled hemlock.

"Madison, you can't sneak up here at this hour." A woman's voice, low and urgent. "It's wrong. What would your grandfather think?"

"I know—but I had this terrible nightmare, and I had to get out of the house. I couldn't breathe! And my mother's not herself since…" The girl coughed, as if she were choking on her own drama. "I can't explain."

"Try," the woman said calmly.

"Do you know Sebastian Redwing?"

Sebastian remained very still. Who was this woman Madison had snuck out to see?

"Not personally. I know he saved your father and grandfather from an assassin some years ago and has his own investigative and security firm. He's widely respected in that community."

"Well, he's here," Madison said, pumping each word full of as much drama as she could.

"Sebastian Redwing?" The woman remained cool. "Really? Why?"

"Mom took us to see him when we were in Wyoming, and—and I didn't think he liked us at *all*. He was such a jerk."

Actually, Sebastian thought, he didn't think he'd been that bad.

"Now he's here," Madison went on, "and I don't know, I just think it's so *weird*. He almost killed himself at the falls the other night. He slipped or something, and Mom found him."

"Sebastian sold your mother your house, didn't he?"

"Yeah, it used to belong to his grandmother."

"Perhaps your visit in Wyoming got him thinking about Vermont, and he decided he wanted to see his grandmother's house again."

"But Mom—she doesn't want J.T. or me going off into the woods alone. She'd *kill* me if she knew I was up here."

Sebastian knew this to be untrue. If Madison really thought her mother would "kill" her for disobeying, she wouldn't have sneaked off. He wasn't sure if this meant mother and daughter really did trust each other or that the kid was a spoiled brat.

"Does your grandfather know Sebastian's visiting your mother?" the woman asked.

The criticism in her voice was almost undetectable, but still unmistakable. Sebastian frowned. This was someone who believed she had Jack Swift's best interests at heart—and believed Lucy didn't.

Madison, however, was oblivious. "I don't think so. She doesn't tell Grandpa much."

"No. I'm sure she doesn't."

Whoever this woman was, she didn't like Lucy Blacker Swift.

"Mom's very independent," the girl said in grudging defense of her mother.

"That she is. Well, you should be running along before she wakes up and doesn't find you. She'll worry."

Sebastian ducked deeper under the branches of the hemlock. He could hear creaking floorboards as Madison and the woman walked, presumably toward the door of the screened porch.

"I can't wait for Grandpa to come up this summer," Madison said. "It'll be so cool. None of my friends believe I have a grandfather who's a United States senator.''

"Your friends in Washington did, didn't they?''

"I mean up here.''

Madison went out onto the deck and took the steps down to the driveway, which was on the opposite side of the house from where Sebastian was hidden.

"Come see me again,'' the woman called from the deck. "You'll keep our secret, won't you?''

"Of course.''

Sebastian didn't like secrets. It was one thing to keep your own mouth shut about something, another thing to ask someone else to keep their mouth shut. Especially a fifteen-year-old. A sure sign of something afoot was an adult telling a child to keep a secret. If it didn't involve Christmas or birthday presents, it usually wasn't good.

He wanted to know about the woman on the deck, but his first priority was seeing Madison Swift safely home. He eased down the wooded hill, making as little noise as possible, and came onto the path several yards behind her. She was walking briskly, practically skipping. Whoever this woman was, Madison certainly thought she was something.

They were almost to the field when Sebastian announced his presence. The girl jumped, startled, then turned sullen. "You *followed* me?''

"Yep. A kid sneaking out of the house at the crack of dawn is asking to be followed."

"That's not true."

She looked as if she might throw a fit. They were out of earshot of the rented house, but not if the kid started screaming and stomping around. Sebastian sighed. "Now don't start yelling bloody murder. It won't go over well if you do."

Madison snorted at him, out of breath and furious at being caught. "What'll you do, tie me to a tree?"

"It's a thought."

"My mother—"

"Your mother would tie you to an anthill."

The girl's mouth snapped shut.

"Who's the woman at the house?" he asked.

She didn't answer.

"Okay, I'll just go up there, knock on her door and ask her myself—"

"No! She'll get in trouble!"

"Is that what she told you?"

Madison obviously didn't care for his tone of voice. "It's what I *know*," she said snottily and marched a few steps ahead of him.

He was still feeling pretty good—she couldn't outrun him. He thought of his hammock in Wyoming. His horses. His dogs. He could pull together a poker game with the ranch hands. Five-card stud, cigars and a couple of six-packs.

Damn, what was he doing here?

"The woman works for your grandfather," he said to the girl's retreating back.

She refused to answer, kept walking.

Sebastian easily caught up with her. "I can call him, find out who's out of town—"

She stopped abruptly and spun around at him, her face pale. "No, don't. Please. I *promised.*"

"Promised what? Your firstborn?"

"No, but I gave my word—"

"Well, you can un-give your word and tell me what's going on."

"Why should I?"

"Two reasons. One, if you don't, I'll still find out, but I won't be as pissed off if you go ahead and tell me yourself. Two, if you do tell me, I can tell your mother and hold her down and let her cool off before she tans your hide."

"My mother doesn't believe in corporal punishment."

This was no surprise. Sebastian kept his cool. "I was speaking metaphorically."

She licked her lips. "Barbara's here renting a house for my grandfather. He's spending August in Vermont. He asked her not to tell Mom. He wanted to make sure everything worked out first, then tell her himself."

"Why?"

"I don't know, that's the way he is. It's a surprise, I guess."

"Barbara who?"

"Barbara Allen. She's my grandfather's personal assistant. She's worked for him forever, since even before you saved his life."

So, as far as Madison was concerned, Barbara had seniority on him, and he wasn't such a big deal. Sebastian was amused. Little snot. But there was real fear in her eyes, not for herself but for a woman to whom she'd given her word. That mix of loyalty and kindness was more like her mother than Madison would probably want to know.

"I accidentally saw her the other day," Madison went on, "and she asked me not to tell."

"Madison, Barbara Allen isn't going to get fired because you caught her renting a vacation house for your grandfather. She must know that." And if she did, he thought, she was deliberately manipulating a fifteen-year-old girl. Why?

Madison nodded, not happy about having to tell him anything. Her blue eyes fastened on him. She wasn't afraid of him any more than anyone else in her damn family was. He was out of practice. People used to be afraid of him.

"Anything else?" she asked sarcastically, as if he were the inquisitioner.

"Nope. Now we can go back and tell your mother."

She said something under her breath. He was pretty sure it was "bastard," but she was only fifteen and shouldn't be using that kind of language. He let it go. Then she said something about being glad he'd tumbled into Joshua Falls. She spoke a little louder, wanting him to hear, wanting him to react. He didn't. In her place, he'd be pissed, too.

Which was nothing compared to what Lucy was.

She greeted Madison at the door, white-faced and scared and too angry to speak. She had on shorts, a T-shirt and sandals. No more little nightgown. She pointed at the ceiling. "Upstairs."

"Mom, I can explain. I—"

Lucy held up her hand, and the girl shut up and flounced off, pounding up the stairs.

"A wonder she doesn't get shin splints." Sebastian slid onto a chair at the table. He was breathing hard; his head was pounding. He needed coffee and food, maybe one more day before he was fit to tackle desperadoes instead of Lucy's kids. "It wasn't a guy, if that makes you feel any better."

Lucy was slightly less pale. "Who was it?"

"A woman named Barbara Allen. She's renting a house on the sly for your father-in-law. He wants to come up in August. Know her?"

Lucy nodded. "*Damn* Jack. He's always doing

things in secret. He says it's because he likes surprises and wants to avoid publicity. He thinks he's the president, I swear.''

''What about Barbara Allen?''

''Barbara? She's been Jack's personal assistant for—I don't know, twenty years or so. She's devoted to him. If he says, 'Jump,' she says, 'How high?' She's always been fond of the kids—she's wonderful to us whenever we're in Washington. Gets us tickets, restaurant reservations, things like that.''

''She shouldn't have told Madison not to tell you—''

''I know.'' Lucy took two mugs down from a cabinet, her movements jerky, betraying her agitation. ''But that's Jack, and Barbara would want to please him. She probably didn't think. And she wouldn't know about the incidents.''

Sebastian made no comment.

She set the mugs on the counter and looked around at him. ''Sebastian, don't even think it. Not Barbara.'' She shook her head. ''I wouldn't want to spend ten *seconds* inside your brain.''

He leaned back and kicked out his legs. The trek up into the woods had done him good, but he could feel it. He smiled. ''No, you wouldn't. Tell me what you know about Barbara Allen.''

''I just did.''

"Her personality," he said, "her sense of loyalty, what she thinks of you, your children, your move to Vermont. Anything."

"I don't know a lot. My contact with her over the years has been mostly about Jack, not her. She's very professional—she's never said much about her personal life around me. I think she has an apartment on the river."

"Not married?"

Lucy shook her head. "She's about my age, maybe a year or two older. Now, don't be thinking she's your weird, mousy, stereotypical spinster, because she's not."

"I wasn't thinking that. I wonder why you did?"

"I didn't. I was just—"

"The thought was there, Lucy. Something about this woman made you think 'weird, mousy, stereotypical spinster.' Think of how many single women in their late thirties and forties you know. Would you immediately warn someone not to think of them in stereotypical terms?"

"I don't know. Maybe."

"I doubt it. Something about Barbara Allen made you want to defend her against stereotype."

Lucy frowned. "I suppose there is a neediness about her. You'd never notice it right off, but I've known her for years. Who knows, I could be projecting."

"There's nothing needy about you."

"I don't know. After you left this morning—"

He grinned. "That's different."

She filled the two mugs with coffee, and with her back to him, said, "Sebastian, I can't be attracted to you. It'll never work, and the timing couldn't be worse."

"I agree."

She spun around to face him. "You agree?"

"Bad timing. Won't work. Can't be attracted. That's pretty much what I was thinking, too."

"After what happened upstairs."

"No, before, actually. I thought about it all night." He walked over to her and picked up one of the mugs, sipped the hot, black coffee. "Obviously I wasn't convinced."

"I am."

"Good. That'll give me ammo for talking myself out of kissing you again."

She nodded. "Right. We can't—" She turned, facing him, and leaned against the counter with her coffee. "I have a sneaky daughter and a son who's worried about forgetting his father, and a business to run, and this person to find—and now Jack Swift coming for August. So, yes, please talk yourself out of kissing me again."

"And what are you going to do?"

"About what?"

"Kissing me. Because if you know I want to kiss you, and would at the drop of a pin, then you don't have the kind of ammo I have. I know you don't want me to kiss you. You don't know that about me."

She stared at him. "You're not making any sense."

"Sure I am. I want to kiss you again. Very much." He touched her hair. "I have for a long, long time."

"How long?"

And suddenly she seemed to know. He could feel it. "Years," he said, and he touched her mouth, traced her lower lip with his thumb.

Her gaze held steady, but he could see her swallow. "I'm sorry."

"I'm not." He smiled. "Now go see about your daughter."

"She's a good kid, Sebastian."

"I know."

He moved aside, and she crossed the kitchen with her mug of coffee. At the doorway, she turned back to him and smiled. "But I am going to lock her in her room for the next hundred years."

While mother and daughter had it out, Sebastian took his coffee to the back steps. J.T. was still asleep; outside the air was warm and still, and the birds were twittering. He thought about Barbara Allen and Jack Swift, a rented house, a dead bat in Lucy's bed, a landslide that had nearly killed him, Darren Mowery, the August congressional recess and blackmail.

And kissing Lucy. He thought about that, too.

Eleven

Madison acted defiant and put-upon when Lucy confronted her in her room. "I'll be a junior in high school next year. I don't have to tell you everything."

"That's true," Lucy said, "and I don't need to know 'everything.' But sneaking out of the house at five in the morning after I specifically asked you—"

"There was *no* reason to worry!" Madison slammed her pillow onto the floor. She was sitting up in bed, looking misunderstood and furious. "You don't make any sense. If you had a life, maybe you'd leave me alone." She caught herself immediately and gasped. "Mom, I'm sorry. I didn't mean that."

Lucy stayed calm, even though she could feel the sting of her daughter's words. "Madison, I have a life. I have my work, I have you and J.T., I have my friends, hobbies I enjoy. I like living here. I get away just often enough. But whether or not I have a 'life,' in your eyes, isn't your concern. My happiness is my responsibility, not yours or J.T.'s.''

"I just—I just don't want you to give up everything for us. I don't want us to stand in your way..." She didn't finish.

"You aren't standing in my way of doing anything."

Madison raised her chin. "Then why can't I spend a semester in Washington?"

Lucy smiled. The kid never missed an opening. "Your brother would miss you."

"No, I wouldn't!"

Madison threw another pillow at her door, where her little brother was eavesdropping. *"J.T.!"*

"J.T.," Lucy said, shooting him a warning look. He laughed without remorse and ran down the hall. She turned back to Madison. "You have lots of time for Washington. Right now, I'd like you to think about what it means to be trustworthy. If I can't trust you here, at home, how can I trust you on your own in Washington or anywhere else?"

"I'd have Grandpa—"

"He's a busy senator, Madison. He won't have time to make sure you're not sneaking off. First, you have to know you can trust yourself to make good decisions. Then I have to know. Then we might be able to discuss Washington.''

"I'm sorry," Madison said simply.

"Find something to do in the house."

Her daughter nodded, if not contrite, at least rethinking her conduct.

Lucy didn't leave. "Madison, I know I didn't convey this adequately the other night—" She breathed, went on, "But I don't want you and J.T. out alone, not because I'm an overprotective lunatic mother with no life, but because I'm afraid you might become targets of someone who's been harassing me."

Madison paled. "What?"

"Right now, I seem to be the only target. And the incidents—I don't know what else to call them—seem to be tapering off. I hope they're over. I hope I've exaggerated their significance. But until I'm sure, I ask you *please* not to go off on your own."

"What kind of incidents?"

Lucy told her. She left out none of the possibilities. "I don't know if they're all related—I don't know if any of them are related."

"That's why Sebastian's here?"

That and something else, which he wouldn't explain. She expected it might have to do with Darren

Mowery, an unnerving prospect. She nodded. "Yes."

"J.T. doesn't know, does he?"

"No." Lucy smiled a little. "He's still young enough that he'll do as I ask without five million questions and arguments."

Madison didn't smile. "This is spooky."

Wrung out, Lucy headed downstairs, refilled her mug with stale coffee and joined Sebastian on the back steps. She sat close to him, but not touching. She sipped her coffee. After a long silence between them, she said, "I'm not Colin's wife anymore. One of the hardest things I did after he died was to take off my wedding ring."

She jumped up before Sebastian could respond and ran into the kitchen. J.T. had wandered down from his room. They made pancakes and sausage, heated up pure Vermont maple syrup and filled the kitchen with homey smells. Madison was allowed down for breakfast, but declined.

This is my life, Lucy thought. It wasn't with a burnout like Sebastian Redwing, a man who'd had to renounce violence, not because he was a pacifist, a gentle man by nature, but because he wasn't. He had killed people. People had tried to kill him. Maybe as recently as two days ago, someone had tried to kill him.

She sat back, stared at her hands. She wore no

rings now. She and Colin had been young and broke, and they hadn't spent much on their wedding rings. But that was okay, they'd had such faith in their future together.

Daisy Wheaton had worn her wedding ring until the day she died. Rob had told Lucy, not that he'd needed to. She'd known, somehow.

I am not Colin's wife anymore.

Her chest was suddenly tight, aching, and she could feel tears welling, because it was real this time, not symbolic. She'd kissed Sebastian. She *wanted* Sebastian. Never mind that he wasn't right for her, he'd somehow managed to set her physically on edge, fill her mind with thoughts of making love to him. It was madness.

But maybe, she thought, necessary.

She didn't want to be known as the Widow Swift. As good as Daisy's life might have been, it wasn't *her* life.

She poured herself a fresh cup of coffee and took it out to the barn with her. Sebastian wasn't on the back steps. She didn't know where he was. Just as well, she thought, and settled in to work.

Barbara went for a run on the main road, past Lucy's house. She'd left her car at the end of the dirt road because she didn't want to walk back up the steep hill. It was Sunday, but no one was around.

Still, she could feel Sebastian Redwing's eyes on her as she ran. She wasn't paranoid. He was *there*. He would wonder who she was. Perhaps Madison had already told him. Barbara didn't know why she was baiting him. Why not stay up on the hill? Why go for a run?

But she knew why, and she kept up her pace, hoping the impulse would subside. She ached with the need to act. She couldn't think, could hardly breathe. She wanted the relief that came, even momentarily, with action.

No.

Pain shot up her shins from pounding too hard. She eased up. She was a strong runner, a fit, disciplined woman.

Did Sebastian Redwing suspect her of toppling him into Joshua Falls? The landslide had worked out even better than she'd anticipated. She remembered her mix of horror and fascination as she'd watched him plunge headfirst over the rock ledge. Oh, God! What if she'd killed a man?

It would have been Lucy's fault. *Lucy's fault, Lucy's fault.* She was the one who'd brought Sebastian Redwing to Vermont.

Barbara turned around at an old one-room schoolhouse, now boarded up, and headed back. Her stomach hurt. She was afraid of throwing up. It was tension, she knew. And hatred. She'd never known such pure hatred, didn't understand it. Lucy had never done anything to her.

But, of course, she had—just not directly. If Barbara followed the winding path to where Jack went wrong, where he'd moved away from openly declaring his love for her to this stubborn denial, it landed at Lucy's feet. She hadn't seen that Colin had a heart condition. She'd stolen Jack's grandchildren away. She'd made him give up Barbara, the one woman who loved him totally, unconditionally. *Lucy's fault.* It was that simple.

Barbara abruptly stopped to pick flowers on the side of the road, grabbing them by the handful, pulling them up by their roots. Black-eyed Susans and daisies, a few purple, spiky things she didn't know the name of. She ran with them, their dirt-laden roots slapping against her shorts and sweaty thighs.

When she reached her car, she grabbed a pad and pencil.

No. She had to do this right.

She dumped the flowers onto her front seat and, panting and sweating, climbed in behind the wheel. She should take time to cool down and stretch, but she didn't.

There was nothing from Darren at the rented house. No messages on her cell phone voice-mail. Nothing from Jack. Nothing from anyone.

She blinked back tears and carefully cut the roots

off the flowers. Some were a little beaten up. She didn't care. She found a piece of string in a kitchen drawer and tied it around the flowers. Downstairs in a closet, she found an old typewriter. She typed a short note. She would have to get rid of the typewriter; it probably could be easily traced. But she didn't touch the paper directly, didn't leave a handwriting sample for Mr. Security Man.

"He should have died in the falls," she said. "He really should have."

Wrapping her hand in a dishtowel, she tucked the typed note into the flowers.

She smiled. "How romantic."

After the sugar and adrenaline of her morning had worn off, Lucy called her father-in-law. She used her portable phone while she deadheaded hollyhocks and daylilies in front of the barn.

"Jack? Hi, it's Lucy. Why didn't you tell me you'd sent Barbara up here to rent you a house? I could have helped! We could at least have had Barbara to dinner." She kept her tone cheerful, half teasing. "I hope you weren't afraid we wouldn't want you."

"No—no, that's not it at all." He sounded tense and awkward, his sonorous voice unable to mask his feelings. "I wasn't sure I could find anything at this late date, and I didn't want to get Madison's and

J.T.'s hopes up. And you know how I love surprises.''

"Well, Barbara's found you a great house just up the hill from us.''

"She told me. That's wonderful. It's okay with you?''

Lucy tossed a handful of wilted blossoms into the dirt and rubbed her forehead. She could feel a headache coming on. Awakened by Sebastian in her room, thrown into fits by his kiss, her daughter acting up, too many pancakes—all had her going. "I've told you before, Jack, you're always welcome here. The kids will be thrilled to have you around.''

"Barbara's rented the house for a month. I'll have to go home a few times—''

"Jack, she could have rented the house for a year. You're family.''

"Lucy…'' He seemed to choke up, but rallied. "Thank you. I'm sorry I went off the deep end on you the other day.''

"Jack, we've known each other too long and have gone through too much together to worry about that sort of thing. Look, you sound tired. Is everything all right?''

"Yes, fine. It's just bloody hot here. Lucy—there's something else I should tell you. Sidney Greenburg will be spending some time in Vermont with me.''

"That's great. Sidney's wonderful." Lucy understood immediately what he, in his almost prudish
way, was trying to tell her. "Jack, I'm so pleased
for you."

"And you? Is everything all right with you?"

Not by a long shot, she thought. "Nothing a few
quiet days won't cure. Is Barbara heading back to
Washington? I can still have her to dinner—"

"I urged her to take a few extra days to relax.
You know Barbara. This place would fall apart without her."

Lucy smiled. "Do you mean your office or all of
Washington?"

He laughed, sounding more like himself.

When she hung up, Sebastian materialized behind
her. "How's the good senator?"

"Eavesdropping isn't polite. I had a talk with J.T.
about that very subject this morning."

"No one's ever suggested I was polite."

She swallowed and pinched off a pale yellow day-
lily blossom. His mood, she sensed, was not good.
He was serious, the teasing sexiness and the depth
of emotion of earlier replaced by a kind of dark
calm.

"He was tense," she said. "This time of year is
always hard in Washington. Everyone wants to get
home, it's hot, and the back-channel pressures and
deals come fast and furious. Jack's a plodder. He

likes to think through issues, not jump on some half-baked compromise."

"I'd like to talk to him."

"Jack? Why?"

He shrugged, but nothing about him was nonchalant. "For the same reasons the local police would want to talk to him if you'd gone to them instead of me. He's a United States senator. If someone's bothering you, maybe it's to get to him."

Lucy tossed more dead blossoms into the back of the flower bed. It needed weeding, too, and a shot of organic fertilizer. "That doesn't make any sense."

"Maybe not."

"You're thinking if he's rented a house here for August, it could mean something's up."

"I'm not thinking anything. I just want to talk to him."

She plunked the phone in his hand. "Go ahead. I'll listen in."

"Lucy—"

"You're hiding something, Redwing. You're not here just because someone shot a hole in my dining room window. So, what is it? What do you know that I don't know?"

"I don't like to talk on the phone with someone breathing down my neck."

"I don't, either."

"You didn't know I was there."

"If you don't want to use my phone and have me listen in, you should have brought your own."

She yanked at a browned, soggy hollyhock blossom, and the plant, which she hadn't staked and was already leaning too far forward, fell. She tore it up and flung it onto the driveway. It lay there like a dead animal.

Sebastian watched her without comment. The man worked on her nerves, got to her senses, made her feel on edge and half-crazy, as if she couldn't think straight—or could think *too* straight. Everything seemed more alive, more energized when he was around. Even deadheading her damn flowers. There were no half-measures with him. No *peace*.

"You're a goddamn liar," she said and marched back to the barn.

He didn't follow her. She kicked a wastebasket and stormed over to a side window, one she'd added in her renovations. He was already dialing. The *bastard*. He'd gotten his way. What did he care if she was in a turmoil?

She picked up the extension.

"Hang up, Lucy. I'm better at this than you are."

"The kids could listen in," she said.

"Not and get away with it. Hang up."

She heard a voice say, "Senator Swift's office."

Sebastian disconnected without a word. Lucy

watched him toss the phone into the flower bed like one of her dead blossoms, then he was coming toward her, taking long strides that put her at a disadvantage.

She was alone in the barn. J.T. was playing Nintendo in his room, Madison was confined to quarters, and it was Sunday, so her staff had the day off.

He was there.

"I was thinking about hiding under a canoe," she said, "but I figure you're the expert. You'd just find me and it'd only reinforce the big, bad wolf ideas you have about yourself."

"Lucy. Damn it."

His voice was ragged, his gray eyes flinty. He caught her around the middle, paused just long enough for her to tell him to go to hell—but she didn't—and his mouth found hers. His hands splayed on her back. She could feel the imprint of his palms and each finger like a hot spike as he drew her against him. He was fully aroused. She could feel him straining, pressing as his kiss deepened, his tongue probing erotically, telling her, in ways that words couldn't, just what he wanted.

He lifted her shirt and slid one hand down her pants, squeezing gently, then easing around the front, between her legs, where she could hide nothing from him. "Don't stop," she whispered. "Don't stop."

"I have no intention of stopping."

And he didn't, until she was quaking against his fingers. It happened so fast, so explosively, she was stunned. But she wasn't embarrassed. He pulled back, let her sink into her chair. She licked her lips, still tasting him. "What about you?"

"I'll wait."

"I don't usually—I haven't—" She cleared her throat; it would take a while before she could think properly. "I'm not usually that reckless."

"That wasn't reckless." He grinned, kissed her softly. "One day I'll show you reckless."

Impossibly, desire spurted through her again, just as searing and furious. He winked, as if he knew, and headed back toward the door. "Where are you going?" she asked.

He smiled. "To make my phone call."

Jack Swift refused to talk details. "I told Plato all you need to know. As it was, I took a huge risk. You know Darren Mowery. You know he'll do exactly what he's threatened to do if I don't cooperate."

"Which is?" Sebastian asked.

"Reveal his lies and filth."

Lies and filth. They were making progress. "Senator, my advice is for you to take everything you have to the Capitol Police. Let them do their job.

They can put a round-the-clock security detail on you. Mowery doesn't have to know.''

"But he will," Jack Swift said.

Sebastian felt fatigue tug at his eyes, settle into the small of his back. He'd done too much today. Kissing Lucy at dawn, chasing after her daughter, damn near making love to Lucy in the barn. He stood in the shade of one of the big old maples in the front yard, her portable phone almost out of range. She was right. He should have brought his cell phone.

The senator went on. "You know I'm right."

"Yes," Sebastian acknowledged. "I know."

"I'm not in any physical danger."

"Did you pay him?"

Jack Swift hesitated. This, too, was more than he wanted to admit. "Two installments."

"How much?"

"Ten thousand each."

Sebastian gripped the phone hard. "Twenty thousand total? Senator, Darren Mowery tried to steal millions last year. He's not planning to settle for twenty grand."

No answer.

"But you already know that," Sebastian said.

"I don't know what he wants. I only know what he'll do if I don't cooperate, and I've already decided that's intolerable." Swift sighed deeply and added, "And now that I've already cooperated twice, the bastard knows he's got me by the short hairs. There's no going back."

"Then what do you want from me?"

"I want you to stop him."

"No, Senator," Sebastian said. "You want me to kill him."

He disconnected while Swift was still gasping. The senator, Sebastian decided, needed a little more time to think over his situation. It was damn cruel to exacerbate his already acute sense of isolation, but from hard experience, Sebastian knew that blackmail victims never liked to divulge what their tormenters had on them. They just wanted all the unpleasantness to go away by itself. Usually, it didn't.

Madison joined him on the porch and sat down next to him with a cardboard box. "I found this in the attic. It's what I do when I'm under house arrest—I poke around in the attic. Look." She opened the lid. "It's quilting pieces. Hexagons. Do you think they were your grandmother's?"

Sebastian lifted out a stack of the hexagons. He nodded, recognizing the soft, worn fabric of his grandfather's old shirts. He remembered Daisy cutting them up years after he'd died. Waste not, want not. But she'd never made the quilt.

"Yes," he said. "They were Daisy's."

"I guess she never got around to piecing the quilt."

"I guess not."

"I was thinking about asking Mom to help me— I've never sewn a quilt before. You wouldn't mind?"

"Why would I mind? Your mother bought the house. She owns everything in it."

"But..." She gave an exaggerated shrug. "If it was my grandmother's, I'd want it."

He smiled. "Consider yourself Daisy's honorary great-granddaughter."

She laughed, delighted. "Of course," she amended, "this is just because I'm bored out of my mind. If I were in Washington this summer, I wouldn't have to resort to sewing a quilt."

"People in Washington sew quilts."

"Only because they *want* to, not because they *have* to because there's nothing else to do."

"Madison, if you could, tell me everything you and Barbara Allen talked about. Just pretend you're a reporter and recorded your conversation."

"Why?"

"Because I don't trust her," he said, giving it to her straight.

"You don't trust anyone."

"I trusted Daisy."

"What about my mother?"

"Your mother?" He leaned back against a step and looked out at shaded lawn. "Well, Madison, I've loved your mother for a very long time. I don't know as I trust her."

The girl gaped at him. Sebastian was unrepentant. The kid needed to learn that if she asked impertinent questions, she'd better be prepared for impertinent answers. Let her figure out if he was serious.

"Barbara Allen," he said.

"Oh. Right." And she told him what she and Barbara had talked about. It wasn't much.

"That's everything?"

She nodded.

"Good report. Thanks."

"You don't think she's the one bugging Mom, do you?"

"I don't know. I like to keep an open mind." He glanced at her. "I suggest you do, too."

She jumped up with her box of fabric pieces. "I've known Barbara *forever*. She's worked for my grandfather since before I was even born. She *couldn't* do those things to Mom."

"Look, under the right set of circumstances, people can do just about anything."

She shook her head, adamant. "Not me."

Sebastian hated arguing with a fifteen-year-old. "Good. Okay. Not you."

She stomped off. She knew when she was being

patronized. He considered going after her to apologize, but decided against it. He'd been nice enough until she started talking about forever. What the hell did a kid her age know about forever?

But he liked her. She was humiliated, annoyed, grounded, probably at least a little scared, and still she was trying to make the best of it. Quilting. The kid had guts. Like both her parents.

He thought of Colin and smiled. His dead friend would have been proud of his family and the way they were carrying on without him.

Lucy found him on the steps. She sat down next to him, folded her hands in her lap. "Looks as if Madison and I will be sewing the quilt Daisy pieced. Madison's at that age where she pushes me away and then pulls me to her, until I don't know what to do. Take it a day at a time and keep loving her, I suppose." She smiled suddenly. "Teenagers really are wonderful."

"You have great kids, Lucy. You've done well."

"So far. Fingers crossed."

"I want to go up and talk to Barbara Allen," he said. "It should only take thirty minutes or so."

"Are you asking me if I'll be okay here by myself? If so, the answer's yes. I'll be fine."

He stretched his legs down over the steps. "I don't know. When Daisy left me here alone, I'd get spooked, especially during a thunderstorm. That thunder would echo in the hills. I'd hide under a pillow.''

"You were just a kid."

"Hell, I was scared of thunderstorms until I was eighteen."

She laughed and placed a hand on his thigh. "Sebastian, about earlier—I'm not embarrassed, and I have no regrets, except that we didn't have more time. I knew when I went to see you in Wyoming that inviting you into my life was a risk. I've never been neutral about you. I'll say that much."

She started to remove her hand, but he covered it with his, keeping it in place. "After my mother died, Daisy said it was a cruel fate to lose both her husband and only child. She was angry, and she thought it would only add insult to injury if she lived a long life. But she was all I had, and she knew it, and she made the best of it. And after a while, she stopped being angry and started living again."

"I was never angry," Lucy said.

"Yes, you were."

She was silent, her hand still under his. She could have slipped it out, but she didn't.

"Colin left you with two small children and a life you didn't want to lead. Then your parents retired to Costa Rica when you needed them most. And Jack Swift was no good to you, wrapped up in his own grief, his work, his ideas about how you should raise his grandchildren." Sebastian paused, but Lucy didn't jump in to correct him, agree, tell him to go to hell. "If I'd shown up for the funeral or had seen you afterwards, I would have wanted to take that anger on."

"I wish you had," she said quietly. "I would have loved to have dumped it on someone else. I guess in a way I did dump some of it on you, in absentia."

"Cursed me to the rafters, did you?"

She smiled. "Pretty much." She wiggled her hand free and gave him another pat. "You're right. I was angry. I didn't know it at the time—I had so much to do, so many emotions to sort out. Anger seemed like the least of my worries. And I felt so guilty. I still do."

"I know."

"Yes. You do, don't you?" She got to her feet, and as he looked up at her, he noticed her slim body, the muscles from her paddling and hiking. She took a deep breath. "It's a gorgeous day. Well, off to Barbara's with you. If you find any dead animals tucked away, you have my permission to haul her to the police station."

"You want to lay odds she's the one?"

"Not me. I've always liked Barbara, and I've always thought she liked me."

"Maybe it doesn't have anything to do with you."

"A dead bat in my bed?"

Sebastian nodded, rising. "You're right. That has everything to do with you."

She crossed her arms over her chest, and he could see she was nervous, rattled at the idea—however far-fetched—that her father-in-law's longtime personal assistant could wish her ill.

"I'm jumping ahead of the facts," he said. "Barbara Allen isn't even a suspect. She could have an airtight alibi, for all we know—or information that could point us in the right direction."

"Well, watch your back. I don't want to have to scrape you off the rocks again."

Twelve

❦

"**I** want out," Barbara said. "I want out *now*."

Darren Mowery smirked at her from his chair in front of the cold stone fireplace. He'd shown up ten minutes ago, without warning. "Barbie, Barbie."

"Don't call me that. I'm Barbara, or Ms. Allen, or Miss Allen. I'm not 'Barbie.'"

She was on her feet, pacing, trying to look calmer than she felt. He'd swooped in so silently, so unexpectedly, catching her coming from the shower. Again, she'd detected no physical interest in her. He was single-minded, totally focused on his mission: the blackmail of a United States senator. Of her boss. She shuddered, horrified.

"Okay, *Barbara*." He drew it out, sarcastic, laughing at her without humor. He wore tan chinos and a white polo shirt, nothing that made him stand out. "You won't call the police."

"I will. If you don't leave me alone, I'll call the Capitol Police. I never should have gone along with you. I wasn't thinking." She'd been caught up in wanting to lash out at Jack, *force* him to acknowledge his love for her. But this was an unholy alliance. There were other ways to get to Jack.

Darren scratched the side of his mouth, looking unworried. "I warned you, if you'll recall. No cold feet, no surprises."

"That's not my problem."

"Oh, it is. You see, Barbie, if you go to the police, they get my pictures of you stalking Lucy Swift."

At first she didn't understand what he meant. Pictures of her stalking Lucy? What was he talking about? She wasn't a stalker. Then she digested his words. Understood. She didn't move, didn't breathe. She could feel him watching her with satisfaction.

"You don't understand—" Her voice cracked, "You couldn't possibly understand."

"Oh, no, I understand. It's simple. You hate her guts, and you took it upon yourself to scare the shit out of her. I tell the Capitol Police how I've been on your case for the past month. I tell them everything, start to finish."

"Jack will know the truth. He knows you're a blackmailer."

"And he'll know you're a stalker, a nutcase lurking in the bushes to get at his daughter-in-law. It'll all make sense to him. He won't say a word about me. You know he won't, Barbie. He's too scared. He doesn't care what I do so long as I don't squeal about Colin and his little shenanigans." Mowery smiled smugly. "I'll be the hero."

Barbara tried to stand up straight. "You followed me? You've known all this time—"

"Barbie." He was chastising, indulgent, arrogant. "You forget what I did for a living for the better part of thirty years."

"Oh, God," she whispered.

Darren crossed one leg over the other, as if to emphasize that he was relaxed, in control. "If I talk, you lose everything. Your job, your reputation, any hope you have of snaring your boss. At best, you get sent to the loony bin for a little head-shrinking. If the jury's like me and doesn't buy a nutcase plea, you're up the river for a good, long stay."

Barbara ignored the pain that swept through her. "There's nothing wrong with my mind."

"So you go for a plea bargain. Barbara Allen, the stalker." He yawned. "I thought the bullet on the car seat was goddamn brilliant, myself. Made Lucy's skin crawl, I bet."

Barbara sniffed, regarding him as if he were an insect on her carpet. "I don't have to explain myself to you. I was merely trying to shock her into doing right by Jack's grandchildren.''

''Uh-huh.''

''I'm hardly the first woman to despise a phony like Lucy.''

''Yeah, right. You hate Lucy because she's everything you're not.''

''That's not true.''

He ignored her. ''She married a Swift, she has Swift children, she has a fun, challenging career, she has a house. You hate her, *Barbara*, because she has a life and you don't.''

''I do have a life! It's Lucy who has no life.''

''When our buddy Jack told you to take a hike, you let your obsession with her get away from you.'' Darren smiled, supercilious, almost enjoying himself. ''It relieves the pressure, doesn't it? Upsetting Lucy, throwing her off her stride. Makes you feel better, at least for a little while.''

Barbara held up her chin, summoning every last shred of pride she had. ''I gave up everything for Jack. I've worked night and day for him for twenty years. I've put his interests ahead of my own. Lucy's not half the woman I am.''

''But she signs her checks 'Swift,' and you don't.''

''Bastard.''

"See? I know these things, Barbie. I'm an expert."

She tried to swallow, but her throat was too constricted. He could never understand. No one could. "I just want out." God, she sounded pathetic.

Darren dropped both feet to the floor and leaned forward. "Get this straight, Barbie." He enunciated each word precisely, as if he were talking to a dunce. "I don't care about your dirty little secret. You can turn Lucy Swift into a babbling lunatic for all I care. You are in this for the long haul. Understood?"

"I hope Sebastian Redwing finds you and kills you."

Mowery grinned. "That'd be kind of fun, wouldn't it? He tried to kill me once. I'd like to see him try again."

"Darren," she said, sinking onto the floor in front of him, knowing she looked pitiful—the obsessed spinster in love with the boss. God! But somehow, some way, she had to get through to him. "Listen to me, I don't care about my share of the money— I don't care about any of it. You can do whatever you want to do. I won't say a word. I just want to stop."

"Barbie."

"Please go on without me. *Please.*"

"I don't think so."

So cocky, so arrogant. She got to her feet, hoping

she wouldn't crack, throw up, cry. Her stomach hurt. She pushed back her hair with both hands and went to the windows that looked out on the woods, the brook. Lucy should have stayed in Washington. *None* of this would have happened if she'd stayed.

"I've gotten all the satisfaction I want from hurting Lucy," she said, and added in a small voice, "And I can wait for Jack."

"Yeah, so?"

She turned back to him. "I'm done. I won't say a word to anyone about what you're doing. Just go on about your business and leave me out of it."

"I can't do that."

"You mean you won't."

"Either way."

She started to shiver. He would see it as a sign of weakness. He had used her, manipulated her. Now there was no way out. It was Lucy's fault. All of it, Lucy's fault. Barbara could feel a fresh wave of rage building. She was trapped, and it was Lucy's fault.

"All right," she said. "What do you want me to do?"

"Right now, you're doing fine just being up here." Mowery walked over to her, stared out the windows at the picturesque scenery. "Vermont gives me the fucking creeps. I hate the woods. You okay, Barbie?"

"Yes. Certainly." No more being mealymouthed. It hadn't gotten her anywhere with him. She would hold her head high. "I have no apologies for what I did to Lucy. She deserved it."

He shrugged. "Sure."

"You've known from the beginning?"

"Why do you think we're in this gig together?"

"You had to have something on me so you knew you could manipulate me when the time came."

"So I could use your fucked-up little mind to my advantage." He winked at her. "So far, so good. You forget, Barbie. I'm better at this than you are."

"That was my mistake."

"There's only one man who's ever outsmarted me. He'll be knocking on your door before too long."

"Sebastian Redwing," she said.

Darren winked at her, patted her on the butt and left.

Fifteen minutes later, as he'd predicted, Redwing walked up onto the deck where Barbara was still contemplating her options. She had few.

Darren knew. Darren would have his way. So, what did she want? *Jack.* At the very least, satisfaction. Lucy suffering. Lucy miserable.

Sebastian introduced himself. He was, Barbara thought, breathtakingly sexy. He wore jeans and a faded polo shirt, but it would be impossible for him to blend into a crowd, even if he wanted to. She was aware of her own prim attire, simple slacks and a blouse, casual yet still professional.

"I'm staying at the house with Lucy and the kids," he said. "It belonged to my grandmother. I sold it to them after Colin died."

"Yes, I know."

His eyes were an unusual mix of grays, she saw. He seemed to take in more of her than she'd have liked—an unsettling quality. But even if he knew she had secrets, he would never guess what they were. That was what was so unnerving about Mowery: he knew, only because he was incapable of trust.

"Do you mind if I talk to you a minute?" Sebastian asked.

"No, of course not." She recovered, reminded herself she wasn't a woman who played up her physical attractions to manipulate men; that was for weaker, less intelligent and capable women. She smiled, poised, professional. "I suppose Madison told you I was in Vermont renting a house for her grandfather?"

"She didn't plan to tell anyone anything. She got caught sneaking up here this morning and came clean."

Barbara nodded. "I never meant for her to lie for me. I suppose asking her not to say anything was bad enough. A sin of omission rather than commission. I hope Lucy isn't too annoyed with me.''

"Madison's fifteen. She knows the score.''

In other words, Lucy was punishing her daughter. Acid rose in Barbara's throat. The woman was disgusting. "How long do you plan to stay in Vermont?'' she asked, keeping her tone conversational.

"I don't have any firm plans. Lucy stopped in when she was in Wyoming, and I decided to come on out, see my old haunts.''

"Had Colin mentioned anything about buying your grandmother's house and moving to Vermont one day?''

Sebastian shook his head. "Not Colin. He loved Washington.''

"Madison's like that,'' Barbara said, smiling to take the edge off her words.

"That's what I understand. I didn't get to see a lot of Colin in the four or five years before he died.''

"It's easy to take the young for granted.''

Barbara couldn't help the subtle criticism in her tone, but Sebastian didn't react. She was thinking of herself and Jack, too, and how he'd taken her for granted for years...and years. She was always there, always capable, always willing to do whatever he asked, without complaint. Unlike too many of his senior staffers, he could rely on her without worrying about her stabbing him in the back.

And what had her loyalty gotten her? Nothing.
Jack *had* to love her.

"When do you go back to Washington?" Sebastian asked.

"In a day or two. I'm open. I'll have to help Jack
tie up a few loose ends before he comes up for August."

"I'm surprised he can manage without you right
now. Isn't this a busy time of year in Washington?"

"Usually, yes."

He didn't comment, and she wondered if he could
see through her. Did he know? Did he suspect?
Lucy, the sniveling coward, would have told him
about the incidents by now. That was why he was
here, of course. Not to see his grandmother's house,
but to protect her. It was sickening.

Barbara didn't need a man to protect her. Maybe
that was why Jack was afraid to admit his love for
her—he knew she didn't need him for protection, an
income, all the things an ordinary woman wanted in
a man. She was different. Stronger.

Sebastian smiled, and it was spine-melting. It
would be so easy for someone as weak as Lucy to
turn her problems, her individuality, over to a man
like Sebastian Redwing. Barbara was more self-
reliant. Tougher. "Well," he said, "I don't pretend
to know the workings of Washington. Lucy asked
me to invite you to dinner tonight."

"How sweet. Please thank her for me, but I have other plans." Of course, Lucy would think Barbara was up here longing for her company, incapable of managing on her own. "And I hope she won't be too hard on Madison. I put her in a difficult position."

"No problem."

He started down the steps, but stopped halfway and glanced back up at her. His expression was impossible for her to read, and she was very, very good at reading people. "A former colleague of mine might be in the area. Darren Mowery. Know him?"

So this was the reason for his visit. Not Madison, not Lucy. "I've heard of him."

"He went bad last year. It's a long story. I hope I'm wrong and he's nowhere near here. If he tries to contact you, find me or call the police." His gaze leveled on her, probing, uncomfortable. "He's dangerous. I can't emphasize that enough."

"I understand. Thank you for the warning."

Lucy, Madison and J.T. had sorted the quilt pieces by color. Now they had three hundred little hexagons in piles on the dining room table. The colors were faded, the fabric worn. "It'll look like an antique quilt when we're done," Madison said happily.

"It's called a 'grandmother's garden' quilt. It'll be pretty."

"It'll be *perfect.*"

Lucy fingered a blue-and-white striped broad-cloth, imagining Daisy carefully cutting her dead husband's shirts into hexagons. Had the work helped her make peace with his death? Or was it frugal Daisy Wheaton making use of what was at hand? "Joshua died sixty years ago. This fabric's old."

J.T., who'd given up on sorting after the first hundred pieces, wandered out to the front porch with a couple of his *Star Wars* Micro Machines. He was making war noises, totally into his own twelve-year-old world.

"Mom!" he called excitedly. "Someone left flowers!"

Madison dropped a stack of hexagons. "Flowers? Oh, cool. I wonder—"

Lucy stopped her in mid-sentence, grabbing her arm. "Stay here."

"Why? Mom, you should see your face. You're white as a sheet! Over flowers?"

"Just stay put."

Lucy ran to the front door and banged it open, catching J.T. by the arm before he could pick up the bouquet of flowers. Black-eyed Susans, daisies. They were scraggly, wilted. If she'd spotted them first, she'd have thought they were from J.T. or Georgie. "Go inside with your sister."

"Mom, what's wrong? You're scaring me!"

"It's okay, J.T. Just go inside."

He started to cry, but did as she asked. Lucy could feel her legs giving way. She had to make herself calm down. She was scaring her children, scaring herself. Maybe she was wrong. Maybe the flowers were Georgie's doing, even if he hadn't been around today. Maybe he'd stopped by while they were inside sorting hexagons and had just wanted to surprise them.

The flowers were tied with a string. There was a note. Lucy plucked it out carefully, unfolded it.

> *To Lucy,*
> *I love you with all my heart.*
> *Forever,*
>
> *Colin*

It was as though the words reached up from the paper and choked her. She couldn't breathe, couldn't see. She tripped on her own feet, stumbled down several steps, reeling.

"Lucy." Sebastian's voice. His arms came around her. "Lucy, what is it?"

She gulped for air. "The son of a bitch. The son of a bitch!" Every muscle in her body tensed. She glared up at him. "Is it Barbara? Is it? Because if it is, I'm going up there now and—and—" She couldn't get the words out. "Goddammit!"

Sebastian half carried, half pushed her to the porch steps. "You're hyperventilating. If you don't stop, I'm getting a paper bag and putting it over your head."

Hyperventilating. Too much oxygen in the blood. She knew what to do. She snapped her mouth shut, counted to three, breathed through her nose, let it out slowly through her mouth.

"Two more times," Sebastian said.

"Madison and J.T."

"Two more times, Lucy. You won't do them any good passed out cold."

She knew he was right. In another minute, she was calmer, breathing normally. He snatched up the note and read it. A slight tightening of the jaw was his only visible reaction.

"I didn't expect it," she said. "I knew it was something, but not this. What kind of sick person would do something like that?"

She got to her feet, held onto his arm to help steady herself. Maybe he didn't have running water or electricity, maybe he'd renounced violence, maybe he had his demons to fight, but he was there, rock-solid.

When she regained her balance, she climbed the

steps. *Forever, Colin*. Sick, sick, sick. She got to the front door. "Madison, J.T.—it's okay, you can come on out."

"I'll get rid of the flowers," Sebastian said.

Lucy nodded. "Thank you."

"And I'll call Plato."

Sebastian's take on Barbara Allen was direct and to the point. "She's up to her eyeballs in something."

Lucy smiled. "Is that your professional opinion?"

"Gut."

They were at the kitchen table, drinking decaf coffee long after dinner. Madison and J.T. had gone up to bed. Lucy asked, "Is your gut always right?"

"About whether or not I want a cheeseburger. With who's lying, hiding, contriving, plotting to rape and pillage—" He shrugged. "It's almost always right. I've been wrong on occasion."

"I sometimes forget what you do for a living. When you're here, you seem so normal."

"I'm not," he said quietly.

She ignored a warm shudder, remembered pulling up to his shack with the dogs and the dust. No, not normal. "How does Redwing Associates manage without you?"

"I hired good people."

"About Barbara." Lucy sipped her decaf, which was a little stale. "Up to her eyeballs in what? You have an idea, don't you?"

Nothing.

"Sebastian, I deserve to know."

"It's not a question of deserving. It's a question of what you'll do with the information."

"You don't trust me."

He frowned at her. "I don't know what that means. Do I trust you to sit back and do everything I tell you? No. Do I trust you to do what you think is right for the sake of your children? Yes."

"That's too specific. I mean trust in general."

"There's no such thing."

"Yes, there is. It's when you trust someone to have an internal compass that will always point them in the right direction, not toward no mistakes—everyone makes mistakes—but toward at least trying to make good decisions."

"I'm not sure your idea and my idea of a 'good decision' are the same."

"That's not the point, either. It's not about thinking alike. It's about trusting a person to be who they are."

He drank his coffee. If he thought it was stale, he gave no indication. "You've been sitting out here in these hills too long and talking to too many crunch-granola types. Lucy, I trust you. There.''

"Good." She sat up straight. "Then tell me what you think Barbara's up to her eyeballs in."

"Blackmail."

She dropped her mug, coffee spilling over her hand and onto the table. He got up, tore off a couple of paper towels and handed them to her. She was shaking. She blotted the spilled coffee, not looking at him. "My God. Blackmail?" Then the realization hit. "Not Darren Mowery. Sebastian, please tell me—"

"I wish I could, Lucy. I've been holding back on you, hoping I could tell you Darren's not involved in what's been happening to you. But he is."

Lucy nodded, breathing rapidly. "I understand."

"No, Lucy, you don't. Darren was my boss, he was my mentor, and he was my friend. He went bad, and I went after him. I knew I might have to kill him." Sebastian returned to his seat; he was calm, as if they were discussing whether the tomatoes were ripe enough to pick. "I should have made sure he was dead or in jail before I left Colombia. I didn't."

"And now—" Lucy frowned, trying to make sense of the bits and pieces she had. She left the coffee-soaked paper towels in a mound on the table. "Is he blackmailing *you?*"

"Would that he were. That'd be easy. No, he's blackmailing your father-in-law."

"*What?*"

"Darren contacted him while you were in Wyoming. Jack paid him off, and when it wasn't enough and Darren came back for more, he got in touch with my office."

"And they got in touch with you," Lucy said, her head spinning.

"Yes."

"When?"

"Before the falls."

"Well, you're a hell of a better liar than I am. Or Madison, even. Jesus. You've known that long?"

"Jack wouldn't give Plato the details. I let him sweat a few days. He still won't budge."

"But you know it's this Darren Mowery character," Lucy said.

Sebastian nodded.

"Then arrest him!"

"That's the thing about blackmail, Lucy. The victim doesn't want to go public. He doesn't care about whether the blackmailer goes to jail. He just wants him to keep quiet."

Unable to sit still another second, Lucy jumped

to her feet. She ran outside, down the back steps, into the grass. It was cool on her bare feet. She could hear crickets as she fought back tears. Blackmail! Jack was being blackmailed!

Sebastian followed her out into the grass, not standing too close. The more he had to think about, Lucy thought, the more he seemed to go deep inside himself and maintain an outward calm. It was a skill she didn't have, except on the water. When a crisis hit while kayaking or canoeing, she operated on training, instinct, skill. She couldn't afford to panic.

But this was what he did, she remembered. He dealt with blackmailers. Blackmail victims.

"How much did Jack pay—do you know that much?"

"Twenty grand in two installments."

"That's all?"

"For now."

She exhaled toward the starlit sky. "I just want to make a quilt with my daughter. I want to take my son fishing. I want to live my life. *Damn.*"

"Plato will be here tomorrow."

She nodded.

"Lucy." He touched her cheek with one finger. "Oh, God, Lucy. If I could make this all go away, I would, even if it meant you never came to Wyoming and I didn't get to see you."

She shut her eyes, squeezed back tears. "Do you think Barbara's involved in the blackmail?"

"Yes."

"Do you think it has anything to do with me?"

"Yes. I don't know how, but yes."

She sank her forehead against his chest and let her arms go around him. He held her. She recovered slowly, stopped crying. "I hate crying," she said. "I haven't cried in years, except when I stubbed my toe last summer, and really, it was more because I was pissed."

"Lucy, you're one of the strongest women I know."

"I'm not. I just get up every day and do the best I can."

"There," he said, "you see what I mean?"

She opened her eyes and saw his smile, and she kissed him lightly, savoring the taste of him, the feel of his hands and the night summer breeze on her back. "If I could," she whispered, "I'd ask you to make love to me tonight."

"Lucy—"

"My children are upstairs in bed. They're afraid, and they need to know where I am."

"I love you, Lucy Blacker." He touched her hair, her mouth, then kissed her in a way that made her know he meant what he said. "I always will."

"Thank you."

He laughed suddenly, so unexpectedly it took her breath away. "Thank you?"

"Well—I don't know. Yes, thank you."

He smacked her on the behind. "Go upstairs to your kids before I toss all honor to the stars and carry you off to bed."

"That's very tempting, you know."

"Believe me, I know."

J.T. was asleep when Lucy entered his room. As if drawn by an invisible force, she turned to the picture of him with his father. "Colin," she whispered, touching his image. "Thank you for what you were to me. For Madison and J.T. and our years together. Thank you."

She went down the hall and listened at Madison's closed door, then slipped into the guest room. She gazed out at the darkening sky, thinking of blackmail and Jack and a dangerous man who wasn't dead, and when she crawled into bed and pulled her quilts up to her chin, she thought of Sebastian. And she smiled. The Widow Swift was falling in love again.

The memo came across his desk late, around nine, and at nine-fifteen, Jack Swift gave up on working until midnight as he'd planned and got a cab home.

It was a routine memo. His staff was aware Sebastian Redwing had once saved his life and had been Colin's friend, and they regularly passed along pertinent information on Redwing Associates.

> Happy Ford, a Washington, DC-based consultant for Redwing Associates, was shot this evening here in the city. She's in critical condition. Prognosis optimistic. Unknown if injury sustained in work-related activity. No suspects at this time.

Mowery.

In his bones, Jack knew Darren Mowery had shot this woman.

He got to his house, ran upstairs, started throwing clothes into his suitcase. Lucy, the children. He had to get to them. Somehow, he'd crossed Mowery. Somehow, he'd screwed up.

"I did everything the bastard asked!"

His suitcase fell off his bed, its contents spilling across the floor. He collapsed onto the thick rug amidst boxer shorts and chinos and sobbed. He pulled his knees up under his chin, wrapped his arms around his ankles and cried like a two-year-old. He couldn't stop. Colin, Eleanor. Gone. Dead. Buried. Everything he'd lived and worked for about to go up in smoke.

He had nothing left. Nothing.

And now Lucy and his grandchildren—he didn't know. He didn't know what Mowery would do.

"Jack?" Sidney's voice, calling from downstairs. "Jack, are you here? I called your office, and they said you lit out like a bat out of a burning cave. What's going on?"

In another minute, she was in the doorway.

She gasped. *"Jack."*

"Oh, Sidney. Sidney, what am I going to do?"

Thirteen

Lucy ignored J.T.'s protests and made him go blueberry picking with her first thing in the morning. "Wild blueberries make the best muffins," she told him. "They're just starting to ripen."

"Why can't Madison go?"

"She's still asleep, and you're right here, bright-eyed and raring to go."

He made a face and slumped his shoulders, dragging his heels. If she'd told him he could go play Nintendo or watch TV, she knew he'd perk up, which only made her more determined. She handed him a coffee can. "You can be miserable or you can be cheerful. Your choice."

"I wish Georgie could come over."

She'd called Rob and Patti last night and suggested they keep Georgie home today. Lucy slung an arm over her son's shoulder. "You're getting so big. Are your feet bigger than mine yet?"

He liked that idea, and they walked up along the western edge of the stone wall that bordered the field, finally climbing over it to a cluster of low-bush wild blueberries. They squatted down, the sun already warm on their backs. It was supposed to rain later on, but now the air was humid and so still that Lucy swore she'd be able to hear a spider move.

"They're still green," J.T. said.

"Not all of them. We only need a cup for muffins. They'll be perfect when Grandpa's here next week. We can have him down for blueberry pancakes, blueberry pie, blueberry ice cream."

"I hate blueberry pancakes."

"J.T."

He smiled at her over the blueberry bushes. He still thought his cute smile could get him out of trouble. Just like his father. Lucy noticed there wasn't the usual pang of regret, the ache of realizing that her son would never really know his father. It wasn't okay—she hated it. But they'd be all right.

"Look! Mom, look, I've got one, two, three—*five* blueberries! Look at this one, it's huge." He plucked them fast, tossed them into his can as he reached for more. "Wow, I'm in the right spot."

"Good for you, J.T. Just keep picking."

He lost interest three handfuls of blueberries later, but Lucy decided they had enough for muffins. They clambered over the stone wall, her life, at that moment, back to normal.

She saw Sebastian walk out onto the back steps and sit down. He waved to her, and her heart skipped a beat, just as if she were a thirteen-year-old with a crush. Except this was different. She and Sebastian weren't kids. She was thirty-eight; he was thirty-nine or forty. Colin was the right man for the woman she'd been, but she wasn't that woman anymore. The past three years had changed her. She'd lost a husband, she was raising two children on her own, she'd started her own business and moved to the country.

J.T. skipped ahead of her. "Hey, Sebastian!"

"Hey, J.T. You're up with the roosters."

"Mom and I picked blueberries." He stuck his can under Sebastian's nose. "Look."

Lucy followed at a slower pace, knowing push was coming to shove. She had a plan. She was tired of waiting for the next shoe to drop. But she knew Sebastian wouldn't like what she had in mind.

"We're making muffins," J.T. said.

Sebastian eyed her as she got closer. It was as if he could sense she was up to something he wouldn't like. "Muffins, huh?"

"Yes," Lucy said. "I thought we'd take some muffins up to Barbara and surprise her."

His eyes darkened just slightly, but enough. She

was right. He didn't approve. "J.T., you've got a few stems in your berries. Why don't you take your can into the kitchen and pick them out while your mother and I talk."

"Don't argue with her," J.T. warned. "She's not in the mood."

He pounded up the steps, never one to make less noise when he could make more. Sebastian stood, his bruises and scrapes even less noticeable today. "You're going to take muffins to Barbara?"

"Yes, it's what I'd do if I didn't suspect her of being involved with a blackmail scheme and leaving me mean-spirited presents."

"They were more than mean-spirited, and the point is, you do suspect her."

"Well, *you* do. I don't know if I do. I'm not the one with twenty years of experience with creeps and desperadoes. I take people on adventures. Fun adventures. Nothing extreme, nothing scary. I mean, the unforeseen can happen and does." She squinted at him against the morning sun. "But we have contingency plans."

"Lucy, whoever left those flowers yesterday knew you were here with the kids. If it was Barbara, she knew I was here. She took a huge risk. When I see something like this escalate, I don't like it."

"I didn't like it when it hadn't escalated. Sebastian, Barbara knows I know she's here. If I don't go up to see her, she's going to wonder why."

"Let her wonder."

"What if she's innocent? Then I'll have hurt her feelings for no good reason."

"No, for a damn good reason. If she's innocent, she'll understand."

"That I thought she was capable of leaving me flowers from my dead husband? I don't think so."

"J.T. was right. You aren't in the mood to argue."

Lucy pounded up the steps almost as hard as J.T. had and tore open the door. She looked back at Sebastian and caught her breath at how the sunlight struck his hair, brought out the hard lines in his face. Maybe she was jumping the gun to think she could have a relationship with him. It was one thing to fall in love, another thing to have a relationship that worked. "I'm bringing Barbara wild-blueberry muffins."

"Plato will be here by noon."

"Good. In the meantime, you can hover."

The door slammed shut behind her.

And he laughed. In another minute, he was making coffee and picking stems out of the blueberries with J.T. as if he'd admitted defeat, which Lucy knew he hadn't. Maybe defeat had driven him out to the edges of his ranch and into a shack, but it hadn't driven him into her kitchen. The man had burrowed under her skin, and he meant to stay there.

She wrapped the muffins in aluminum foil and drove up the dirt road while they were still warm, because that was what she ordinarily would have done. She wouldn't have walked for fear of squishing the muffins, and she wouldn't have waited until they were cold, because they were no good cold.

The only difference was not taking Madison and J.T. with her. They stayed at the house with Rob.

Sebastian, she knew, was on the prowl in the woods. Hovering. She could almost feel his presence when she got out of her car at the rented house. There still was no breeze, the air warm and humid even up on the ridge. She followed a shaded gravel path and took the stairs to the deck. Sebastian had suggested she not go inside. Made sense to her.

"Barbara? Hello, it's me, Lucy!"

"I'm here," Barbara said from the screened porch.

"Oh, I didn't see you. J.T. and I made muffins this morning, and I brought you some. We picked wild blueberries bright and early."

"Sounds lovely."

Barbara pushed open the screen door, smiling as she came out onto the deck. She looked perfectly normal to Lucy. A bit formally dressed for Vermont, perhaps, but that wasn't out of the ordinary for Jack Swift's assistant. Lucy tried to place when they'd first met. It was when she and Colin were dating, for sure—not long after the assassination attempt. Barbara Allen had been a fixture in Jack's office for as long as Lucy could remember. Could she feel taken for granted and resent it?

But when Barbara smelled the muffins and seemed so genuinely delighted, Lucy couldn't imagine her stalking and harassing anyone, much less her boss's daughter-in-law. If nothing else, it would be dumb, and Barbara wasn't dumb. "Thank you so much," she said, "I love wild blueberries."

"There might be a few bushes up here." Lucy noticed blueberry and flour stains on her T-shirt and wished she'd changed. "You could probably get enough at least for a batch of pancakes."

Barbara laughed. "I'm afraid I'm not that domestic."

"I don't know, just about anyone can manage Bisquick and a handful of blueberries. Well, I hope you enjoy the muffins. Are you here long?"

"Just another day or two, I imagine. Thank God for cell phones. Otherwise I wouldn't be able to spare so much time away from the office."

"Yes, I know what you mean."

But Lucy regretted her words, irritated at herself for being defensive. She enjoyed making muffins and pancakes, picking berries, puttering in her garden, hanging out with her children; she had a business, she worked, she knew her way around Washington. She had nothing to prove. So what if Barbara had to make sure Lucy knew how important and indispensable she was? Why get defensive?

"I hope I didn't get Madison into trouble," Barbara said.

"You didn't." Madison, Lucy thought, got herself into trouble. "She's looking forward to her visit to Washington this fall. We all are, actually."

"Fall's my favorite time of year in Washington. It's so vibrant, so alive. I love the country, but—" She looked around at the still, quiet woods, and smiled. "I guess all this peacefulness would get on my nerves after a while."

"My first few months here, I was so restless, I didn't know if I'd stay. Then, I don't know, I started to enjoy the pace of life. Vermont isn't as isolated as it sometimes seems. There's so much to do."

"With so many tourists and second-home owners from the city, I imagine so. Your adventure-travel business is going well?"

Lucy nodded. This woman was driving her nuts. Maybe Sebastian's suspicions had colored her perceptions, made her hypersensitive to what she might ordinarily have treated as a normal conversation. "It's going very well, thanks. I have a great staff, and we have so many ideas. Did Madison tell you we're putting together a Costa Rica trip?''

''No, actually, we didn't really get a chance to talk about you.''

It was as if Lucy had just been stuck with a thousand poison needles. This woman did not like her. ''My parents retired there, you know.''

''Jack told me. An odd thing to do, don't you think?''

So, now not only was she selfish and inferior, but her family was odd, too. She shrugged and made herself smile. ''A natural thing for them, considering their background. I'm trying to get Jack to go with us on the dry run. Wouldn't that be fun? Maybe Sidney Greenburg can go, too. She and my parents are friends—''

''Yes, I know.'' Barbara set the muffins on an Adirondack chair and took in a long breath, staring out at the woods. For a moment, she seemed to forget Lucy was there, but she caught herself. ''I'll check Jack's schedule. I don't know if he can spare any time for Costa Rica.''

For frivolities, her tone said. Lucy pretended not to notice. ''I hope he can, although I understand. Life as a senator must be awfully hectic and demanding.''

''Well, one must prioritize. Jack would spend all his time with you and his grandchildren if he could.

You know that. Unfortunately, I have to rein him in, help him stay on track. There's very little thanks in telling someone no all the time, but he understands.''

"You don't think he should spend August up here?''

"Not the entire month, frankly, no. Personally, I can understand. You're his only family. Professionally—he's a Rhode Island senator, not a Vermont senator.'' Barbara smiled sweetly. "If you'd moved to Providence or Newport, it would be a different story.''

If she'd been a good daughter-in-law, in other words. Lucy gave a lighthearted laugh. "No one offered me a house on the cheap in Providence or Newport. Well, I should be going. We're pulling together the last details for a father-son backpacking trip.''

"It must be nice to have such a flexible schedule,'' Barbara said. "I'm so used to my dawn-to-dusk hours!''

"Nice seeing you, Barbara.''

"You, too.'' When Lucy was halfway down the steps, Barbara added, "Oh, and I'd keep my eyes wide open around Sebastian Redwing.''

Lucy turned. "Sebastian? Why?''

"I think he has another agenda aside from seeing his childhood home again.''

Yeah, Lucy thought. The blackmail of a United States senator. "I'm not worried. I've known Sebastian for the better part of twenty years."

Barbara walked to the top of the steps. She was a handsome woman, Lucy thought, but annoying. "It's obvious, Lucy. You're his hidden agenda."

"What?"

"He's been in love with you for years. Everyone knows but you."

"Washington." Lucy laughed off her uneasiness. "I sure don't miss the gossip. See you, Barbara. Enjoy the muffins."

When she got back to her car, Lucy got in behind the wheel. She was furious with herself, furious with Barbara, and sickened by the idea of what this woman had done to her. "I wish I had proof. I'd drag the bitch by the hair down to the police," she said aloud.

"Well, well, well." Sebastian grinned as he opened the passenger door and slid in. "I like your spirit, Lucy Blacker."

"You weren't supposed to hear that."

He slumped low in the seat. "Eavesdropping is an unappreciated art."

"You listened in on my conversation with Barbara?"

"Yep. Female version of a pissing contest."

"I don't know what got into me." Lucy started

the engine, backed out in a fury. "I don't care if she works twenty-four hours a day and thinks I'm a frump. Really, I don't."

"She sucked you into measuring yourself by her standards instead of your own."

Lucy shifted into drive, hit the gas pedal and tore off down the dirt road. It needed grading, and her car bounced over the washboard ruts. "It's tempting to say she has to make more of her position with Jack and work 'dawn to dusk' because she has no life." She gulped for air, relaxed her grip on the wheel. "But then I'd be as bad as she is, judging her for her choices. Well, you're right. It was a pissing contest."

"You want to slow down? If we get wrapped around a tree, Plato will end up raising your kids." Sebastian leaned back in his seat, not looking as if her driving bothered him at all. "You don't want that. He used to jump out of a helicopter in the middle of a nor'easter."

She slowed, but not because she was worried about hitting a tree or Plato Rabedeneira raising her children. She glanced over at Sebastian. He had on a black polo shirt and jeans that fit closely over his thighs, and even the fading scrapes and scratches on his arms struck her as sexy, evidence of his hard life, his hard thinking. His choices. She sighed. "What are we going to do about Barbara?"

"We?"

"She's not going to stop. Whatever she has against me, I'm pretty sure I just made it worse."

"You couldn't have said or done anything to make it better. She's determined to hate you. She likes it. Hating you makes her feel better about herself."

"Do you really think she's in cahoots with Mowery?"

"I'd say there's a high probability."

"Meaning," Lucy added, "whatever he has on Jack could be something that would also hurt me."

Sebastian regarded her with a steady, reassuring calm. "Would Jack jeopardize his reputation and his bank account to protect you?"

"Yes. Yes, I think he would."

"Because of Madison and J.T.?"

"No, not just because of them—but they're a factor, absolutely. We're all the family he has. After Colin died—" She stepped on the brake, stopping the car. "Oh, my God. Sebastian, what if it's something to do with Colin?"

"If you know something," Sebastian said quietly, his tone professional, deadly, "if you even suspect something, now's the time."

"I don't. There's *nothing*. Jack and Colin both— with both of them, what you see is what you get. Colin had no secrets, not from me. He died suddenly, without any warning at all. We had no idea he had a heart condition. He didn't have time to hide anything. I went through all his stuff.''

"Did he keep a journal?"

She nodded.

"Did you read it?"

"No. I burned it without reading it. Wouldn't you?"

"Probably not."

She shot him a look and realized he wasn't kidding. "You'd read a dead person's journal?"

"I might. I wouldn't rule it out and just burn it. What if it contained the secret to cold fusion?"

She found herself biting back a laugh. "You're full of shit, Redwing."

He grinned at her. "You needed to lighten up. What about Jack? What could he have to hide?"

"He might have some unpaid hospital bills. That's about as nefarious as he'd get." She took her foot off the brake and stepped on the gas pedal. "Maybe Mowery and Barbara made up something."

"That's possible," Sebastian said.

She sighed at him. "How can you be so calm?"

"Who says I'm calm?"

When they reached the house, Lucy put Madison and J.T. both to work with her in the barn. Rob wore a look that told her he wanted to interrogate her, but he wouldn't do it in front of her kids. So they actually managed to get some adventure travel work done.

And at noon, on schedule, Plato Rabedeneira arrived.

"Holy shit," Rob breathed, peering out the barn window at Plato and his big, shiny black car. "You know, Lucy, sometimes I start thinking you're just this ordinary adventure travel person, this widow with two kids, and then the cavalry rolls in."

"This is nothing. You should see what would happen if I called Washington."

"Grandpa Jack."

She nodded.

Plato got out. Apparently he'd parked his plane next to Sebastian's at the local airstrip and had the car waiting. He wore a black suit and dark glasses, and his limp was more pronounced, probably from the long hours in the plane.

"Think he's armed?" Rob asked.

"To the teeth."

Lucy went out to the driveway and practically felt Rob's shudder when Plato kissed her on the cheek. "Hey, kid."

"Hi, Plato. Thanks for coming out here. Just one thing before I let you into my house." She crossed her arms and gave him the kind of look she'd given J.T. and Georgie when she caught them playing war with her tomatoes. "I can't believe you sicced Sebastian on me knowing—'' She faltered, realizing she was already in over her head, and finished lamely, ''Knowing what you knew.''

Plato grinned. ''You mean that he's a reprobate or that he's in love with you?''

''Both.''

''I was thinking I'd sicced you on him.''

''Ha.''

His dark glasses made him even harder to read. ''He's still the best.''

''I hope so. I need the best.''

''Where is he?''

''Right here,'' Sebastian said, walking down from the front porch. ''What's with the car and the dark glasses? You're lucky I didn't shoot you.''

''You don't have a gun,'' Plato said, ''and you wouldn't use one if you did.''

''Maybe I've changed my mind.''

''Good. Your sabbatical's over. You can get back to work.''

''Sabbatical. Jesus, Plato.''

But the joking ended, and Plato said, ''I have news.''

He glanced at Lucy, who shook her head, adamant. ''Oh, no, you don't. I'm not going anywhere. Whatever you two have to say, you can say it in front of me.''

''Sebastian?''

Lucy gritted her teeth but didn't jump in and argue her point further. Technically, Sebastian was Plato's boss, and his military training would compel him to follow the chain of command—but they were *friends,* and who the hell had given Sebastian the last word? She was agitated, frustrated, and it was entirely possible what they were discussing was none of her business.

"Go ahead," Sebastian said.

"It's not good news," Plato said. "Happy Ford was shot last night in Washington. She's critical, but she should pull through."

Sebastian had no visible reaction. "She's getting everything she needs?"

"Everything."

He looked out across the road at the lush, wooded hills. "Mowery?"

"We haven't been able to talk to her."

"Then we don't know where he is," Sebastian said.

"No. She thought she'd picked up his trail yesterday afternoon. That's the last we heard."

"If she dies, it's my fault."

Plato shook his head. "If she dies, it's the fault of whoever pulled the trigger."

"I should have killed Mowery a year ago."

"Only a year ago? Why not fifteen years ago? Why not the day you met him?"

Madison and J.T. bounded out from the barn. Lucy felt her heart flip-flop at their energy, their youth, their obliviousness. Her babies. Dear God, she had to protect them!

Sebastian's eyes had narrowed into slits. "You're on kid watch."

Plato grimaced. "I was afraid of that."

"Take them out of here. Keep them safe."

Sebastian walked back up the porch steps and disappeared into the house. The door banged shut behind him, and Lucy jumped. She tried to smile. "I'm a little on edge."

"Good," Plato said. "It'll keep you alert."

"What do you want me to do?"

"Help your kids pack up. Two changes of clothes, two pairs of shoes, no animals."

"Sleeping bags? I have a ton of freeze-dried provisions—"

His unsmiling mouth twitched. "I'm not taking them into the outback, Lucy. We'll find a motel somewhere."

"You'll call me?"

"No. If I call you, it means there's trouble."

Her knees went out from under her, but she held steady. "Plato, I don't know if I can..."

"You can come with us."

She shook her head. "No. I have to figure this out. I trust you."

He tucked a finger under her chin. "Trust Sebastian."

"Mom," Madison said, and Lucy could feel her terror. "What's going on?"

"Cool car," J.T. said.

Lucy didn't know how to explain. She composed herself, and plunged in. "I want you two to go with Plato. It could be for a few hours or a couple of days, until I get things sorted out around here. He'll take care of you."

The color drained out of Madison's face. "*Mom.* What about you?"

"I'll be fine. I'll be here with Sebastian, and with any luck, I'll just get a lot of work done."

J.T. was still enthralled with the car. "Can I ride up front?"

Plato grimaced. "Sure, kid."

Madison tried to smile. She was older, and she knew more, guessed more. But she was determined to be brave. Lucy could see her struggling not to panic. "Um—can I take my quilt?"

Lucy knew she meant the hexagons she'd found in the attic.

Plato didn't. He sighed. "Quilt? Yeah, sure. Take your quilt."

Fourteen

Plato leaned in the doorway of J.T.'s room. "Kid's packing for the new millenium," he said to Lucy. "Your daughter's worse. Maybe you better go on downstairs and pour yourself a glass of lemonade, Lucy. I'll supervise."

She nodded. "They're nervous."

"They're packing too much. I didn't bring the moving van. Go on. We'll get it pared down in no time." He unfolded himself from the doorway and joined J.T. by his bed. "J.T., where'd you get all this crap?"

"It's not crap, it's my stuff."

"Well, it's a shitload of stuff." He picked up a Micro Machine. "Hey, I like this little helicopter here. I used to jump out of one of these babies."

"Really?"

Lucy could see her son was smitten. A tough,

handsome ex-parachute rescue jumper who swore and knew helicopters—Plato would end up paring him down to a change of undershorts. He'd probably find some way of working his charms on Madison, too.

Lucy slipped downstairs to the kitchen. She didn't know where Sebastian was. Rob had gone off to Manchester on a supply run.

There was no lemonade made. She took out a frozen can of concentrate and set it in the sink, turning the hot water on to a trickle.

The phone rang, making her jump.

"Lucy? Thank God. It's Sidney Greenburg." She paused for air. "Jack's in trouble."

Blackmail trouble, Lucy thought. She wondered what her father-in-law had deigned to tell Sidney. "What kind of trouble?"

"He told me about the blackmail. How much do you know? Damned little, right? He's such an ass. He thinks he's being noble. Lucy..." Sidney groaned. "I hate this. I hate every single minute of it."

"I know." Lucy calmed herself by watching the ice melt on her can of frozen concentrate. "Tell me, Sidney. I can take it."

"Of course you can. I told Jack you could. Some jackass named Darren Mowery is blackmailing him over an affair Colin may or may not have had shortly before he died. There are supposedly pictures. If Jack knows the name of the woman, he won't tell me. I assume it's someone who'd interest the media, but who the hell knows."

Lucy stuck her finger in the hot trickle, ran it over the top of the still-icy can. An affair. Colin. "This is ridiculous. Colin didn't have an affair. Even if he did, he's dead, and it was a private matter."

"I know! That's what I told Jack! He said once something like this gets out in Washington, it can take on a life of its own. I said bullshit and told him to call you at once. He was so upset. He really thought he was protecting you and the kids by paying this bastard."

"I don't need him or anyone else to protect me from the truth. He can protect me from lions, tigers and bears if it comes to it, but never the truth."

She could almost feel Sidney's sad smile. "He meant well. He cares about you and his grandchildren so much. He'll never get over Colin. He couldn't save him on the tennis court—he can at least save his reputation."

"Where's Jack now? Did he put you up to calling me?"

"Lucy, there's more." Sidney took a deep breath. "Jack showed me. This Mowery character put up pictures of you on a secure Internet site. Recent pictures. Like from last week."

"Jesus," Lucy whispered.

"Jack was horrified. He took it as an implied threat that if he didn't cooperate and follow instructions to the letter, this guy could get to you."

Lucy shut off the hot water. "Sidney, he can get to me if Jack *does* cooperate!"

"I know. I have to say, when I saw those pictures of you, I didn't think, either. I'd have cut Mowery a check for every dime I have. Now——" Her voice faltered, and she fought back a sob. "Lucy, Jack's missing. I don't know what the hell to do."

"Missing? What do you mean, missing?"

"He was supposed to meet me at my office an hour ago. We were going to call you together. He didn't show up. I called his office, and he never showed up there today. I went to his house—that's where I am now—and he's not here."

"Call the Capitol Police, Sidney. Tell them *everything*. Okay? Tell them to send someone up here right away. Damn it. *Damn it.*" Lucy scooped up the frozen concentrate and banged it down onto the counter. "Jack and I both waited too long, trying to protect ourselves, Madison and J.T., each other. Colin. Oh, Sidney...I'm so sorry."

"Lucy?"

"I've got a stalker," she blurted. "I thought it was Barbara, but now—I don't know, maybe someone's using her as a decoy." She rubbed her forehead, tired, frustrated, too much coming at her at once. "I can't figure it out. I've got Plato Rabedeneira and Sebastian Redwing here. They're like a couple of big, mean guard dogs."

"Listen to me, Lucy. Listen!" Sidney spoke briskly, taking charge. She was a brilliant, kind woman Lucy had always admired. "A couple of weeks ago, Barbara Allen went a little nutty on Jack and told him she's been secretly in love with him for twenty years."

"Oh, no."

"I wouldn't be surprised if this Mowery character had taken advantage of her. She thinks she's tough as nails, but she's kind of like a turtle. Her hard outer shell protects a soft, mushy inside. She won't be happy when she realizes Mowery's manipulated her. My bet is, she'll lash out before she admits a weakness. She'll do anything to keep people from seeing that mushy inside."

Lucy managed a smile. "I'm impressed."

"Forget it, my mum's a shrink, and I'm an anthropologist. I come from a family that thinks too goddamn much. You take care, do you hear me?" She spoke fiercely, her intensity palpable. "I'm counting on Costa Rica."

Sidney hung up, and Lucy stood in the middle of the kitchen, shaking.

Sebastian fell in behind her. "I don't know about

you, but lions, tigers and bears would be fine with me right about now."

Lucy whirled around at him. "You listened in? Goddamn it, Redwing! How dare you? How—" She slammed her foot into a cabinet. "That was a private conversation. *Damn* you!"

He grabbed her wrists and held them up close to his chest, nothing about him calm, nothing retreating deep inside him. "Damn me all you want, Lucy. I'm not here to make you feel comfortable or to live according to your rules. I'm here to keep Darren Mowery from killing anyone else."

"This isn't about you!"

"It is about me. It's about me and a mistake I made a year ago. Mowery isn't blackmailing Jack Swift over an old affair he and Barbara Allen cooked up. He isn't after twenty grand or Jack's vote on legislation. Jack doesn't know this man. *You* don't know him."

"And you do?"

"Yes."

"He wants you," Lucy said abruptly. "Oh, my God. This is about revenge, isn't it?"

Sebastian's grip softened, and he released her, caught up one hand and kissed it. "Lucy, when I'm whitewater kayaking, I'll do everything you say. I promise."

She nodded, tried to smile. "I'll hold you to that. Any guess where Mowery is?"

"Not here. Not yet. My guess is he's already reined Barbara back in, recommitted her to the program. Sidney's calling the Capitol police. They'll get things into motion."

"We should call the local police. They're not a bunch of yokels. If I tell them to be discreet—"

"Lucy, I know who they are. I went to school with half of them. Let the Capitol police get them involved. Right now, if Mowery does have Jack, he has the advantage."

"He'll kill Jack—"

"He'll kill everyone if it suits him."

Lucy started for the back door. "I'm going up to warn Barbara she's in over her head."

"She won't thank you for it."

"I don't care."

She plunged out the door, leaped down the back steps even as she fought for calm, for control, for one quiet space in her mind where she could think.

Sebastian followed her. He didn't seem to be moving as fast as she was. Longer legs, she thought, but she felt like a whirling dervish, spinning, spinning, but not centered.

"I'll go with you," he said.

She ground to a sudden halt in the warm grass. Dark clouds were sweeping in from the west, and she could feel the humidity gathering around her. "You only want to come along because you don't want me going alone. You're a loner, Sebastian." She tilted her head back, gave him a long, clear-eyed look and saw him as he was. "It's easy to love me from a distance."

He touched her mouth and, with no warning whatsoever, he kissed her, a quick, passionate kiss that almost sank her to the ground. He stood back and smiled. "It's not easy to love you at all."

"Sebastian—"

"Later. Let's go." She saw he'd grabbed her cell phone off the counter. He dropped it in his pocket. "Tough to believe Larry the Lump from ninth grade is the chief of police."

Barbara slipped through the back door of Lucy's converted barn, past the canoes, kayaks, life vests, rescue equipment and office supplies, and into her work space. How pathetic. Lucy had given up a job with a prestigious Washington museum for this, Barbara thought. Her desks were nothing but hardware-store doors set onto handmade trestles. Cows and horses had once trod across the wide-board floor. There was a woodstove to supplement the electric heating unit, and the walls were covered with posters of northern New England, the Canadian Maritimes, Costa Rica. Only because of her Swift connections in Washington could Lucy have survived in business this long.

She had one of those plastic cubes on her desk, filled with pictures of Madison and J.T. None of Colin, Barbara saw. None of Jack. It was as if Lucy had wiped them out of her life. She'd come to Vermont to start over, and start over, she had.

Now she had Sebastian Redwing wrapped around her little finger, and no doubt Plato Rabedeneira, too. Didn't they see through her? But Barbara knew better. People were stupid. Men were particularly stupid. Twenty years in Washington had taught her that much.

If only Jack would admit he loved her, Barbara thought. If, when she'd finally come forward, he'd had the courage to say, as she'd fantasized countless times. "Oh, Barbara, I've been waiting all these years for you to give me the slightest hint you cared. Even when Eleanor was alive, I dreamed of us being together one day."

Sentimental nonsense, of course. In real life, Jack had patted her on the head and sent her off. Good Barbara. Reliable Barbara. What if he were just another stupid man, after all? Twenty years of her life, gone!

She stroked the barrel of the Smith & Wesson .38 she'd appropriated from her father years ago. It was the same one he'd used to teach her and her sisters how to shoot with. He still wandered around the house, grumbling about what had happened to it. "I hope some stupid bastard doesn't hold up a gas station with my goddamn gun!"

A crude man, her father. It was an old gun, hopelessly out-of-date in a world of semiautomatics. But she had a silencer that fit it, and she knew it would do the job.

Plato Rabedeneira.

Madison had called from the phone in her room. "I'm packing," she'd told Barbara. "Don't tell anyone I called, okay? I just didn't want you to think we were ignoring you. All kinds of weird things have been going on around here, and my mom's friend Plato's taking J.T. and me off somewhere."

"Are you scared?"

"I'm trying not to be. We're leaving in a few minutes."

Barbara eased to the front entrance of the converted barn. Plato was out by his car. He was so handsome, but slowed down by his limp and out of his element in the hills of Vermont. She remembered his dropping to the ground when he was shot during the assassination attempt on Jack and the president. He hadn't made a sound.

She tucked her gun into her waistband and pulled her shirt over it. She didn't have a focused plan. She'd seen Sebastian and Lucy walking up along the edge of the field. Did they all suspect her? Had Lucy poisoned them against her?

Refusing to rush, Barbara walked out of the barn and across the yard toward the front porch. She would say she'd come to thank Lucy for the blueberry muffins. Maybe she'd invite them to dinner. Spaghetti. Kids always liked spaghetti.

They couldn't leave.

She wouldn't let them.

Madison stomped down the front porch steps. The hanging petunias needed watering. Lucy neglected them, just as she did her children.

The girl was complaining bitterly to Plato. "You're not making J.T. leave his Micro Machines."

Plato swore under his breath. "All right. Hurry up."

"I'll only be ten seconds." Victory sounded in her voice. "This is going to be a *fabulous* quilt."

A quilt? Dear God, Barbara thought. Madison would never be ready for the real world if she stayed here sewing quilts, snapping beans, wandering off in the woods by herself. *Someone* had to bring these people to their senses.

Barbara removed the Smith & Wesson from her waistband. She didn't know why. A precaution, a necessity. She was following her instincts.

Plato saw her. "Madison, get down!"

The girl leaped at him, pulling on his arm as he reached for his gun. "No, no, it's Barbara! She's a friend!"

Plato backhanded the girl into the dirt. "Stay put."

She scrambled to her feet, wild, out of control, then charged him. "You're a maniac! You're all maniacs!"

Barbara fired before Plato could get to his weapon. With the silencer, the shot hardly made a sound. Madison screamed, her interference and Plato's quick reactions throwing off Barbara's aim so that she only caught his upper right arm. She fired again, grazing the side of his head.

The girl went nuts, shrieking when Plato, semi-conscious, collapsed onto the dirt driveway. Blood streamed down his face.

Barbara marched over to Madison and snatched her by the elbow. "Get up. Stop your screaming."

The girl sobbed, her face streaked with tears. "You killed Plato!"

"I *will* kill him if you don't shut up and come with me. Right now." Barbara inhaled. Her head ached, but now she had a clear purpose. She knew what she needed to do. "Where's your brother?"

"J.T.! Run! Run get Mom and Sebastian!"

Barbara slapped the girl across the face, half with her hand, half with the butt of her gun. Madison gulped back a scream. Barbara could see the fierce anger behind her terror. So like Colin, but corrupted by her mother.

Plato lay motionless on the driveway, blood from his wounds spilling into the dirt.

How like Lucy to abandon her children to a stranger.

There was no advantage to killing him. Barbara was more interested in the missing boy. He could be a problem.

Madison's teeth were chattering. "Don't—don't kill Plato. *Please.* I couldn't live with myself. It's my fault. I *trusted* you!"

"Well," Barbara said, "let's not give Plato a clear shot so he can kill me, shall we?" She placed her father's Smith & Wesson at the girl's head. "Your mother doesn't care about you, Madison. I'll prove it to you. She rescued Sebastian Redwing from Joshua Falls. Do you think she'll rescue you?"

Madison squared her jaw. "I'll rescue myself."

"There, you see? You're used to being on your own, even at fifteen. Come on, Madison. That's it. One step at a time."

Jack held up his head, trying to retain his dignity. "You will never get away with kidnapping a United States senator."

Darren Mowery grinned at him. "So?"

He was driving, and he was armed with a semi-automatic. They were within minutes of Lucy's house. Jack still didn't know exactly what had happened. A Senate colleague and personal friend had loaned him his private plane, which Jack, an experienced pilot, would fly to Vermont, where he planned to tell Lucy what had been going on and discuss their options.

Instead, Mowery intercepted him at the airport, and blackmail quickly turned to kidnapping. He'd piloted the plane. He had a car waiting in Vermont.

His threat to keep Jack in line was simple. He repeated it now, as he had every ten minutes since the start of this ordeal. "I'm the expert, Jack. You're the pompous senator. If you try anything, it'll just piss me off. I'll kill you. Then I'll kill Lucy. Then I'll kill your grandchildren."

"What do you want?" Jack croaked.

"You haven't figured that out yet, have you, Jack?"

"If it's money—"

"If it was money, I'd have fucked with a senator with a bigger trust fund than you have. Jesus, Jack. You're not worth much by Washington standards, you know?"

"I have devoted my life to public service."

"Yeah, and it pays shit."

"Then what is it? Power? My vote? Is someone

else paying you? If I knew, maybe we could work something out.''

''Nope. I had my chance at the brass ring. It was a once-in-a-lifetime deal. I knew it when I started down that road.'' He drove smoothly, steadily; nothing seemed to bother him. ''Redwing Associates had already cut into my business. Sebastian put the word out I was losing my edge.''

''That's not what I heard,'' Jack said.

''Who the hell ever tells a senator the truth? That's why you have all those goddamn hearings. You have to dig through everybody's bullshit to get at something.'' He glanced over at Jack. ''Doesn't that get to you after a while?''

''No. No, it doesn't.''

''Well, aren't you fucking holier-than-thou. So, here I was, going broke, that son of a bitch I trained pulling in millions—I mean, we are talking *millions*. He lives like a goddamn monk, but he's worth— well, shit, he didn't have to borrow a plane to get here.''

Jack thought Mowery was exaggerating, but he chose not to say so. The man seemed to relish how put-upon he was. ''It's an old story, isn't it? The student bests the master.''

''The bastard didn't understand. I got wind of a kidnapping and ransom scheme and dealt myself in,

but I always planned to make sure the real bad guys
didn't get away."

"Weren't you one of the 'real bad guys'?"

"No, asshole, I was going to see to it the family
got back safe."

"What about the ransom money?"

"That was my only sin—wanting to take the
money. I figured I'd deserve it for saving the family."

"But if you put them in danger in the first
place—"

They'd come to Lucy's road. Darren made the
turn. "You know, Jack, why don't you shut the hell
up?"

"It's Sebastian you want?"

"Well, Jack, you did it. You figured it out. If I
ever move to Rhode Island, you get my vote. Now,
shut up."

Fifteen

Lucy touched Sebastian's arm, but he'd already stopped on the steep, narrow path. A few yards above them, through a screen of trees, was the dirt road. "I thought I heard something."

"I did, too."

A car sounded on the road. Sebastian shot up the path and crouched down as it passed above him. It wasn't Barbara's sturdy rental, and it wasn't Plato's shiny black car.

Lucy dropped low. "Did you see who it was?"

He eased back down to her and placed the cell phone in her hand. "It's Mowery. Lucy, he has Jack." He curved her stiff fingers around the phone. "Call the local police. Tell them they've got a probable hostage situation with a U.S. senator. Have them get in touch with the Capitol Police."

"Jack—was he okay—did he look—?"

"He was in the passenger seat. He looked fine."

She nodded. "Should I tell Plato?"

"If he's still there. If not, get your butt over to the police station or a friend's house and stay put." He smiled grimly, a glint of humor coming into his eyes. "Not that I'd tell you what to do."

"Under the circumstances, feel free. What about you? If Mowery's bent on revenge, you'll just be playing into his hands. You don't even have a gun."

But he'd already slipped into the woods, off the path. Lucy watched him make his way around a huge boulder and disappear. She quickly retraced her steps down the path, dialing the police as she went. She got patched through to Larry, the chief of police, and gave him the facts as succinctly as she could. "I'm on my way back to my house," she said.

"Good. Stay there."

"For God's sake, don't come up here with guns blazing. This guy will kill my father-in-law."

"Jesus Christ," Larry said. "All right, I'll meet you at your place. Where you live, it's going to be a while before we can get there."

"I know. I'll be okay."

She disconnected and picked up her pace, coming soon to the stone wall on the far edge of the field. Plato materialized out of nowhere and caught her around the middle. "Lucy." Blood poured down the side of his head. He'd ripped off his suit coat, and blood had soaked through his white shirt; the fabric on his upper right arm was torn. He was sweating and ashen-faced, and he was heavily armed. "Lucy, she's got Madison, maybe J.T., too, by now."

"Oh, no. Oh, God." Lucy held onto him, pushed back the panic. "You mean Barbara? Where?"

"Waterfall. She shot the shit out of me. I'm going to pass out. Call the police." He grimaced, catching his breath. "Where's Sebastian?"

"He took off."

"Good."

Lucy shook her head. "Mowery's got my father-in-law."

Plato sank into the ferns growing up close to the stone wall. "Shit."

"The police are on their way. Go meet them."

"Your kids—"

"You're in no condition to help them, and you don't know the way. I'll go. I know a shortcut from here to the falls."

"I screwed up," Plato said. "I didn't realize Madison knew Barbara, liked her. I should have."

"I didn't think to tell you. I'm sorry."

"Luckily the bitch is a lousy shot."

Lucy quickly checked his wounds. They were unpleasant, but she didn't believe they were life-threatening. She shoved the cell phone at him. "I just called the police. Call them again. Can you make it back to the house? You'll be okay?''

He pushed her toward the path. "Go. The woman's a nut. Be careful. Buy time for the police to get here." He held up his gun—a black, sleek thing—with a shaking, blood-spattered hand. "Take this."

"And do what with it?"

The barest ghost of a smile as he dropped the gun. "You're right. You'll just shoot your foot off. Now, go."

Barbara's legs ached from the steep climb up to Joshua Falls. "You'll see your mother doesn't care about you. You'll see."

Madison was still defiant. "My mother never held a gun on us."

"She's done far worse. If she hadn't brainwashed you against me, I wouldn't have to hold a gun on you. It's her fault. And I'm just doing this for your own good. You have to see what she's done to you."

This time, Madison kept her mouth shut. She was even worse now that they had J.T. with them. Barbara had caught him hiding in the back of the barn. She'd had to fire at him. He got the point. He hadn't said a word since. He was scared. Brainwashed. Barbara would make sure he and Madison both got appropriate therapy in Washington. She didn't want them to have lasting scars from what their mother had done to them.

Yes, she thought, she could see a future for herself. She would take care of Colin's children, Jack's grandchildren. She would see to their upbringing, their education. She would raise them the way Swifts should be raised.

Lucy's fault they were frightened and defiant now. All Lucy's fault.

She could hear the water rushing over the falls. The rain had started, a steady, cold drizzle. Madison and J.T. didn't seem to notice. Country bumpkins.

J.T. slipped on a wet rock and skinned his knee, but he scrambled back to his feet and didn't complain. Barbara was pleased. He was stoic, like his father and grandfather. "Good boy."

"Just keep going, J.T.," Madison whispered to him. "It'll be okay. I promise. I won't let her hurt you."

Barbara resisted the impulse to strike the girl. "You sound like your mother. Don't fill the boy with negative ideas about me, poison him against me."

"I don't need to poison him against you. You've poisoned him yourself!"

That mouth. Barbara gritted her teeth and called upon her heroic self-discipline. She remembered her purpose. They had to see the truth. Both these children did.

"All right." They'd reached the top of the falls; the rain was steadier now. And colder, autumn-like. She preferred Washington heat to this dank misery. She nodded to the children. "Stop. Now, listen. Madison, I want you to take the rope." She tossed the length of rope she'd removed from Lucy's supply room. "If you do anything stupid, I will shoot you or your brother—possibly both of you, if it's really stupid. Do you understand?"

The girl nodded, pale, the rain glistening on her coppery hair. Barbara liked its color. So pretty. They'd have to get it trimmed at a good salon.

She pointed to the rope. "Take it and tie one end around your waist. Your mother taught you knot-tying, I assume? I hope so. You won't want to get this wrong."

"Let J.T. go," Madison said, shivering now as she tied the rope around her waist. "This is all my fault, he didn't do anything. If I hadn't tackled him, Plato would have shot you. J.T. didn't know anything—"

Barbara waved her gun. "Tie the rope."

J.T. stood on the rock ledge, trembling and sobbing. Oh, Lucy, Barbara thought, look what you've done to your little boy!

Madison secured the rope. She tested it, and even

Barbara, who admittedly knew nothing about knots, could see it was tight. "Very good," she said. "Thank you for cooperating. You'll see I'm a fair-minded, disciplined professional. Now, tie the rope around that tree right there." She pointed with her gun at a thick, misshapen hemlock, its roots growing out over the abyss of the waterfall. "Be careful. Don't slip."

"Why do you want—"

"Just do it."

The girl nodded. The rain had soaked through her shirt and shorts and was making her shiver even more. She crouched down and tied the rope to the tree.

"I thought about getting a rock-climbing line with one of those harness things," Barbara said, "but I think this will do. It's more dramatic. You'll see." She leaned forward, over Madison's shoulder. "Don't dawdle."

"You've made your point." Madison looked up at her, her blue eyes and spray of freckles heart-stoppingly like Colin's, like Jack's. "My mother's awful. I hate her."

Barbara smiled. "I know, love. I know. Now, lower yourself over the edge."

"First let J.T. go."

"Madison, you're not in charge. I am. I've been doing the bidding of the Swifts for twenty years. It's my turn." She stood up straight, ignoring the rain pelting down on them, and leveled the gun at the girl. "Now lower yourself over the falls."

Barbara stepped back while Madison dutifully stood up and eased herself to the edge of the hemlock's twisted, gnarled roots. She took a breath, so pale, and gave herself more length on the rope. She tugged at it, making sure the end on the tree held.

"Don't take forever," Barbara said. "If you make me push you, it'll hurt more. The rope will cut into you. You'll smash into the rock."

The girl nodded. "I know. I'm just a little scared. My stupid mother should be here."

"Yes, yes, that's right."

Madison edged her heels out over the abyss. Barbara could hear the water rushing, swirling beneath them. She wasn't quite sure how long the rope was, but she thought it wouldn't reach the water. Madison would dangle several feet above the deep, cold pool. She and Barbara would just have to take it from there.

What to do about J.T.?

"Madison, *don't,*" he cried. "Don't."

Such a big baby, Barbara thought. They'd have to work on that. It was good for him to see his older sister be brave in the face of adversity.

"J.T., listen to me."

Madison's voice was calm and intense, and Barbara expected she was rallying her brother to the cause. Instead, she swooped out from the edge of the roots, kicked herself off the tree and used her momentum to carry herself toward Barbara. She kicked wildly, knocking Barbara flat onto her behind. Her gun went flying.

"Run, J.T., run! Get Mom! Go, go, go."

Barbara pushed the monster off her. The cold rain made her slippery. "I trusted you!"

"My brother's smarter and faster than you are, you *bitch.*"

Barbara recoiled, seeing this stupid girl for what she was. Poisoned. Too far gone. She caught the rope with both hands and pulled hard, shoving Madison back to the edge of the ledge. The girl kicked and fought and struggled, but Barbara was too strong, too furious for her to prevail.

She went down fast. Barbara could see her trying to get her balance to rappel, but she banged against the rock wall, hitting her arm and shoulder. She yelled out in pain.

"It serves you right," Barbara called down to her.

She sank onto the wet ground. Her hands and wrists were rope-burned, stinging and bleeding as if she'd been in a violent tug-of-war. She was exhausted, but she remembered the boy. She had to rally, find him.

She reached backward, feeling for her gun, rain pouring into her eyes.

Lucy. Holding Barbara's gun. The rain pelted down on her. "You'd better pray my daughter isn't badly hurt."

Barbara saw the fear in Lucy's eyes. It wasn't fear for Madison. It was a selfish fear—fear for herself and what she would lose. From the way she held the gun, it was obvious she didn't know how to use it. She peered over the falls.

"Mom," Madison sobbed, "oh, Mom, thank God!"

Barbara sighed. She was right. The girl was lost.

"Are you hurt?" Lucy called. "Can you find a handhold?"

"My arm. I think it's broken."

Lucy glared at Barbara, her .38 steady. "Why? What did she ever do to you?"

"Not her," Barbara said. "You."

"Jesus," a man's voice said behind them. She looked up, and Plato, bloodied and soaked, fell against a hemlock. "You're one sick puppy, you know that?"

Lucy was obviously relieved to see him. Of course, Barbara thought. A man to the rescue. Lucy nodded to the rope still tied around the tree. "Madison's hanging over the falls. I have to get her out. J.T.—did you see him?"

Plato shook his head. "Lucy, all hell's breaking loose down at your house. Cops're everywhere. We can get a rescue team up here to pull her out."

"Call Rob. He's the best." She peered down at her daughter, the rain easing to a drizzle. "Madison, how's the rope? Will it hold?"

"Mom, I can't hang on. My arm. I *can't.*"

Barbara was disgusted at the girl's whining. "I could have killed you and Madison when I had the chance," she told Plato.

"Well, you didn't. It's okay, Lucy," he said softly. "I've got a gun on our Ms. Allen. She's not going anywhere."

Lucy placed the .38 next to the hemlock root and dropped onto her hands and knees. She hung herself partially out over the rain-soaked ledge, inspecting, as if she knew what she was looking at. Barbara wasn't impressed. This was all for show.

"Madison." Lucy cleared her throat. "Here's the situation. I can't come down there and get you, not without equipment. I wouldn't do you any good. And I don't have the strength to pull you up by myself. Plato's here, but he's injured. You can either wait for Rob, or you can try to work your way up a little higher, then I can help."

"I can't. My arm hurts."

"What about your other arm? Use it and your feet. Find hand and footholds. Steady yourself."

Barbara sniffed. "Of course, you're too much of a coward to go after her yourself."

"You know, Ms. Allen," Plato said, dropping down beside her. He was a bloody mess. "Seeing how you've shot me twice today, I wouldn't do or say one damn thing that's going to piss me off. Right now, consider yourself lucky I'm good with pain."

"You wouldn't shoot me. You're a professional. You only shoot to kill."

"I'm right-handed. You shot me in my right arm. Holding a gun in my left hand—who knows?—it could just go off and put a bullet in your bitching leg."

"I loathe your kind," Barbara said.

"Yeah, you hold that thought. What's your pal Mowery up to?"

Barbara snapped her mouth shut. She wished it would stop raining. It was so damn cold.

"That's it," Lucy was saying, still hanging over the falls. "One step at a time. God, I'd give anything to be there instead of you."

"Tell her to pretend her injured arm got cut off," Plato said. "That's what I did with my leg when I got hurt."

Lucy glanced at him dubiously. "Thanks, Plato. She's doing fine."

Barbara could feel the cold of the rock seeping

into her, the dankness of the day. She held herself stiff against shaking and shivering. In another minute, Lucy was pulling on the rope with all her might. Plato transferred his gun into his right hand, his wince of pain barely detectable. He edged over to the tree, grabbed the rope with his left arm and pulled, adding his strength to Lucy's.

Madison came up and collapsed into her mother's arms, sobbing. "J.T.," she said. "I told him to run. Is he all right? Oh, God, this is all my fault!"

"It's not your fault, Madison. You're *fifteen*."

Plato touched Lucy's shoulder. "Go ahead. Cops'll be here in no time. Find your kid."

Barbara sighed. Of course, of course. Lucy would abandon the daughter for the sake of the son. Of course.

Sebastian had the situation under control, if not to his liking. He was tucked behind a nice, fat sofa inside the house Barbara Allen had rented. Darren Mowery and Jack Swift were out on the screened porch, discussing her.

"Barbie made up the affair with Colin just to get back at you," Mowery said. "And you fell for it. Makes you feel kind of stupid, doesn't it?"

"Where is she now?"

"My guess, she's making Lucy's life miserable.

Hates her guts. Totally obsessed with her. Amazing. Miss Super-Professional with a deep, dark secret.''

"You used her. You manipulated her."

"Don't feel sorry for her."

"I don't," Jack said.

"Sebastian Redwing hasn't done you much good, has he?"

"If I'd told him the truth from the beginning—"

"Yeah, well. You didn't."

Sebastian didn't plan on letting them leave. He'd already disabled Mowery's car. A clump of mud in the exhaust pipe did the trick. Now, he would wait. So far, Mowery hadn't made a move against the senator. If he did, Sebastian would act. If he saw his window of opportunity, he'd act. Otherwise, he'd wait for Larry and the Capitol police to get there. Whichever came first was fine with him. With the situation stable, he had no intention of lighting a fuse.

Then J.T. came screaming up out of the woods. "Grandpa! Grandpa!" He pounded up the deck steps. "She's got Madison!"

Sebastian reacted instantly, shooting out through the sliding glass door onto the deck. He had to get to J.T. before Mowery did, even if it meant he'd lost his advantage. He grabbed J.T. The boy was hysterical, traumatized, gulping for air. He clawed Sebastian's arms. "J.T.," he said. "It's okay. I've got you."

"Madison—we have to save her. Barbara's going to kill her. She hung her over the waterfall. She'll cut the rope. Sebastian!"

Sebastian stayed between the boy and the screened porch, where he knew Mowery would be quickly calculating his options. "Listen to me, J.T. Go back down the road. Run your ass off, you hear me? Your mother will be looking for you."

Being Lucy's son, he argued. "Grandpa—"

"I'll take care of your grandfather. Go, J.T. Trust me. Your mother will be there." That much Sebastian knew. Lucy would be there for her kids.

"Well, well, well," Mowery said behind them. "Daddy Redwing."

Sebastian stayed focused on the boy. He grabbed J.T. up and dumped him off the deck, several feet to the ground. J.T. scrambled to his feet, and yelled, "Grandpa! He's got a gun!"

Jack Swift pushed away from Mowery and leaned over the rail. "Run, J.T. I'll be fine. *Go.*"

J.T. hesitated, then darted into the woods, down the hill, moving fast. He was twelve and energetic, and he knew the woods. Sebastian had done his job. J.T. wasn't in Mowery's hands.

"What?" Mowery said. "You two think I'd shoot a kid?"

"I know you would," Sebastian said, turning to Mowery. The minute he'd heard J.T., Sebastian knew Mowery had him. He had a gun, a Glock. "It didn't used to be that way."

"Sure it did, you just never noticed. And I wouldn't shoot a kid in the back. In the head, as part of a business arrangement, only if necessary. I'm not a fucking monster."

Jack Swift, gray and breathing hard, collapsed against the deck rail. "I can't—if anything happens to Madison or J.T. I don't think I could go on."

Mowery snorted. "Enough votes, you'll go on." He walked over to the senator and put the Glock at his temple. "No whining, okay? I need to think."

"Darren." Sebastian didn't move; he was centered, focused. Plato was right. This was work he knew, even if he'd come to hate it and distrust himself. "You're on a dead-end road. I've disabled your car. The local police are probably here by now. The Capitol Police are on their way. Everyone's coming. Let Jack go and get out now while you can."

"Why would I do that?"

"Because you're good. You know my first priority is saving the senator and his family. This is your best chance to get away."

"Sebastian, in case you haven't noticed, I'm the only one here with a gun. Suppose I just shoot you both and take off?"

"If you'd wanted to shoot me, you could have come out to my place in Wyoming and shot me in my hammock." Sebastian sat on an Adirondack chair and stretched out his legs. "You don't just want me dead, Darren. You want me ruined, the way I ruined you. You want me to suffer, the way you've suffered."

"I want the senator dead. I want Lucy and her kids dead and you held responsible, ridiculed, run out of business."

"Well, Darren. If you shoot both the senator and me, you have no hostages left. Then what? You're still on a dead-end road with no car."

"Up on your feet."

Sebastian did as instructed. He wondered where Lucy was, what had happened to Plato if Madison was dangling from Joshua Falls and J.T. was tearing through the woods on his own.

Mowery got Swift to stand beside Sebastian, then he marched them both off the deck. Sebastian wasn't too worried. He figured he had about ten minutes to figure something out before J.T. found Lucy, and all hell broke loose.

Lucy charged down the path from the falls, slipping in the wet pine needles, oblivious to her fatigue, the pain in her side from running.

"Mom!"

"J.T." She sank onto her knees, caught him in her arms as he almost ran over her. "Are you all right?"

"Sebastian," he croaked. "Grandpa. Mom!"

She realized he was incapable of talking. He was out of breath, in shock. "It's going to be okay, J.T. The police are on their way. Come on."

She half carried, half pulled him up the path back to the falls. Plato, pale and bloody, had two guns on Barbara Allen, his and hers. Madison was shivering next to him, cradling her arm in pain, not looking at the woman who'd nearly killed her.

Lucy knew that, for her children's sake, she had to appear to have command of the situation. She urged J.T. down next to Madison. "Sit here by your sister. Don't move. Don't look at Barbara."

"Mom, that man had a gun pointed at Grandpa," J.T. said breathlessly. "And Sebastian—he—he was right there."

"Don't think about it. Just think about breathing." She put her palm on his chest. He was wet and cold with rain, terrified. "In, out. Come on, J.T. Think about it. Breathe in, breathe out. Slow and controlled."

But he whimpered like a lost puppy, and her heart broke. Madison, gray-faced, fell back on a bed of hemlock needles as she dealt with her terror and the pain of her injuries.

Lucy steeled herself against her own rush of emotions. She had to think. "Plato, I need to borrow one of the guns."

"Better idea." His voice was soothing, steady, professional. "You stay here, I go with the gun."

She shook her head. "You won't get three steps before you pass out."

He smiled feebly. "Bet I get six steps."

"Plato…"

"Go, kid." He flipped her Barbara's gun, barrel first, and kept his. "Mine's high-tech. You'll shoot up the woods with it. You know how to pull the trigger?"

"I think so." She felt the weight of the gun in her hand. "I've seen a lot of movies. Is there a safety or anything? Do I have to cock it?"

Plato looked at her with his bloodshot eyes. "Just pull the fucking trigger."

Lucy nodded. "I will if I have to."

"And trust Sebastian." Plato cleared his throat; he was weak, in need of medical attention. "He does things in his own time, and in his own way. Trust him, Lucy."

"If he's renounced violence—"

"He's renounced gratuitous violence. If Mowery's got a gun on him and a senator, we're not talking gratuitous. Lucy, if Sebastian can't go through a brick wall, he'll go around it. He'll find a way.''

She blinked back tears. "I hope you're right."

J.T. shivered violently. His lips were purple, and dark circles had formed under his eyes. "Mom, don't go. I'm scared."

Lucy looked at her son and daughter. Their father was dead, their grandfather was being held hostage. If something happened to her, Madison and J.T. would end up in Costa Rica with her parents. She couldn't be reckless or take unnecessary chances. It wasn't a question of courage. It was a question of responsibility.

She had to trust Sebastian, the way she'd had to trust Madison to get herself into a position from which Lucy could pull her up out of the falls.

"I love him," she said to Plato. "Sebastian. I love him."

Plato leaned against his rock. "I don't know which one of you has it worse. Sebastian, loving you, or you loving Sebastian. You're both a couple of stiff-necked pains in the ass."

Lucy smiled and bit back tears. "I'll go down and meet the police, make sure they get the rescue squad up here."

He nodded, satisfied, too spent to talk.

"J.T. can come with me. You up to it, kiddo?"

He sniffled and put his hand in hers, and she

kissed her daughter and told her it wouldn't be much longer. "Hang in there, okay?"

Madison didn't open her eyes. "Sure, Mom."

Barbara Allen didn't say a word, didn't acknowledge Lucy's presence or her own imminent arrest.

Plato was sinking fast. He managed one last smile. "Tell your local yokels to hurry it up. I'm about ready to push Ms. Barbara here over the falls and call it a day."

In spite of his fatigue and terror, J.T. kept up with Lucy. She took the path to the dirt road, assuming the police would come that way instead of along the brook path.

When they emerged onto the dirt road, J.T. gasped and tightened his grip on his mother's hand. Then she saw, too. Just down the road, Jack and Sebastian were walking a few feet ahead of another man who she presumed was Darren Mowery.

"That's him," J.T. whispered. "That's the man—"

Lucy bent down to him. "Go back and tell Plato."

Plato was in no condition to help, she knew, but he could hold onto her son. J.T. hesitated. She gave him an encouraging hug, and he summoned his last reserves of energy and ran back up the path.

Mowery must have heard them or sensed their

presence. He half turned to her. "Put the gun down, Lucy, or I shoot Sebastian."

She'd almost forgotten she had a gun. She glanced up the path. She raised it. "If you shoot Sebastian, I'll shoot you."

Sebastian eased around slowly, without a word, and Jack inhaled sharply. Lucy didn't know what to do. She wasn't a marksman. She hated guns. She held her breath, met Sebastian's eyes just for an instant. He didn't speak. He didn't give her even the smallest sign as to what she should do.

Mowery moved, and she fired.

Blood spurted from his right buttock, and he swore viciously. Sebastian pounced, tackling Mowery with blinding efficiency and ferocity, knocking the gun from his hand as if he'd been waiting for just this moment, just this mistake.

Jack snatched up the gun. Lucy kept Barbara's gun pointed in their direction, in case she was misreading the situation and Sebastian wasn't winning.

Sebastian pushed Mowery facedown on the ground and yanked his hands behind his back in what looked like a professional hold. He shook his head at her. "You shot him in the ass?"

"I guess I did."

"Lucy, for God's sake. You don't shoot someone in the ass. If you're in a situation that requires you to fire your weapon, you're shooting to kill."

"I was shooting to shoot. It's not like I was aiming!"

"Well, hell. That makes me feel better." He motioned to her with one hand. "You want to lower that baby, then?"

She lowered the gun. She knew Sebastian was half teasing, half lecturing to keep her mind off what she'd just done—how close they'd all come. She saw how serious his eyes were. "Did you have the situation under control?" she asked.

"No." He grinned. "But I was working on it."

Jack handed Mowery's gun to Sebastian and turned to his daughter-in-law. "Lucy," he sobbed. "Oh, God, Lucy."

"The kids are okay." Suddenly tears were streaming down her face. "Madison, J.T.—they're okay."

Sebastian held the gun on Mowery, moaning in pain. "Go, you two." He spoke to Lucy and Jack without looking at them. "Go to your kids."

Lucy walked over to him, the dirt road squishy under her feet. The rain had stopped altogether now; the air was close and yet refreshing, as if it had been washed clean. Her eyes met Sebastian's. His were still deadly serious. This, she reminded herself, was his job, work he knew how to do—work that had brought her to him in the first place.

"Are you okay?" she asked quietly.

"You mean, am I going to put a bullet in Mowery's head the minute you and Jack turn your backs?" He gave her a ragged smile. "I'm the one who renounced violence, remember?"

Lucy managed a smile back. "Well, don't tell *him* that."

"Go on. I'll get Mr. Mowery to the police. No loose ends this time."

Jack took her hand, and together they walked up to the falls. She told him what Barbara had done.

"My God, Lucy." His voice cracked, tears spilled down his wrinkled cheeks. He squeezed her hand. "I had no idea. I didn't put it together. I should have spoken up sooner."

"Water over the dam now, Jack. We both made mistakes."

"I'm shattered," he said, "and I'm stunned. I never expected this. Never, not in a million years. I'd have done anything—anything—to spare you and the kids this ordeal."

"I know you would. That's the hardest thing, isn't it?" She pictured her injured daughter, her terrified son. "Realizing no matter how much you want to, how hard you try, you can't protect your kids from life."

"It is. It's the hardest thing." He tucked his hand into hers. "But you've given Madison and J.T. the skills they need, the good judgment. Lucy, when I saw J.T. running up those steps straight at Mowery—"

She shuddered. "It's over, Jack. It worked out."

"Thank God."

As they came to a curve in the path, Lucy glanced back. Sebastian was in the same position, alone with his gun drawn over an enemy who had once been his friend.

"He won't shoot him," Jack assured her.

"No," Lucy said, "he won't. But I think it's how he likes life best, don't you? Alone with a gun on a bad guy."

"Actually, no. I think he likes life best with you. I think he has for a long, long time." Her father-in-law pulled her arm around him and hugged her fiercely. "It just wasn't possible until now."

Sixteen

—◦◦◦◦—

The Capitol Police and the local police weren't too happy with the Swifts. "They chewed my ass off, too," Rob said, as he and Lucy lined up supplies for the father-son backpacking trip. It was four days later, and they had work to do.

Lucy sighed. "Well, I was right about them crawling all over the place, wasn't I?"

Rob grinned at her. "A kidnapped senator does bring the men with guns out of the woodwork."

The Capitol Police had assigned a detail to Lucy, Madison and J.T., until they completed their investigation and were satisfied Darren Mowery and Barbara Allen had no other accomplices. Straightforward greed, one detective told Lucy, was often an easier motive to sort out than vengeance and obsession.

Sebastian had found another car—a getaway car

Mowery had put in place—in a small clearing on the western edge of Lucy's property. He'd meant to use Jack as a shield until he no longer needed him, then shoot him, shoot Sebastian and take off. Mission accomplished, Sebastian Redwing dead and discredited. Money was never the point. The freedom from hating Sebastian was.

Rob stood over a row of water bottles. "I wish J.T. could come with us."

"Next year."

He smiled gently. "Maybe Sebastian will take him."

Lucy couldn't think that far into the future. Right now, it was enough to count water bottles. Madison and J.T. were with their grandfather and Sidney Greenburg, who'd flown up from Washington. They were all picking wild blueberries—even Madison with her broken arm in a cast. "We all need simple, healing tasks," Sidney had said in that kind, firm way of hers.

After Rob headed for home, Lucy walked across her yard to her front porch. She paid attention to the soft grass under her feet, the warmth of the sun, the smell of the flowers and the sounds of the birds. Simple, healing tasks. Walking across the yard. Breathing in the clean summer air.

Plato Rabedeneira was sitting on a wicker chair on the porch. He looked less ashen and weak, but still wasn't a hundred percent. The bullet wound on his head was lightly bandaged, bruising at its edges.

Lucy laughed as she came up the steps, delighted to see him. "I didn't know you were getting out of the hospital. When did this happen?"

"I fought my way out this afternoon." He grinned at her. "I thought the bastard'd never spring me. I hate hospitals."

"How did you get here?"

"An FBI detective I know."

"The FBI's here, too?"

"Lucy, everyone's here."

"Well, they can all go home. I want my life back."

His dark, handsome eyes settled on her. "Do you?"

She knew he meant Sebastian. "I can't leave here," Lucy said quietly. "This is my home. Madison and J.T. need to be here."

"Lucy, Lucy." Plato shook his head at her. "There are two things in Sebastian's life that are permanent. This place and you."

"His ranch—"

"He almost lost the damn thing in a poker game."

"Redwing Associates," she said.

"He's done his bit. He can do something else, maybe leadership training. You get the right kind of leadership in place, you can prevent a lot of trouble down the line." He stretched his long legs. "Of course, sometimes you just run into bastards and wackos. Keeps us in business, I guess."

"Bastards and wackos. Are those technical terms?"

"Absolutely." But his grin faded, and he said softly, "Lucy, I'm sorry I didn't do better by your kids."

"You did fine by my kids. Madison's got good-looking men with guns watching over her, and J.T.'s named one of his Micro Machine helicopters after you. I'm sorry you got shot looking after them."

"Yeah. Not your everyday baby-sitting job."

"You're welcome to stay with us as long as you want."

But he shook his head, rising stiffly to his feet. "I need to get down to Washington and check on Happy Ford."

"She's okay?"

"She's got a long recovery ahead of her, but she's tough."

"Then it's back to Wyoming?"

"Work's piling up." He took both her hands and pulled her to her feet. His dark eyes sparkled with a humor that was pure Plato Rabedeneira. "Don't tell Sebastian, but I had his cabin bulldozed. Packed up his poetry and maple syrup and mowed that sucker down."

Lucy bit back a smile. Plato, Sebastian and Colin had always had an unusual friendship, the rules of which she didn't understand. "What about his dogs and horses?"

"Moved them up to the main part of the ranch. I think the yellow Lab might do okay out here. The other two are western dogs. Sebastian can get new horses."

"Plato…"

"He's staying, Lucy. Trust me."

"I don't know. It's as if he's gone inside himself. I don't even know where he is."

Plato laughed. "Are you kidding? He's out playing detective with the big boys and checking out the talent in case he sees any good prospects for the company. I said he was staying, Lucy. I didn't say he was quitting."

Sebastian took them up to the falls that evening after dinner. Jack and Sidney promised to have hot cocoa and cookies waiting when they got back.

The sun was low on the horizon; the air warm and dry, without a breeze. At Lucy's side, Madison shook visibly. "Mom, I don't know if I can do it."

"You don't have to do it. We can turn back."

She nodded. There didn't seem an inch of her that

wasn't bruised. Her cast was already covered with signatures, drawings of hearts and flowers, smiley faces. When the news of her ordeal spread through town, her friends came up by the carload.

"I'll do it," she whispered.

Up ahead, J.T. held Sebastian's hand. He had his Plato helicopter in his other hand. He kept looking up at Sebastian, as if taking his cue from him. Sebastian focused on the task at hand. Mind the tree roots, step over the rocks. He'd been thoroughly nononsense since the police had carted off his former mentor and friend, a man he'd thought he'd killed a year ago.

They stopped when they could hear the falls. "Listen," Sebastian said.

Madison frowned, then managed a small smile. "It's beautiful."

J.T. looked around at her. "What?"

"The sound of the waterfall."

"It's just water," he said.

Sebastian tugged on his hand. "Come on."

They walked all the way to the top of the falls, to the ledge where Barbara Allen had dangled Madison. The scraggly hemlock was still scarred from the rope. Madison was breathing rapidly, and Lucy worried about her going into a panic attack or hyperventilating. But she said nothing, and her daughter squared her jaw and pushed ahead of her mother,

her brother and Sebastian. Madison placed a hand on the tree and looked down into the deep, cold pool.

"*Don't,* Madison," J.T. sobbed. "You'll fall."

"It's just water and rock," she said over her shoulder at him. "Come on, J.T. I didn't fall the other day. I was pushed."

Tentatively, he went and stood next to his sister, but kept back from the very edge of the ledge. Sebastian looked at Lucy, his hard gaze impossible to read. "What about you?"

She remembered her terror and helplessness at seeing her daughter hanging over the waterfall, knowing she was hurt, frightened, one wrong move away from not coming out of there alive. Her baby. She blinked back tears, could almost feel Madison's little head against her shoulder as she'd rocked her as an infant. Madison wasn't a baby anymore.

"Come on, Mom," J.T. said.

Lucy walked up the sloping rock and stood next to her children. The water of Joshua Falls ran clear, a mix of sunlight and shade dancing on the surface. "We did good that day," Lucy said. "All of us."

Madison smiled at her mother. "It's beautiful here. It's just so beautiful."

On the way back, J.T. skipped ahead to catch tree toads, and Madison counted the names on her cast.

Lucy smiled at Sebastian. "At least we managed to do that without the Capitol Police on our tails."

"No, you didn't."

"You mean—"

"They shadowed us. I just didn't tell you." He grinned at her. "Jack's leaving in a couple of days. They'll go then, too."

"Good."

"I will, too."

She swallowed, kept walking. "Back to Wyoming?"

"Yes. I have things I need to sort out, Lucy."

"I know you do. I'll be here."

He smiled and said nothing, and Lucy decided not to tell him Plato had had his cabin bulldozed.

"Lucy has a good life here," Sidney said, "a damn good life."

Jack nodded, holding Sidney's hand as they sat on the back steps waiting for Lucy, Sebastian and the kids to return from their trip to Joshua Falls. "Yes, she does. I'm happy for her."

"But you weren't, not for a long time."

"No," he admitted. "I guess I thought if she stayed in Washington and didn't move on with her life, somehow it kept a part of Colin alive. I miss him, Sidney. Some days it's so hard, even now."

She turned his hand over and kissed his palm.

"You'll have those days for the rest of your life. Be grateful for them. They tell you how much you loved your son. They tell you that you don't have to be afraid you'll ever forget him."

"I couldn't protect him, Sidney. I couldn't protect Eleanor."

"No, you couldn't."

He smiled and brushed her cheek with the tips of his fingers. "How did you get to be so smart?"

She laughed, her dark eyes crinkling. "By not really and truly falling in love until I was fifty. Now." She sprang up and dusted off her bottom. "If you don't mind, I'm not your romance-in-the-country sort of person. Too damn many mosquitoes."

"You're not going to want to move to Vermont?"

"God, no." She grinned, and Jack's heart melted. "Don't look at me like that, Senator Swift. I am not making love to you in the pumpkin patch."

He pulled her close. "Does this mean you're willing to hang your panty hose in my bathroom?"

"Jack, *Newsweek* has us as an item. The cat's out of the bag. I'll hang my panty hose in your Senate office."

"I don't know about that."

She laughed and kissed him. "I do."

His heart jumped. "Sidney?"

"Yes, Jack. I'll marry you."

* * *

"Goddammit, Plato," Sebastian said two days later when he arrived back in Wyoming. They stood in the dust where his cabin had been. "You bulldozed my place."

"Not me. I'm the boss. I delegated the job."

"To whom? I want a name."

"I promised anonymity."

Sebastian glared at him. They'd met in Washington to visit Happy Ford, now recuperating at home, and Plato had never mentioned the cabin. "My stuff?"

"Packed up."

"Where?"

"In your truck. I figure you'll have to drive back to Vermont. The yellow Lab won't take to flying."

Sebastian nodded. "I'll need a truck in Vermont."

The other two dogs rolled on their backs in the dust. They wouldn't do well with kids and easterners. Definitely western dogs.

Sebastian grinned at his friend and partner. "I'll let this one go, seeing how you got shot in the head."

"That barely counts as a bullet wound. Now, the one in my arm hurt. Lucky there was no nerve damage. Do you know that crazy bitch thought she was an expert marksman?"

"Ms. Allen had a lot of lofty ideas about herself."

"She operated according to a logic all her own." Sebastian knelt beside the shepherd and rubbed the old dog's stomach. He breathed in the cool, dry air. He loved this place—it had restored his mind and body. But his soul wasn't here. "If Lucy hadn't shot Mowery in the ass, I'd have killed him."

"If you had no other choice. You're a professional, Sebastian. This was personal, but you kept your cool. Your mistake," Plato said, "was in letting Mowery take the credit for thwarting that assassination attempt all those years ago."

"Thwarting?" Sebastian got to his feet, grinning at him. "What kind of word is that?"

Plato's eyes darkened. "You know what I'm saying. Darren Mowery didn't have it. The instincts, the keen sense of right and wrong, the ability to stay focused and not get cynical. He just didn't have it."

"He wanted to, at least in the beginning."

"You, on the other hand. You never wanted it."

"No, I never did. I wanted to be happy the way Daisy was happy, with a patch of dirt, her birds, the woods." He squinted out at the incredible Wyoming landscape. "I suppose I needed the last twenty years to sort that out."

"Yeah, well, you're not throwing in the towel. I figure, a nice addition to Lucy's barn, and we've got our eastern leadership training center. Invite me to the wedding?"

"I'll need a best man."

Plato rocked back on his heels. "You have a ring? You can't be asking Lucy to marry you without a ring. I know she does all this adventure travel stuff, but she'll want a ring. Trust me."

Sebastian sighed and dug in his jeans pocket, producing a simple diamond ring. "There."

Plato frowned. "That's it? You can afford a bigger rock than that."

"It was Daisy's. My grandfather gave it to her. They didn't have much money."

"I thought you didn't take anything of Daisy's after she died."

Sebastian shrugged. "I didn't. I appropriated this from the attic before I left."

"You mean you stole it?"

"It wasn't stealing. Daisy meant for me to have it, only I was too stupid to take it."

"You never thought Lucy would fall for you," Plato said. He shook his head. "You're right, you were stupid."

"Keep it up, Rabedeneira. I've already got you earmarked for kid duty during the honeymoon."

"Ha. Me and what army?"

"They adore you."

"Yeah, well, those two get me shot again, that's it for me and kids."

* * *

Sebastian arrived in Vermont unshaven, jittery from too much road food and sick of his damn dog. The dog was sick of him, too. When Sebastian opened the door of the truck, the dog bounded out and immediately laid ruin to Lucy's hollyhocks and daylilies.

Well, what the hell. They'd plant more.

Lucy walked down off the front porch. She had on a long sundress and sandals, and her hair was down, shining in the late-afternoon sun. "I heard you were in town."

"Spies everywhere."

"You stopped at the store for something. My spies wouldn't tell me what. They recognized your Wyoming plates. They didn't recognize you. They said you were—" She pretended to search her memory. "Disreputable looking. That was it."

"Am I?"

"Around here, disreputable is a euphemism for sexy."

"Ah. I see."

She glanced over at the yellow Lab, now chasing a gray squirrel across the yard. "Think he'll ever learn the rules?"

"Not a chance."

"Hell of a nerve, bringing your dog."

Sebastian leaned against his truck. She wasn't twenty-two anymore, and neither was he. But she was the woman he'd always loved. "Where are the kids?"

"Rob and Patti Kiley took them to their place for the night."

"Convenient."

"Hmm. The feds have finally left us to our own devices. The media have decamped. The bad guys are in jail without bail." She smiled at him. "I'm alone."

"No, you're not."

He kissed her, long and slow and gently, and after a while he got the champagne out of the truck. It was what he'd bought in town. He'd told the woman at the counter, who had a spying-for-Lucy look about her, to keep her mouth shut. It was probably all over town by now—Daisy's grandson and the Widow Swift having champagne together up at the old Wheaton place.

They went into the kitchen, and he popped the cork and filled two glasses.

"What are we celebrating?" Lucy asked.

"Well, we can celebrate anything we want. We can celebrate getting the bad guys. We can celebrate living another day. Or," he said, "we can celebrate Lucy Blacker falling in love again, or making love again, or anything you want, because I'll take whatever you can give me."

She smiled. "Can I celebrate all of the above?"

He didn't think he could manage to carry two glasses of champagne and her, but it wasn't far to the bedroom. Then she threw back her head and laughed; it knocked him off balance and the champagne spilled all over her. Both glasses. He started to lay her on the bed.

"My antique quilt," she said.

He whisked it off, the old wedding-ring quilt Daisy had stitched so long ago.

Lucy dangled her arms around his neck. "I smell like champagne."

"You taste like champagne, too."

"You taste like...dog hair."

He laughed, kissing her. "Do you want me to shower first?"

"No, shower second."

"We'll shower together."

"I was just kidding." She rubbed the back of her hand on his beard stubble. "You taste like a man who's driven hard across country to—" She smiled, her eyes alive, happy. "To make love to me."

"It's all I've thought about for days."

"Years, I think."

He could see the shape of her breasts against her champagne-soaked dress. "You've a fine opinion of yourself, Lucy Blacker."

"Of you," she said. "I love you, Sebastian. I think I always have in one way or another. You've been there for me all along. It's different now. I love you as a partner, not just as a friend. I love you as an equal, not just as my protector. I love you up close." She pulled him to her and said as her mouth found his, "Never again from a distance."

He licked the champagne from her throat, and when they dispatched with her dress, he licked it from her breasts and stomach, until she was quaking with urgency. He made short order of his clothes, too, and when he came back to her, curving his hands over her hips, her stomach, her breasts, he could feel his own urgency, his unstoppable desire for this woman he'd loved for so long.

"I can't hold back, not anymore."

"Then don't," she said, and pulled him into her.

It was cool in her room, and he could hear the birds outside, his dog panting after a fresh scent, and in the distance, Joshua Brook tumbling out of the hills. He was home, and when he made love to Lucy, he knew this was where he belonged.

"I've always loved you," he whispered. "I always will."

Somewhere just east of Peculiar...
Hannah is learning to expect the unexpected.

Suzann Ledbetter

*H*annah Garvey has had enough: of the fast track, the corporate ladder and chronic love-gone-wrong. So she's traded in the rat race of Chicago to become the resident manager for Valhalla Springs, an exclusive retirement development nestled in the Missouri Ozarks.

*B*ut Mondays happen even in Paradise. And in this community of delightful oddballs and endearing buttinskis, Hannah finds more than she bargained for. She certainly didn't expect murder...or a sexy lawman seven years her junior...or a mystery that puts her wits and wiles, not to mention her patience, to the test.

East of Peculiar

"From her sharp descriptions to her crisp dialogue, Ledbetter tickles the jaded palate of any reader."
—*Colorado Reverie*

On sale mid-May 2000 wherever paperbacks are sold!

Visit us at www.mirabooks.com

MIRA

MSL597

From the critically acclaimed author of
Iron Lace and *Rising Tides*

EMILIE RICHARDS

Once a struggling community of Irish immigrants, Lake Erie's Whiskey Island has a past as colorful as the patrons who frequent the Whiskey Island Saloon. A local gathering place for generations, the saloon is now run by the Donaghue sisters, whose lives and hearts have been shaped by family tragedy and a haunting mystery.

Then an act of violence sets the wheels of fate in motion. As an old man struggles to protect a secret as old as Whiskey Island itself, a murder that still shadows too many lives is about to be solved—with repercussions no one can predict.

WHISKEY ISLAND

Emilie Richards is "a careful storyteller who uses multidimensional players to lend credibility to storybook situations."
—*The Cleveland Plain Dealer*

On sale mid-June 2000 wherever paperbacks are sold!

MIRA

Things are heating up...

MARY LYNN
BAXTER

SULTRY

Since her mother's tragic suicide, Lindsay Newman has watched her wealthy Mississippi family spin out of control. Tired of being a pawn in men's games, Lindsay is determined to become a rebel in her own life—and Mitch Rawlins ignites that first white-hot spark.

But the Newmans' new groundskeeper isn't interested in playing games with a spoiled rich girl...yet he wants Lindsay more than anything. But, like everyone else in the Newman household, he's got something to hide. Something that could tear Lindsay away from him forever.

On sale mid-June 2000 wherever paperbacks are sold!

MIRA

MMLB588

CARLA NEGGERS

66541	ON FIRE	___	$5.99 U.S. ___	$6.99 CAN.
66485	KISS THE MOON	___	$5.99 U.S. ___	$6.99 CAN.
66266	CLAIM THE CROWN	___	$5.50 U.S. ___	$6.50 CAN.

(limited quantities available)

TOTAL AMOUNT	$_____
POSTAGE & HANDLING	$_____
($1.00 for one book; 50¢ for each additional)	
APPLICABLE TAXES*	$_____
TOTAL PAYABLE	$_____

(check or money order—please do not send cash)

To order, complete this form and send it, along with a check or money order for the total above, payable to MIRA Books®, to: **In the U.S.:** 3010 Walden Avenue, P.O. Box 9077, Buffalo, NY 14269-9077; **In Canada:** P.O. Box 636, Fort Erie, Ontario, L2A 5X3.

Name:_____

Address:_____ City:_____

State/Prov.:_____ Zip/Postal Code:_____

Account Number (if applicable):_____

075 CSAS

*New York residents remit applicable sales taxes.
Canadian residents remit applicable GST and provincial taxes.

MIRA

Visit us at www.mirabooks.com

MCN0600BL